The Italian Girl

Also by Patricia Hall

# THE
# ITALIAN GIRL

## Patricia Hall

St. Martin's Minotaur ❧ New York

ISBN 0-312-26489-5

First published in Great Britain by Constable & Company Ltd

First U.S. Edition: May 2000

10 9 8 7 6 5 4 3 2 1

# 1

If the skull had not fallen from the maw of the digger and skittered jerkily down the pile of wet rubble to land almost on the toe of Pete O'Halloran's mud-caked wellington boot, the skeleton might have been buried again beneath the concrete foundations of the new factory and forgotten for good. O'Halloran kicked the spherical object gingerly, turning it over so that the eye sockets, full of drier earth, gaped at him. Their blank gaze dispelled the last faint vestige of doubt he had clung to as the object had tumbled towards him down the heap of wet earth and rock.

'Oh, shit,' he said, glancing around the site before shrugging wearily and waving to the digger driver to stop his engine. His eye had rested on young Gobbler Clark, tall, broad and muscle-bound in a grubby singlet in spite of the chilly wind which whistled down the valley from the high Pennines bringing the first heavy spots of rain. And it was obvious that Gobbler's fascinated eyes had fixed on the skull and recognised it for what it was.

O'Halloran knew that what Gobbler saw he would be trading for pints around the pubs and clubs of the town within hours. He glanced at his watch and saw that it was not yet midday. But the skull could not be ignored, penalty clause or no penalty clause, he thought with considerable bile, knowing who would take the blame for the delay.

'Gobbler,' he said. 'Don't stand there gawping. Go and phone the effing police, lad. There'll be nowt more done here till we get this little lot looked at. And put t'kettle on while you're about it. We might as well have a brew while we're waiting.'

Within an hour Chief Inspector Michael Thackeray stood warming his hands around one of the construction workers' substantial mugs of tea as he watched a team of blue-overalled police officers painstakingly trowelling sticky mud away from

5

the patch of earth which the digger had disturbed. He was a burly, broad-shouldered figure, hunched inside his dark trench-coat, his black hair blowing in the wind, his face impassive as he watched the progress of the search several feet below in the waterlogged foundations of the new building. He was joined by a slimmer, slighter man, wearing the same police issue gum-boots with considerably more aplomb as he stepped with fastid-ious caution through the bog.

'It's definitely human remains, then, is it, Guv?' Sergeant Kevin Mower asked sceptically as they watched their colleagues working like agitated hippos in their baggy overalls at the bottom of the pit, sloppy with mud which ran in yellowish rivulets down the steep sides of the excavation.

'Not some kids having us on with a plastic skull?'

'It's human,' Thackeray said. He glanced at the Sergeant's stylish suit and jacket and smiled faintly. 'You'd better get some overalls on. I want you down there if they find anything else.'

'Terrific,' Mower said, though without much rancour. Mower's sharp edge had seemed slightly blunted since he had returned to duty a month ago with nothing but two small scars to show for a knife attack which had almost killed him. 'Is Amos on his way?' he asked.

'He's been informed,' Thackeray said. 'Though there's not much for him to see yet. We need the rest of the body.' He glanced impassively at the small cordoned off area where the skull still lay, the rain beginning to wash away the mud so that the bone gleamed white here and there through its mantle of earth. 'I doubt that a skull alone will get us far with an identification.'

The police were being watched from beyond the cordon of blue and white tape by a handful of construction workers in donkey jackets, collars turned up against the now driving rain, half pleased, half perturbed at their sudden enforced idleness. The site itself, three acres on a plateau halfway up one of the hills which surrounded the manufacturing town of Bradfield, had been ploughed and churned into a sea of dereliction by the diggers and heavy trucks that now stood abandoned close to the entrance. The rain came in great grey gusts from the surrounding hills, obliterating the view of the town below and finding cracks in every waterproof defence which the huddled watchers had devised.

Thackeray wiped the water from his face with a sodden handkerchief and brushed his drenched hair out of his eyes. The workmen gave an ironic cheer when one of the officers below raised a hand to indicate that he had found something and Thackeray turned in some irritation to Mower.

'Get rid of them, Kevin,' he said. 'Make sure we've got names and addresses and keep the foreman, O'Halloran, here and the driver of the JCB, for statements. The rest can go. I'll see you back at HQ.'

It was several more hours before the pathologist, Amos Atherton, eased his considerable bulk down the slippery slope from the firm grip of one police officer above to the waiting arms of another below.

'By 'eck,' he said breathlessly as he regained his balance and squelched gingerly through the mud to join Mower in the tent of white plastic sheeting which had by now been erected over the site of the police excavations. He glanced out at the leaden sky and the still pitiless rain. 'You've chosen a grand afternoon for playing wi' buckets and spades.'

He loosened the fastening on his heavy waterproof, shook back the hood and wiped the dampness from a broad, unfurrowed brow with a large khaki handkerchief before he cast a sharp eye at the collection of fragments which the police had so far assembled in a box on a trestle table. Just feet away a group of officers were still painstakingly scraping in the sticky mud. Atherton poked an impatient finger amongst the bones.

'Aye, they're human remains,' he said glumly. 'Such as they are. You're not going to need anyone to certify death, are you?'

'Can you tell anything from just looking?' Mower asked, with an almost equal lack of enthusiasm.

'They're old,' Atherton said. 'But God knows how old.'

'Archeology old or just unsolved murder old?' Mower asked, but Atherton shrugged.

'You're going to need a virtuoso performance from the forensic lads to pin that down.' With stubby, sensitive fingers, he riffled amongst the muddy fragments in the box as if they were toys.

'You've not got anywhere near the complete set,' he said. 'Though if you pressed me I'd say that bit of pelvis was female.'

'Surprise me,' Mower said, with just the faintest note of disbelief.

'It's too hefty to be a bloke,' Atherton said kindly. 'Why do you think girls have big bums, lad? They hang off big bones, don't they? See here? This is a femur, thigh-bone to you, do you see?' Mower fixed his dark eyes almost reluctantly on the long stick-like object Atherton picked up and waved in his direction. 'That's too slight for an adult male, any road. Possibly a young lad, but you wouldn't get a pelvis like that on a young lad. So if this isn't some prehistoric relic they've disinterred, I reckon you need to look for missing women or girls. Bones survive an amazingly long time, you know, if they're not disturbed.'

'But the skeleton's not complete yet?' Mower asked.

'Nowhere near,' Atherton said cheerfully. He picked over the contents of the box again. 'You're short of most of the spine, the tibia, fibula, small bones of hands and feet. And teeth, if you can find them.'

'Teeth?' Mower said faintly.

'That skull up there's missing most of its teeth. They must have been knocked out when the digger hit. If this is a modern skeleton your best chance of identifying it is probably through dental records. You need to find as many of the teeth as you can.'

'In this bog?' Mower muttered, looking down at the soft, almost liquid earth beneath his boots and at the search team whose blue overalls were now caked with the stuff. Their sergeant looked questioningly in Mower's direction.

'Keep going. We need the teeth,' Mower called and turned away, with Atherton, from the incredulous stare and unspoken discontent the instruction provoked.

'Where's your boss, then?' Atherton asked after the two men had scrambled to the higher ground above the workings.

'Taken himself back to the office,' Mower said bitterly. 'How do we know when we've collected all the bits, then?'

'Take what you've got to the mortuary and I'll do a preliminary assembly, then you can bring the rest in as you work and

I'll let you know when to stop,' Atherton said with cheerful matter-of-factness. 'It's only like a jigsaw puzzle, after all. But unless you come up with more than you've got there you'll never get an identification, or even know whether there's one body or more. These days they very often come in batches, after all.'

Mower gave the slightest shudder of distaste at that but Atherton snuggled himself into his roomy waterproof against the gusting rain and gave the Detective Sergeant a beaming smile.

'It's good to see you back on duty, lad,' he said. 'I thought you might have had enough after that last little caper.'

Mower glanced away at the town in the valley below, where a single shaft of weak sunlight suddenly caught the curiously shortened stump of a church tower against a backdrop of boxy modern buildings, a flash of golden light which lasted only seconds before the rain swirled in and obliterated the view again. What was left of St Jude's church reminded him sharply of the menace which occasionally lurked in this obstinately surviving little town with its heart down in the valley between its seven surrounding steep hills. He was seized with the Londoner's sense that this was a foreign country and felt a stab of nostalgia for the warm, stale air and self-absorbed crowds of the Underground, where the weather was an irrelevance.

'Being in hospital certainly gave me time to think,' he said bleakly. 'Now, if I can get the blasted traumatic stress counsellors out of my hair, I'd quite like to forget it, thanks very much.'

'Giving you a hard time, are they?'

'You could say that. As for getting out, I suppose when it comes down to it, I don't know how to do anything else, so I guess I'm stuck with it. And with bloody Bradfield.'

Going back to London as a copper was, he knew, impossible but time seemed to be doing nothing to dim the exile's sense of injustice at being wrenched from the familiar bustle and glitz, particularly as his departure had been more forced than voluntary.

'Aye, well, stay long enough, Sergeant, and we'll have you drinking Tetleys and laikin' cricket like a native,' Atherton said heartily. 'Your Superintendent Jack Longley, who had the misfortune to be born in Derbyshire, reckons it takes about thirty years to be accepted. You've nobbut another twenty-eight to go.'

'God help me,' Mower said under his breath.


'What's all this then?' Ted Grant, the editor of the *Bradfield Gazette*, asked, stopping short on his post-prandial amble around the newsroom and leaning over Laura Ackroyd's shoulder, breathing heavily and alcoholicly down her neck. Laura inched away from the steamy gust just enough to avoid passive intoxication and not enough to cause offence. She cursed herself for her carelessness in opening the bulky package in front of her at her office desk.

'John Blake,' Grant went on, picking up one of the glossy publicity photographs which Laura had been studying. 'Flippin' 'eck, I thought he was dead.'

'He's not that old,' Laura said mildly, ever aware that after lunch Grant's volatile temper was even more uncertain. She pushed her cloud of copper hair away from her face and turned slightly to face her boss, her eyes level with the white shirt front which strained over one of the more substantial beer bellies to grace a profession in which there was still fierce competition. She was wearing an open-necked green shirt which she instantly knew she had unbuttoned one button too far when she saw Grant's eyes glancing downwards. She took hold of the gold chain around her neck, conveniently blocking off the view Ted evidently appreciated so much.

'He's coming to Bradfield to open this new cinema museum they're putting into Fosters' Mills,' she said, willing Grant to move away. 'He's had some part in setting it up, apparently. Part of the Tourism Initiative.'

'Tourism Initiative!' Grant's contempt was massive. 'I've never been able to see who'd want to come touring to Bradfield. What's it got to offer, for God's sake, apart from curry restaurants and a Mickey Mouse university?'

Laura swallowed the first riposte which sprang to mind and counted to ten as, to her relief, Grant stepped slightly to one side and leaned his bulk against the side of her desk, hands in pockets, pale blue eyes in florid face now showing signs of interest as well as antagonism.

'He's also planning to look for locations for his new film, according to this PR stuff,' she said. 'He's going to play Mr Rochester in a version of *Jane Eyre* and he's particularly keen to film parts of it in Yorkshire. We should get some good copy out of it.'

'I thought John Blake's filming days were long done,' Grant said. 'I never liked him, myself. I could never see what all the fuss was when he made that Western they all raved about. But the ladies seemed to like it. What was it called?'

'*Sierra Farewell*, 1961,' Laura said. 'Shades of Gary Cooper.' She shuffled through the sheaf of photographs to uncover one of a much younger John Blake in black shirt and stetson, sideburns and sidelong smile. 'Before my time, but he was certainly quite a hunk in his day.'

'Huh. He must be sixty-odd, now,' Grant said, putting the black and white picture alongside the more recent colour shot of the actor, a comparison which was not flattering. Blake had all too obviously put on some weight around the jowls and the eyes, dark and amused in youth, had lost their sparkle in late middle age.

'That hair's dyed, and he must have had a couple of face-lifts by the look of him. Sixty if he's a day.'

'A bit old to play Mr Rochester, I'd have thought,' Laura said.

'*Jane Eyre*,' Grant said thoughtfully. 'Another of these costume sagas they're so keen on just now, is it?'

'Charlotte Brontë,' Laura said circumspectly. 'You know? Haworth? *Wuthering Heights* – though that was the other sister.'

'Aye, I know all about them,' Grant said quickly. 'It was Blake I was interested in. Wasn't there some Hollywood scandal, nearly finished him off? What was it? Drink? Drugs? You'd best look him up in the cuttings. Those publicity people'll only tell you what they want you to know.'

'You want me to do a feature?' Laura asked carefully, hardly able to believe that she had been so conveniently unhooked from what threatened to be a serious embarrassment.

11

'Well, you better had, if he's coming to town. There's always a bit of copy about when they make a film – actresses throwing tantrums, actors looking for new wives, backers backing off, that sort of thing. When's he arriving?'

'Next week. He's coming up to do his recce and then the museum opening is on the following Wednesday.'

'Right, well, pencil summat in for the Tuesday on your feature page and then we'll give it some news coverage when the museum opens.'

'Right,' Laura said faintly as Grant levered himself upright again and continued his beady-eyed perambulation between the reporters' desks and into his own office at the other end of the room. Carefully she extracted a letter from the heap of photographs and publicity material which Grant had riffled through and which his sharp eyes had fortunately missed. She folded it and put it into her handbag, before making her way as unobtrusively as she knew how into the library on the floor above. She was well aware, as she usually was, that more than one pair of male eyes followed her progress to the newsroom door, feasting on her long dark-stockinged legs beneath the short black skirt.

The library file on John Blake was not a bulky one. Recent cuttings spoke of the 'former Hollywood star' almost as if he were dead. The explanation came in a bundle of yellowing but more extensive articles that outlined acrimonious divorce proceedings in California in the late 1970s during which Blake's estranged wife had accused him of an interest in under-age girls. There were a lot of sins the famous could get away with in Tinsel Town, Laura thought, but even in the licentious seventies that was probably one of the tougher accusations – it never appeared to have been substantiated – to live down.

Whatever the reason, John Blake's career had begun a downward spiral from that moment on. His last film – given an unenthusiastic review even in the *Gazette*, whose film critic, Paddy Stanford, watched the screen through a permanent alcoholic haze and seldom overestimated the intelligence or discrimination of his readers – had bombed in 1985. After that, as far as the *Gazette*'s record went, John Blake's Hollywood career had ended.

Laura took the covering letter which had arrived with the package of publicity material out of her bag and read it through again with some elation. It was from a colour magazine editor for whom she had done some freelance work before, asking her to do a major feature on John Blake's return to England and his attempt at a film comeback in *Jane Eyre*. The commission looked like being a meatier one than she had at first realised, she thought with satisfaction. And it could just possibly be the one which offered her the key to her cell in Ted Grant's capricious prison.

She went back to her desk, picked up the phone and dialled a London number.

'Is that Lorelie Baum?' she asked when she was connected. 'I want to arrange an interview with John Blake when he visits Yorkshire next week. Can you fix that for me? It's for a profile in the *Sunday Extra* magazine.'

2

It was so long since Michael Thackeray had had anywhere to call home that he had not got used to it yet. He put his key into the front door of the tall Victorian villa, walked slowly up the three flights of stairs to Laura Ackroyd's top-floor flat and let himself in with a mixture of apprehension and delight. But even before he stepped over the threshold he realised that Laura was not there.

His disappointment at finding the flat empty was piercing. He stood for a moment looking round the small living room, taking in the familiar signs of her presence: the untidy pile of newspapers on the shelf underneath the television, the flamboyant gold silk poppies in the jug on the narrow hearth in front of the small black cast-iron grate, the book left open on the coffee table where Laura had put it down the previous evening when he had enticed her to bed. Gradually he felt soothed by her presence even in her absence.

He still felt half a stranger here in a home which Laura had created not for him but for herself, but he did not mind that. He had no talent in that direction and less inclination. His only other home since he had left his parents' farm to go to university had been created for him by another woman whose youthful face he now sometimes had difficulty in recalling. He had never had the heart to try to emulate what he regarded as a uniquely feminine gift. When he had lost its benefits he had simply gone without, camping out in a series of bleak and utilitarian lodgings upon which he made no effort to imprint his personality or taste. It was not until he had moved in with Laura a couple of months before that he had become aware of what he had previously lost and now painfully and tentatively regained.

He put a Billie Holiday CD, his own, on Laura's stereo and stood for a moment as the strains of 'Stormy Blues' filled the flat. There were times when he woke in the middle of the night with a sense of shock at finding Laura's warm body curled in sleep against his own. He could not believe his good fortune and in the dark watches of the night expected it to disappear in the miasma of cruel memories which still haunted him. More than once he had put an arm around her and half wakened her simply for the reassurance of her sleepy voice and the comfort of the arm which she invariably twined around him as she settled herself for sleep again.

'You are an untidy wretch,' he said softly to himself as he went into the kitchen and began to stack the scattered breakfast crockery in the sink. He turned on the hot water, squeezed washing up liquid into the bowl and contentedly watched the foam rise and sparkle. He had finished drying the dishes and stacked them away methodically in the kitchen cupboards before he heard the front door open and close.

'You're late,' he said, helping her off with her wet coat and taking the opportunity to lift her hair and kiss her neck gently just below the ear. She pulled him close and kissed him on the lips.

'You,' she said tartly, 'are bloody early. When did you ever get back at six? Your performance indicators will be through the floor if you're not careful, Chief Inspector. Your arrest rate will be bottom of the league. All the little toe-rags up at Wuthering will be laughing all the way to the dealer.'

She pulled away from him, knowing that if she didn't she would need to kiss him again, and then again, and there would only be one end to the encounter.

'I thought you'd found a brand-new skeleton to play with, anyway,' she said. 'That's what Bob Baker, my esteemed crime colleague on the *Gazette*, has been telling the public all afternoon. Isn't it right?' She dropped a copy of the last edition of the *Gazette* on the coffee table and indicated its bold black headline: DIGGER UNEARTHS SKELETON.

'He is, and we do,' Thackeray acknowledged. 'But for all we know it might be Piltdown woman. It's just a collection of bones so far. We won't know any more until the forensic labs have had a good look at them.'

Laura shivered slightly although the room was warm.

'We haven't got another Fred West at large, have we?'

'I hope not,' Thackeray said soberly. 'There's coppers in Gloucester who'll never recover from that.'

'Reporters too, from what I hear,' Laura said softly. 'That's a trial I'm glad I didn't have to cover.' Avoiding his eyes, she took off her coat and hung it up. There were aspects of his work, the worst of it, that he resolutely refused to share with her and she did not think this was the moment, as the remnants of some long-buried horror were dragged from the grave, to try to exorcise his demons.

'I went to see Joyce on the way home,' she said.

'How is she?'

'Not good,' Laura said, unable to keep a note of deep anxiety out of her voice. Her grandmother, fiercely independent and occasionally obstreperous, had suffered a fall, broken a leg and was languishing in a bed at the Bradfield Infirmary.

'She's not seriously ill, is she?' Thackeray said sharply, knowing how hard Laura would take that, but she shook her head.

'Physically she's mending fine for someone her age. Every other way she's creating merry hell. They need her bed, want her moved, but they say she's not fit enough to go home unless the council comes up with some care – which they won't – and she refuses point blank to go into a private nursing home. Says she worked all her life to get a decent health service and she's bloody well not going private now.'

Thackeray smiled. Both in looks and temperament there was more than a touch of Joyce in her grand-daughter and he sympathised with medical and social workers who had come up against that streak of Ackroyd obstinacy which showed no sign of diluting itself down the generations.

'They suggested I should bring her here,' Laura said. 'But I told them that was crazy – three floors up in a wheelchair and no possibility of her getting out on her own. She'd go bananas stuck up here on her own all day.'

'This isn't a sensible place for someone disabled,' Thackeray said. 'I know what it's like. She wouldn't be able to get a wheelchair into that tiny kitchen of yours.'

Laura glanced at him sharply. He seldom talked about his family or the mother who had spent years in a wheelchair before she died. The fact that he had even mentioned her in passing was, she thought, a good sign, a sign that perhaps their often tense relationship might one day achieve normality.

'You think I was right to say no to that then?' she asked anxiously. 'Joyce backed me up, said it was impossible, because of my job, but I wondered if she was hurt . . .'

'You can't bring her here, Laura,' Thackeray said flatly, putting his arm around her. 'You're right, she's right, there has to be another solution and it's their job to find it.'

'I think I'll ring my father,' Laura said slowly. 'Joyce doesn't want me to but I think he should know what's going on.' She glanced at her watch, casting her mind a thousand miles to her parents' retirement home in Portugal. 'They'll just be changing ready for an aperitif on the terrace,' she said. 'That would be the best place for Joyce to recuperate, you know. A villa all on one floor, a shady terrace to sit out on, a view over the bay to Cascais . . . Fat chance. But I'll tell him just the same.'

But before she could pick up the phone, it rang.

'It's for you,' she said, handing Thackeray the receiver, unable to resist a small satisfied smile of acknowledgement that he now left her number as his contact. She had recognised Sergeant

16

Kevin Mower's voice at the other end, and the subdued excitement in it. But she watched Thackeray with a sense of foreboding as he listened to Mower without speaking. She saw his jaw tighten. His work consisted almost entirely of news which was more or less bad. There was no reason for her to suppose that this call brought tidings any worse than he handled daily, but she was sure it did.

He hung up and gave her a rueful smile.

'I need to go back to the office,' he said. 'Not for long, but they've found some more remains at the building site, not just bones this time, some bits of jewellery, pretty modern, not old . . . I need to see.'

'Not Piltdown woman, then,' Laura said more lightly than she felt.

'I'm afraid not, no,' Thackeray said. 'It looks as though she's maybe a whole lot younger than that.'


The plastic evidence bag contained a small gold cross, still attached to a fragment of chain. Thackeray picked it up and felt the shape through the protective film as if to make sure that it was real.

'Is that it?' he asked Sergeant Mower, who was sitting at his desk, shirt-sleeves rolled up and tie loose, his hair still wet from his long muddy stint at the building site.

'There were some more bones,' he said. 'Still not a complete skeleton. They've been taken down to the infirmary to help Amos with his jigsaw. I've called the team off until the morning now. They're not going to find anything else unless we can extend the search area and that's best done in daylight. Whoever she is she's been buried long and deep. Another few hours isn't going to make much difference.'

'No indication of the cause of death?'

'No, nothing obvious. And no remnants of clothing, no shoes,' Mower said sombrely. 'That could all have rotted away with the rest of her or she could have been put into the ground naked, Amos says. But my guess is that whoever she is, she's been there a very long time.'

17

'And there are no recent suspicious disappearances which would fit? Murder cases still on file?'

'Well, nothing since I've been here, Guv,' said Mower, who had arrived in Bradfield from the Metropolitan Force two years previously. 'You know West Yorkshire better than I do. I've asked around the station but there's nothing anyone can recall, nothing that instantly springs to mind. Obviously there'll be more people here in the morning. We can search the files properly then. And Superintendent Longley's due back tomorrow, isn't he? Someone might come up with something.'

Thackeray nodded. He had been in the county, though not until recently in Bradfield, for the whole of his career, but he could not remember any case of the suspicious disappearance of a young woman which could easily be identified with the body that had turned up that morning, or the small cruciform piece of gold which he still held in his hand.

'The Super won't be in a very good mood after three days of management theory down at County HQ,' Thackeray said. 'They'll be wanting to know why he hasn't completed his policing plan, and I know for a fact he's got no reason at all except sheer bloody-mindedness – I reckon he'll have had a rough time. So watch your step if you're thinking of picking his brains.'

'Right, Guv,' Mower said thoughtfully.

'How far back do the missing person files go?' Thackeray asked, turning his mind once more to the problem in hand.

'On computer, ten years, Guv,' Mower said. 'Any further back and you're into dusty paper in the basement. But there'll be thousands of names, most of them girls and women who simply decided they wanted to be somewhere else.'

'Well, this one ended up in a muddy grave and I've no doubt she was somebody's wife or daughter,' Thackeray said. 'So we may have to blow the dust off a few files. In the meantime, what about the area where she was found? It's just a bloody great hole in the ground now, but what used to be there?'

Mower reached across his desk with a faint smile of self-satisfaction. He had never found Thackeray an easy master to please but reckoned that as he got to know him better he was at

18

least beginning to anticipate his moves. The folded sheets of paper he pulled towards him should earn him a few Brownie points, he reckoned.

'This is a map of that part of Bradfield before they started the demolition work three or four months ago,' he said. 'The site they're working on used to be allotments at the end of Peter Street, which led off Peter Hill. Here look.'

Thackeray pulled up a chair and bent over the map, following Mower's finger.

'This is a derelict clothing factory, went out of business in eighty-six,' the Sergeant said, pointing to a rectangular site on one side of the narrow street. 'And this terrace is boarded up now, empty and waiting for demolition.'

'The tall Victorian houses we passed on the way into the site?' Thackeray said.

'That's right. They've been multi-occupied and deteriorating for years, apparently. The houses and the factory are due to come down in the second phase of the redevelopment.'

'So if the body was local we'd have the devil's own job finding people who used to live round there?' Thackeray said. 'How long have the houses been empty?'

'Eighteen months, according to the site foreman, O'Halloran. But they weren't nice stable family homes, in any case. "A right dump," he called them. Split up into flats and bedsits with short-term tenants. "Winos and druggies" O'Halloran said.'

'The more you tell me, the less I like the sound of this,' Thackeray said gloomily.

'Do I set up an incident room in the morning?' Mower asked.

'No, you don't,' Thackeray said flatly. 'Until we know just how old the bones are we'd be wasting our time and sending the overtime budget through the roof for no useful purpose. We'll just take it a step at a time, wait for some sort of answer from forensics, before we go rushing in. This could be some little Victorian housemaid who got in the family way and was bumped off by her lover. It could be a bomb victim they never found during the war. There were one or two bombs fell on Bradfield, I seem to remember my father saying. Mistook it for Manchester, or something daft.'

'Or it could be another prostitute knocked off by whoever's been knocking them off all over the north for years,' Mower objected. 'Or a runaway who never made it out of town ... I could start looking through the files, Guv. That wouldn't do any harm.'

Thackeray put the evidence bag with its bright trinket, undimmed by time or mud, carefully down on Mower's desk. The Sergeant was right, he knew, but that did not prevent him harbouring a deep reluctance to admit it. If he was honest with himself, he hated murder investigations, however satisfactory the conclusion. More than any other crime, he thought, murder damaged the innocent as well as the guilty, casting suspicion on blameless lives that had touched the victim's, casting a shadow which might never be lifted over families and individuals who were brushed by grief or the slimy finger of suspicion. He had no more idea than Mower how the unknown woman who had been dragged back to the surface of the earth that morning had died. But he nurtured a fervent hope that it was so long ago that it need not concern him or anyone else still living.

'Wait,' he said more sharply than he intended. 'There's nothing we can do but wait. Just concentrate on the burglaries in Southwell tomorrow, and wait for Amos Atherton's report. Whoever she is, she's long gone. She's one woman in your life who really won't mind if you keep her waiting.'


# 3


John Blake stood at the window of his suite at the Dorchester, gazing at the traffic sweeping down Park Lane and smiled a self-satisfied smile. Across the road the broad expanse of Hyde Park stretched almost as far as the eye could see, acres of undulating green sward dotted with clumps of trees and scattered with deck-chairs where a few early summer sun-worshippers were already stretched out amongst the morning strollers and joggers.

Blake was a tall figure, his hair still dark and worn slightly longer than was considered fashionable in nineties London, his face showing few signs that his sixtieth birthday was just months away. Only a close examination would have revealed that his classic good looks owed much to the cosmetic surgeon's skill and trichologist's art.

He had kept his body in good shape though. In fact he had made almost a religion of it during the later, fallow years of his career. Not for him the classic Hollywood props of booze or drugs. Working out had kept him lean enough, the Californian sunshine had kept him tanned, the claret silk dressing gown, which was all he had put on for the late Continental breakfast still spread on the mahogany dining table behind him, was cinched in tightly around a still enviable waist with no hint of a belly. The fans who had idolised him as a much younger man would not have had any difficulty in recognising him had he chosen to leave the sybaritic embrace of the hotel and take a stroll through the throngs of West End shoppers just streets away.

In the park, a pair of glossy chestnut horses trotted past on the sandy shingle bridle-path which followed the curve of the road, their riders immaculate in black jackets and hard hats, bottoms in skin-tight jodhpurs rising rhythmically in the style you did not often see in America. He liked tight little bottoms, he thought with a faint smile. He liked Lorelie's bottom encased in its tight Lycra mini-skirt.

His attention was caught by a Rolls which had drawn up outside the hotel's main entrance below and he watched entranced as a tall Arab in snow-white traditional robes and a red and white banded head-dress got out, followed by two women veiled to the eyes in black. They were welcomed promptly by the uniformed flunkey on the door. He had been too long away, he thought. He had almost forgotten the sheer cosmopolitan elegance of this part of London, the still restrained display of wealth, so unlike the brash extravagance of the California where he had, he thought regretfully, perhaps spent too much of his life.

Not that he had been able to appreciate these sorts of attractions when he had worked in the city as a young actor. All he could remember almost forty years on were the endless queues of the post-war capital. Queues at the dole office where he signed on most weeks and at the scruffy little employment agency specialising in kitchen skivvy jobs to which he resorted occasionally in financial desperation; queues in the wings at theatres as he waited for one audition or another, never sure whether what was required was a cut-glass accent or his native northern vowels as drama lurched from Rattigan to Osborne.

There had been queues for buses and queues at Underground stations, even queues at his agent's, more often than not, as he waited impatiently to discuss a career which seemed to have taken the down escalator without ever setting foot on the up.

The chasm between his chilly, dismal digs in Kentish Town and the Dorchester had been as deep as any he had ever crossed. He might take the Tube back up to Tufnell Park, he thought, just for old times' sake, to see if the tall brick house where he had rented a damp top-floor room was still there. But then again, he might not. Nostalgia, he reckoned, was a dangerous emotion to indulge in, especially on this side of the Pond. Better to leave the past strictly undisturbed.

It was only the chance of publicity for the Brontë project which had persuaded him to ignore the determination of the best part of a lifetime never to return to England. But Rochester was a part he desperately wanted to play, the tragic romantic lead he felt he deserved after years of dismal 'cameo' roles or no roles at all. If Newman and Eastwood could keep going at his age, he saw no reason why he should be any different. But this was his last chance of a comeback, of that he was quite sure. And with the current, slightly astonishing surge of interest in costume drama and a writer of the calibre of Brad Bateman with a screenplay already written, it was a chance worth taking a risk for.

Behind him he heard Lorelie Baum put the phone down. He turned and picked up the tall flute of Buck's fizz he had left on the breakfast table.

'Well?' he asked, in the voice, deep and rich and just slightly husky, which had caused thousands (if not the millions he imagined) of feminine hearts to flutter in the early 1960s. He knew his voice at least was surprisingly untouched by the years.

'Well, not bad, honey,' Lorelie said, glancing down at the clipboard of papers on which she had been making notes. She was perhaps half his age, with the emaciated figure of a model, breasts of silicone voluptuousness and the eyes of a tiger. She wore a skin-tight black mini-skirt and a peacock-blue silk shirt open to her cleavage, with chunky gold jewellery at the neck and ears and weighing down long slim fingers with nails as red and glossy as her lips. She waved her pen at her notes.

'*The Globe* will go for an interview. So will *Movietime*. We lunch with them today. The *Evening Mail* will get back to us. So will the *Courier*'s show-biz person. And then when we get up to York-sheer . . .' She pronounced it as if the syllables were separate words and she knew the meaning of neither. 'Up there we've got this interview arranged with a local hackette, been commissioned for the *Sunday Extra* magazine. They want to concentrate on the prodigal returning angle, you know? A bit like that artist going back to his home town to see his old Ma. What's his name? The one with all the swimming pools and the gays in the shower? Wasn't that in York-sheer too?'

'Hockney,' Blake said shortly, flattered by the comparison but still self-aware enough to know that his return to his native turf was not quite in that league. 'But you can forget all that prodigal son stuff. As far as my fans are concerned I'm an adopted American. That's the way I've always preferred it.'

'Right,' Lorelie said dubiously. 'So, we've the two days here for interviews, then I've rented you a limo for the trip to the north and you'll have a week before the museum opening. That will give you time to do your recce for locations before you need to come back to London to meet the backers the next Friday. And we can fit in the interviews with this local journo – Laura Ake-royd . . .'

'Ackroyd,' Blake said irritably. 'You pronounce it Ackroyd.'

'Sure,' Lorelie said easily. 'And you can fix a visit to your aged Ma on the way. That should make a good photo-call for the local press . . .'

'Nope, no pictures of my mother,' Blake said sharply. 'She's very old and she doesn't like her picture taken. Has always hated it.'

'But John, honey, that's a real shame,' Lorelie protested. 'That's a great angle for us. A really great angle.'

'You can work on a story, but no pictures,' Blake said, the once famous dark blue eyes as cold as a winter pool. 'What you've got to remember, Lorelie, is how darned depressed and miserable that part of Yorkshire was when I was a kid – dark, dirty, puritanical ... Why do you think I got away as soon as I could and never went back? I hated those grim little towns we lived in – Bradfield, Millfield, Eckersley. Here today and gone tomorrow. Hated them, always did and always will. The last thing we want is someone crawling out of the woodwork to tell the press how I spent most of my youth working out how I could break loose. It's not as if I was even born there. I hardly know where I was born, for Christ's sake.'

'Gee, I didn't realise it was as bad as that,' Lorelie said, her lips taking on a faint pout.

'It's nothing you can't handle,' Blake said easily, running a hand through her hair and down the long neck, not stopping at the collar of her shirt. She shuddered as his fingers reached her breasts, although a watcher might have been hard pressed to judge whether in anticipation or fear.

'Why do you think I brought you with me?' he asked, unbuttoning her deftly.

'I thought there were other reasons,' she said, letting her clipboard slide to the floor and hitching up her short skirt over silky underwear.

'Those too,' he said, but his voice was muffled as he slid off her French knickers and buried his face between her legs. She closed her fingers tightly on the back of his thick hair, taking care not to disturb his toupee.

'Cool,' she sighed and shut her eyes. Then she screamed.


Superintendent Jack Longley walked into Bradfield police head-quarters that morning in a mood so dark that it could have extinguished every light in the building. It was another wet morning and on the hillside site a mile away a dozen of his officers were still scrabbling in deep mud and occasionally coming up with a relic which would be tentatively identified as human. Up above them Pete O'Halloran watched gloomily, clutching his mobile phone and trying to reassure the main contractor's office that it would be possible to recommence work some time soon.

Once back in his office Longley skimmed through the reports on his desk with simmering irritation before picking up the phone and summoning his DCI peremptorily.

'A good conference, sir?' Thackeray asked cautiously as he responded promptly to the call he had been expecting.

'Bloody awful,' Longley said shortly. 'Those beggars seem to think that if we clock up arrests of a couple of dozen kids with spliffs in their pocket rather than concentrating on banging up the six or seven serious villains we've got in this town we've done summat useful for society. All they're bothered about is number-crunching. The sooner I get out of this mad-house the better.'

Thackeray nodded. He shared Longley's conviction that much of the management culture being imposed on the police service from above was profoundly misguided but did not have the option of a swift exit into retirement open to him yet.

'Any road – you're my crime manager. How's crime managing? What's all this about a body?' Longley asked, flicking a finger at the report which lay on top of the pile. 'Recent, is it?'

'Amos Atherton thinks not,' Thackeray said. 'I've got a team still working up there and gradually Amos is piecing together a skeleton, though it seems unlikely we'll find everything he'd like. They've not come up with much this morning. And there's no trace of anything except bones – no remnants of hair, clothing, shoes, anything of that sort, which leads Amos to think she's been there a long time.'

'She? It's definitely she, is it?'

'Amos reckons so from a quick examination of the remains,' Thackeray said. 'Female and relatively young, he says, though he needs more time and specialist tests to be sure. And then there's the crucifix and chain. It may have nothing to do with the body, may simply have been lost in the area by someone else, but it was found close to the bones, so I'm working on the hypothesis that they belong together.'

'Any likely missing persons?'

'Mower's done a quick run-through and come up with half a dozen names – two prostitutes who've not been seen for years, a sixth-form girl who went missing in 1981 and has never turned up, though there were suggestions that an unsuitable boyfriend might have gone away with her, a mother of two who apparently walked out on a sticky marriage in eighty-four, and another woman who disappeared in the family car in eighty-nine, leaving a note saying she'd had enough. But she was in her forties and Amos reckons this is a relatively young girl.'

'But he can't tell you how old the remains are? When she was buried, I mean?'

'No. And it's not easy to work that out, he says. There are chemical tests the labs can do on the bones and the surrounding soil but they're not very accurate and they'll take time. He's going to consult some expert forensic anthropologist in Manchester when he's completed his own examination. He reckons he can give us sex and a rough age but he's unlikely to come up with a cause of death unless there are obvious injuries like a bullet wound.'

'Bloody hell,' Longley said. 'So what we've got is an unknown female who died on an unknown date from an unknown cause. I can't see that improving our performance indicators much, can you?'

'I think we should leave it alone until the forensic tests are completed,' Thackeray said slowly.

'Aye, we'll play it down with the press for the time being,' Longley said. 'You've enough to do without chasing ghosts. Though there is one line you could get that sharp young beggar Mower to follow up. A bit of desk research to keep him out of mischief.'

'And that is?' Thackeray asked, intrigued in spite of himself.

'It's a long shot on the basis of where this lass was found. There was a girl went missing on Coronation Day – when was that, Nineteen fifty-three? Fifty-four? I remember it because I was about the same age myself and desperate to join the Force. I saw the pictures of this pretty Italian lass who went out with a gang of lads when they got bored with watching the crowning on the telly and never came back. She lived there on Peter Hill somewhere. I remember going up there while they were searching for her, mooching about watching the coppers going house-to-house and thinking what a grand start it'd be if I could find her. One of those daft things lads do. But they never did find her. It's a long while back and it'd be the devil's own job to trace anyone who remembers the case, but it'd be worth digging out the file if it still exists.'

'Do you remember her name?' Thackeray asked, intrigued at the thought of a young Jack Longley smitten by the photograph of a pretty girl.

'No, I don't,' Longley snapped, picking up the incautious glint of amusement in Thackeray's eyes. 'But the date sticks in my mind. And the fact that she was Italian. It wasn't that long after the war, and the notion of an Italian family paying less than total attention to the Coronation didn't go down too well, I remember. Her father was an ex-PoW who stayed on and brought his family over, as far as I can recall. There was still some prejudice around in the fifties.'

'I can imagine,' Thackeray said feelingly. Prejudice against incomers was not something which had faded much over the last few decades in this part of England in his experience, and the opportunity to display it had grown exponentially as a trickle of post-war refugees from Europe had turned into a flood of immigrants from Asia.

'Italian, therefore Catholic, therefore wearing a gold crucifix,' he said thoughtfully. 'It's a possibility.'

'Aye, well, a possibility but no more,' Longley said dismissively. 'Don't waste your time on it until you get some forensic evidence. If there's a chance she's been there forty months rather than forty years there's no point in taking the difficult option before you have to. If it is the Italian lass the chances are whoever buried her's long dead too. So it's hardly worth fretting over, is it?'

# 4

'Mariella Bonnetti,' Joyce Ackroyd said firmly.

'What?' her grand-daughter said abstractedly, kneeling down awkwardly to try to fit a pile of books into the small locker beside Joyce's bed.

'Mariella,' Joyce repeated sharply. 'She disappeared on Coronation Day. They never found her. Your father was always out playing with her.'

Laura knelt back on her heels and looked at Joyce in astonishment.

'Playing with her?' she exclaimed. 'Playing what, for God's sake?'

'Cricket,' Joyce said, wincing as she tried to move herself into a more upright position against her pillows. She had been delivered under protest to the Laurels Nursing Home by ambulance that morning, wheeled into the tiny single room which Laura was presently trying to make a little more homelike, and, complaining loudly, had been put to bed. In spite of her protests Laura had found her asleep soon after lunch, looking frail and every inch the old woman she resolutely refused to admit she was. She had clutched the bedclothes with arthritis-gnarled hands as she woke, and Laura thought she caught her blinking away tears, though more of frustration than self-pity, she was sure.

But now Joyce's eyes were sparkling with glee and her face was alive with interest.

'Cricket?' Laura said faintly, scrambling to her feet and pulling the room's single, not very comfortable chair into the narrow space between the bed and the wall. 'What on earth are you talking about?'

Joyce looked at her grand-daughter in triumph, astonished as always at seeing so clearly a resurrected version of herself, slim-hipped, green-eyed and with that unruly mop of red hair which she guessed attracted as many admirers now as it had done when she had been young. One of the sadnesses of a life almost without vanity had been watching her crowning glory fade away with the years to its present snow-white.

'This skeleton they've found at Peter Hill, of course,' Joyce said, aware of a sparkle in Laura's eyes which matched her own. 'It was all over the front page of your newspaper yesterday afternoon. Don't you read what your colleagues write? Didn't I ever tell you I lived there for a while after the war? Me and your dad. We had rooms in one of those houses in Peter Street, the ones they're going to pull down.'

'Good lord,' Laura said. 'I thought you lived up at the Heights, before it was the Heights of course, before they pulled the old terraces down and built the flats . . .'

''That was later,' Joyce said impatiently. 'Immediately after the war you had to take what you could get. When your grandfather was killed I couldn't afford the house we'd been renting. I was lucky to get the Peter Street place. It wasn't a palace, but it wasn't a slum either. Not then, any road. Those places got very run down later.'

'And this girl? What did you call her? Maria?'

'Mariella,' Joyce said. 'There was an Italian family living two doors down, father, mother and a whole tribe of children. Of course they weren't very popular, being Italian, so soon after the war.' Her eyes went blank for a moment and Laura let her compose herself. The photograph of her grandfather in his army uniform was as familiar as those of her own parents. It stood now on Joyce's bedside table, and Laura guessed that the young soldier who had left her to go to war was as close to her as the day she had married him. Joyce sighed and Laura touched her hand gently.

'Mariella?' she said softly.

'Her father had come over here as a PoW – a prisoner of war – and decided to stay. Mariella was the oldest of the children. She'd been born in Italy before the war and came over here afterwards when her father sent for her and her mother. The other children were much younger, born here when the family was together again. Mariella and her mother spoke poor English, spoke Italian to each other most of the time, as far as I can remember. She was fifteen that year, the year of the Coronation, the year she disappeared. A lovely looking lass, very dark, dark eyes, dazzled all the young lads, including your father.'

'But Dad must have been much younger than that,' Laura objected, doing a few quick sums in her head.

'Oh, yes, he was only twelve or so. He was the baby of that little gang.'

'Gang?' Laura said faintly.

'Not a gang in the sense you mean it now, drugs and knives and joy-riding,' Joyce came back sharply. 'Playmates, more like. There were four, maybe five lads, teenagers you'd call them these days, and your dad who was younger. Mariella and her little brothers used to tag along, though they were more hangers-on, really. Not really accepted. But they went around in a group, played cricket in the summer, in the winter too if it was fine, kicked a ball around the street after school if it wasn't, came begging for extra points to buy sweeties, made a damn nuisance of themselves on Mischief Night. And the bonfires. You've never seen owt like the bonfires they built for Guy Fawkes. They collected wood and rubbish for months ahead. A huge great fire they had, on the allotments, making up for all the ones they'd missed during the black-out, I dare say.'

'And Mariella disappeared?'

Joyce closed her eyes for a moment and lay back against her pillows. Laura watched the flickering of her eyelids and thought for a moment her grandmother's energy had deserted her after the tense transfer from the infirmary and she was drifting back into sleep. But eventually she opened her eyes again and gave Laura a faint smile.

'It's all so long ago, it's hard to remember what it was like. We were packed into those terraced houses, you know, all higgledy-piggledy, one family on top of another, all of us refugees of one sort and another. In some ways that made folk even more anxious to keep themselves to themselves. There were a lot of mothers on their own, single parents they'd call them now but then of course some of us had lost our husbands in the war so that was all right, quite respectable it was, to be a war widow.

Though there was always the odd jack the lad who thought we were fair game if we didn't have a man about. But it wasn't the sort of cosy community people like to tell you existed in those days. There was a lot of unhappiness. A lot of despair.

'But on Coronation Day people did get together. Everyone crammed into one of the flats to watch it on telly. The Parkinsons, they were called. Her lad was the oldest, I think. Just about ready to leave the grammar school. I'm blowed if I can remember his name. They weren't there long. And there was a little lass, Pamela, I think. A big gap between them, because of the war, I suppose. Any road, Mrs P. was the only one who had a TV, so we all went there. The kids sat on the floor with the adults crammed in behind. Thought she was a cut above, she did, but I persuaded her she should invite the neighbours in.

'You couldn't see much, to be perfectly honest. The picture kept disappearing in a snow-storm and the youngsters soon got bored and started whining and got sent out to play. We were supposed to be having a street party at tea-time but it was so wet it had to be cancelled. Everyone just took the sandwiches and things home with them to eat there. But Mariella never came home. The parents came round later in the evening looking for her, but the youngsters said that she'd left them playing in the yard of Brewster's mill opposite. There was a sort of covered part of the yard where they could play even when it was wet. No one had seen her since she set off home. They'd been teasing her again, I dare say. They had a go at all the Italian children when the mood took them.'

'Poor girl,' Laura said softly, recalling a time when she had been an object of derision in a school dormitory because her accent did not fit. Just as she had flattened out her Yorkshire vowels to meet southern expectations she had no doubt that this long-forgotten Italian girl had forced her tongue around English in an attempt to fit in.

Evidently Joyce shared her lively sense of old injustice. There was no doubt about the tear which crept down her paper-thin cheek this time.

'They never found her,' she said so softly that Laura could barely hear.

31

'And you think this body they've found could be her?'

'Well, it's in the right place, isn't it?' Joyce said. She leaned back against the pillows wearily as if talking had tired her out, her eyes taking on a distant look after shifting back forty years to revisit old sorrows. Laura watched and waited, not wanting to press her yet consumed with curiosity about this ancient tragedy in which her own father had apparently been involved.

'They never found a trace of her, you know. No one who said they saw her after she left the other children,' Joyce continued eventually. 'Where they're digging is where the allotments used to be. You could have hidden a hundred bodies there over the years, I should think, and no one would have known the difference.'

'Did the police never arrest anyone?' Laura asked.

'I don't think the police were right interested,' Joyce said, not meeting Laura's eyes. 'Reckoned she'd run off. Reckoned she was no better than she ought to be. A little Eye-tie tart, I heard one officer saying when he didn't know I could hear. Her parents were devastated.'

'Was she?' Laura asked. 'A little tart, I mean.'

'I've no idea, love,' Joyce said wearily. 'I shouldn't think so in those days. Once the war was over they tried to lock sex up in a cupboard again and throw away the key. It didn't work, of course, but nineteen fifty-three wasn't a good year for a young lass to find herself in the family way. And fear's a good contraceptive.'

'You'll have to tell the police, if you think the body could be hers,' Laura said.

'Aye, I reckon I will,' Joyce said without enthusiasm, her face pale and strained again, all the suddenly excited interest draining away as quickly as it had come. She lay back against the pillows, her eyes half closed.

'Shall I bring Michael to see you?' Laura asked gently. 'Tomorrow? When you're feeling stronger?'

'Aye, leave it till tomorrow, love,' Joyce said. She suddenly clutched the sheets convulsively and half sat up again. 'You're sure you're not paying owt for me to come to this place?' she asked fiercely. 'They're not charging you?'

'No, no, I promise,' Laura said with literal accuracy, although she knew that even though her grandmother had nothing but her pension to live on, the social workers who had found her a bed for her convalescence were more than eager to find a relative they could charge for care the hospital had refused to provide.

'Nye Bevan wouldn't have put up with any of this nonsense about paying,' Joyce said with a brave attempt at the ferocity of her old political hero. It was her proudest boast that she had once met the charismatic Welshman who had launched the National Health Service.

Laura took her hand. 'Rest and get yourself fit again,' she said. 'You don't have to worry about anything, I promise.'

'Did we fight all those battles for nothing?' Joyce asked plaintively. 'Have those beggars undone it all? Set us back half a century? Can this new lot really not put it right?'

The door opened before Laura could think of another reassuring reply she only half believed and a uniformed nurse came into the room, grim-faced and abstracted.

'You're still here,' she said to Laura with a note of accusation in her voice. 'We like them to rest after lunch, you know. This is the medical ward. You can visit again after five.'

Laura glanced at Joyce to find that she had closed her eyes. She kissed the soft, wrinkled skin of her cheek and gave her hand a final squeeze before turning to leave, suddenly overcome with a desperate fear for her future. She had never heard her normally combative grandmother so close to despair before.

Amos Atherton, his green apron stretched tight over his stomach, a surgical mask hanging loosely beneath his several chins, gazed in some satisfaction at his jigsaw of bones. He had arranged them neatly on a white Formica work-bench, away from the gleaming steel of the pathology tables under the harsh lights in the centre of the room. This was not a job for his scalpel and kidney dishes or even his hovering blood-splashed assistant who was clearing up after a post-mortem behind him. This was a puzzle Atherton had determined to solve alone.

There was little enough left of the body which had been

unearthed at Peter Hill, and nothing that needed his surgical skills. At one end lay the skull, the cranium intact and washed clean, but missing the jaw-bone and most of the teeth. As far as possible in their correct anatomical places he had arranged a collection of vertebrae and a collarbone, two portions of humerus, one for each arm, but only one painfully thin radius with none of the other arm-bones or the small bones of the hand to complete the upper limbs. Both wings of the pelvis were in place, if a little jagged round the edges where time and erosion had done their work, and the two strong thigh-bones were in place. But again the skeleton was less complete as the bones became smaller and more liable to disintegration under the weight of earth and the scatter effect of the jaws of a JCB. A small collection of so far unidentified fragments lay to one side.

Atherton barely glanced up as the door opened and DCI Thackeray came in, took off his coat and jacket, loosened his tie and crossed the room towards him, grim-faced. Atherton re-aligned one of the vertebrae to his satisfaction and wiped his hands to clear them of the slight grittiness which adhered to his skin.

'Well, Amos?' Michael Thackeray bleakly surveyed the pathetic remnants of a human being. 'What have we got?'

'Just the one body,' Atherton said. 'There's no duplicates amongst the bones. And it's a young lass. The pelvis and the skull give you a good idea of the sex of a skeleton. The pelvis here is not large but it has distinctive female characteristics. The angle between the bones here is too large to be male. And if that wasn't conclusive then the skull is. Women have a much less prominent ridge of bone here over the eyes and here ...' He turned the skull over and ran a finger along the base.

'But young, you said. How do you know that?' Thackeray asked, fascinated in spite of his distaste.

'I've been studying the text books on this one,' Atherton said, waving a hand towards a pile of books and journals which lay scattered further along the bench. 'It's not a problem you come up against that often. But the crucial thing to remember is that bones change as you get older. You know what a baby's skull's like when it's born, the throbbing gap at the crown which closes up gradually?'

Thackeray winced slightly. It was not an image he chose to recall, but Atherton ploughed on, oblivious to the policeman's discomfort, captivated by the problem in hand.

'Those sutures in the skull fuse by the age of about five. But there are changes in the skull and pelvis, the more marked sexual characteristics, which don't develop until puberty. And there are other bones which take even longer to reach their full adult shape, well into the teens in fact. A small child has about three hundred bones altogether, but an adult only has two hundred. The difference is where they've fused, two or three small child's bones going to make one adult one. The long bones of the limbs take anything up to eighteen years to fuse at each end. This girl had reached puberty but judging by her thigh-bone here . . .' He picked up the humerus and put a finger lightly on the rounded end which was marked off from the stem by what looked like a deep crack. 'Judging by this she was not yet fully mature. I would put her age between fourteen and eighteen.'

'Anything else?' Thackeray asked, casting a professional eye the length of the re-assembled skeleton in an attempt to judge the height from head to toe. Atherton picked up his train of thought easily.

'Well, there's research which tells you how to judge a person's height from the length of some of the bones, the humerus in particular, but I'll have to do a bit of research myself to find out what the formula is. But you can see from what's left of her she wasn't tall. Under five three, at a guess. But it is only a guess at this stage.'

Atherton stood back from his work-bench and flashed Thackeray a glance of some excitement.

'There is one identifying feature though,' he said.

Thackeray waited. He knew better than to rush Amos's big moment.

'Look here,' the pathologist said, picking up the single bone which had survived below the elbow. 'This has been broken at some time.' Thackeray squinted at the rough, stained surface and convinced himself that he could see a slight irregularity which could just possibly have been a break.

'Are you sure?'

'Oh, aye, quite sure,' Amos said comfortably. 'This lass broke her arm at some time and it wasn't reset that well. There's a tiny misalignment. There's no doubt about it. You can feel it. If you get anywhere near identifying her, that might be a crucial bit of evidence. But that's about as far as I'll be able to go. To find out how long she's been there we'll have to send samples away to the labs. If you want to know what she looked like you'll have to go in for some pretty expensive facial reconstruction – and even then, unless the jaw turns up, it won't be easy. Are you still searching the site?'

'No,' Thackeray said. 'I've called them off. I'm not sure they're going to find much else. The place is like a quagmire in this rain. But the contractors have agreed to leave that area undisturbed for a week at least so we have the option of going back if we need to.'

'Aye, well, unless you're lucky and come across the rest of the jaw, I'm not sure you'll find owt which will add much to what we've got,' Atherton said. 'If nowt in the way of clothes has survived with her you can reckon she's been there a long while and she'll be difficult to identify. But she certainly broke her arm at some point.'

'To be honest I don't think Jack Longley wants a murder investigation going back years if he can avoid it,' Thackeray said.

'Cost too much, won't it?' Atherton said cheerfully. 'I dare say I'm running the hospital up a pretty bill just by standing here nattering to you like this. Can't be cost effective, can it?'

Sergeant Kevin Mower stood close behind Laura Ackroyd with a feeling of faint regret. She had fastened her hair up today and he particularly admired the curve of her neck, a column of pale cream beneath the copper, which met the dark green of her shirt like the breast of a swan meeting deep water. She continued to ignore him, though hardly unconscious of his closeness and his

36

steady breathing, in the dusty recess which the *Gazette* dignified with the name of an archive. She turned over the pages of yellowing copies of the paper determinedly.

They had the heavy and dog-eared file out for 1953 and had turned to the month of June. It had been a broadsheet then, not the compact tabloid of recent years, which made it even more difficult to handle. The pages crackled ominously as they were turned and here and there a few flakes detached themselves from the edges and floated down to the dusty floor.

'They should have put all this on micro-film years ago but they're too mean,' she said.

The editions for most of Coronation week were overwhelmingly filled with special features about the royal occasion: page after page of photographs of Westminster Abbey, the processions, Queen Elizabeth and her most extrovert guest, the Queen of Tonga, the crowds in the Mall and the doggedly cheerful street parties around the country which had mostly been held in the rain.

But what they were looking for was there, hidden away at the bottom of a column on page three.

'Here you are,' Laura said. '"Girl goes missing at Coronation celebration. Fifteen-year-old Maria Bonnetti was reported missing yesterday after leaving a local Coronation party at 32A Peter Street, Bradfield." No suggestion of foul play, but maybe that's all they had room for. I think the editions went to press much later in those days but even so that story did well to get into that day's paper. There should be a fuller story the next day, I should think.'

She turned to the next edition, handling the fragile newsprint gingerly. When Mower had arrived at the front office asking to look through back copies she had been surprised to find that the *Gazette* had kept its files for so long. But she could only suppose that they had survived intact simply because so few people had ever referred to them in the intervening forty-four years.

'Here we are,' she said. 'It's graduated to the front page now. "Fears grow for missing girl." The police are involved now and Maria's been amended to Mariella. Your man in charge seems to have been an Inspector Jackson. He's issued a description and asked for anyone who has seen her to contact him urgently. Don't you have any of this in your own files?'

'Apparently not,' Mower said. 'They say they never close a murder file, but there seems to have been some doubt that this was murder at the time. They never found a body and there was a suggestion from the parents that she'd taken some money. In which case she could have run away.'

'Well, if she ran, it must have been the shortest run in history, if your skeleton really is Mariella. Do you have any evidence?'

'Not a lot,' Mower said. 'Just a hunch from Superintendent Longley, a man not usually given to hunches. He's old enough to remember the case, apparently. Old enough to retire, if you ask me. We don't even know yet if the girl's parents are still alive. This Inspector Jackson is long dead. Killed in a car accident years ago.'

'You know my grandmother knew the family?' Laura said. 'Michael's going out to talk to her this afternoon.'

'He said so,' Mower said shortly. He had not been pleased to be excluded from the visit in favour of further enquiries into the series of burglaries which was preoccupying CID. 'Can we copy these cuttings?'

'Yes, of course,' Laura said, realising she was treading on dangerous ground with Mower who, she suspected, resented her relationship with his boss more than he would ever admit. 'I'll get one of the secretaries to do it for you. I've got to get on. I'm seeing that old has-been John Blake this afternoon. He was a heart-throb of my mother's, for God's sake, and seems to think he can still make a comeback in *Jane Eyre*. Can you see him as Mr Rochester?'

'I'm not even sure I know who John Blake is and I never read *Jane Eyre*,' Mower said shortly. 'I went to a crummy comprehensive, remember?'

'You're very twitchy this morning, Kevin,' Laura said, knowing perfectly well that Mower had gone on from his London comprehensive school to take a degree.

'Let's just say I don't like being used as an office junior either, shall we?' Mower said, picking up the heavy bound volume of the *Gazette* and moving towards the door.

Laura looked at her dusty hands and grinned. Serves you right, she thought.


# 5


Laura stood at reception at the Clarendon Hotel drumming her fingers slightly impatiently on the polished mahogany counter. She had announced herself some ten minutes earlier, sat for a while in one of the soft armchairs arranged around coffee tables in the lounge, rebuffed the attentions of several waiters anxious to bring her coffee or tea, and finally gone back to the young woman at the computer to repeat her request that John Blake should be informed of her arrival.

'They said they'd be down in a couple of minutes, madam,' the receptionist said somewhat sniffily.

'They?'

'Mr Blake has his publicist with him. Ms Baum. She took the message when I called up to their suite.'

Oh, God, Laura thought irritably. The last person she wanted at this initial interview was Blake's American PR person interposing her view of what she should write between her and her subject. Laura seldom thought about her future career. It was a topic best avoided, she had concluded some time ago. Her personal life, in which she veered between hope and despair over her relationship with Michael Thackeray, and despair and hope about her grandmother's health, was so uncertain that the tiny flame of ambition which she nurtured at the core of her being occasionally seemed to die away to a mere ember.

But the feature articles she had been commissioned to write for the *Sunday Extra* magazine were, she knew, her best hope of escaping from an increasingly frustrating life on a local newspaper. They could, if they went well, just possibly allow her to have the best of both worlds: an entry into national journalism and a means of remaining, for some of the time at least, in Bradfield. So she felt a certain anxiety in the pit of her stomach as she waited to meet John Blake. It was not every day that she had the chance to write about even a slightly faded international fim actor. She did not intend to mess it up.

He stepped out of the lift in a cloud of expensive aftershave, immaculate in a dark blue silk shirt and a beige Armani suit, the jacket slung over his shoulders, perfectly coiffed and, Laura suspected, made-up, and every inch the star. He acknowledged the turning of heads in the lobby as no more than his due. In spite of herself Laura was impressed. She had a deep suspicion of anything which could remotely be described as charisma, but she had to admit that was precisely what John Blake had.

'Miss Ackroyd?' he said, striding towards Laura, closely followed by a stick-thin person in mini-skirt and high-heeled shoes who Laura supposed must be Lorelie Baum. The star's dark, assessing eyes did a sweep from Laura's own lace-up boots, taking in her inexpensive black trouser suit and silky shirt with a certain disdain but pausing with just a flicker of admiration when he reached her perfect oval face and fiery hair.

'I am so pleased to meet you. I am so delighted that you're doing this piece for the *Extra*. Absolutely delighted.'

The voice was deep and slightly husky without a trace of his native Yorkshire, but with just a touch of acquired American, and every word was spoken as if he meant it for her alone.

'I knew some Ackroyds once when I was a kid,' he said.

'It's a common name in these parts,' Laura said, surprised and slightly appalled at the effect Blake's charm had on her. Blake nodded and dismissed the subject, turning quickly to his companion.

'This, by the way, is my publicist, Ms Baum, without whom I never, but never, speak to journalists. She is indispensable.' He put an arm round Lorelie's gaunt shoulders and pulled her into the conversation.

'Lorelie,' he said in a voice deliberately projected to reach the furthest corners of the Clarendon's lounge. 'Lorelie has never been to Yorkshire before. I intend to show her the delights of the county.'

Lorelie gave the assembled company the benefit of a smile which revealed an acreage of too-perfect white teeth.

'Shall we take afternoon tea, Miss Ackroyd?' Blake went on. 'An English custom I haven't introduced Lorelie to yet. Shall we take tea and cucumber sandwiches and seed-cake and scones? Can the dear old Clarendon lay that on, do you think?'

'I'm sure they can,' Laura said quietly, realising that not only was she being patronised but that the whole of Bradfield, if not the whole county of Yorkshire was too.

They took a table in the corner of the lounge and waiters appeared as if by magic to meet John Blake's every whim. Laura watched him in some fascination as he specified the exact type of tea he required, the thickness of the bread and butter and the precise selection of cakes. Only when all that had been attended to did he finally lower his voice and turn to her with a satisfied smile.

'And now, Miss Ackroyd, let's talk about your article. Just exactly what is it you intend to write?'

'And will we able to have sight of your copy before you submit it?' Lorelie added sharply, in what Laura tentatively identified as the New York twang. 'Those are our usual terms.'

Laura took a sharp breath, and a mouthful of tea to give herself time to think.

'I don't think that's what *Sunday Extra*'s editor is expecting,' she said. 'I'm not at all sure he'll give you a right of veto on what I write. It's not usual in this country.'

'Well, it's sure as hell usual in LA,' Lorelie came back quickly. 'We don't co-operate with reporters who want to say just anything. Only the gossip papers get away with that and everyone knows they make most of it up.'

'Well now,' Blake said, flashing Laura his most brilliant smile, revealing perfectly even white teeth which were as much a tribute to his dentist's art as Lorelie's were. 'Don't let's fall out about this. We all know that we have a mutually beneficial arrangement here, don't we, Miss Ackroyd? May I call you Laura?'

Laura gave an infinitesimal nod of acquiescence while Lorelie glowered.

'You know I want as much publicity as I can get for my Brontë project and I'm sure you are thrilled to pieces to have been asked to write for a national magazine. Am I right?'

'It's not the first commission I've had from them,' Laura said, trying to keep the irritation out of her voice.

'Oh, we know, we know,' Blake agreed quickly and Laura realised that they had taken the trouble to check and were quite aware that while it was not the first commission it was only the second. 'Lorelie showed me the very interesting piece you wrote about young women victims of incest. Very nicely done, I thought. Very powerful. Very sensitive. I was impressed.'

'Thank you,' Laura said without feeling the slightest trace of gratitude. She was painfully aware now that she was playing with the grown-ups and the feature she envisaged might not be as easy as she had anticipated.

'What I wanted to do was to take you back to some of the places you remembered from your childhood around here,' she said, hoping that the suggestion did not sound as tentative as she felt. She could feel Lorelie's unforgiving eyes watching her every move. 'Your school, the places you used to live, that sort of thing. And perhaps talk to anyone you're still in contact with, family, old friends?'

Blake's smile was as fulsome as ever but he shook his head slowly.

'It's not easy as all that,' he said. 'I lived in Bradfield very briefly as a small boy. I can hardly remember it, to be honest. Obviously the connection is useful for the publicity – but my mother and I moved around so much when I was a kid that I never felt I belonged anywhere. I went to grammar school in Sheffield. Someone told me that was amalgamated into a comprehensive long ago. I went into the army when I was eighteen – National Service, you know. Then I went to drama school and never came back to the north. My mother moved away too. I think the area where I lived when I was eight or nine is long gone, pulled down and redeveloped. All those wonderful little *Coronation Street* terraces, such a warm community . . .'

And a bloody good thing too, Laura could almost hear her grandmother saying, having been largely responsible in her political career for those same wholesale demolitions. She did not believe Blake's sentimental view of Bradfield's Victorian legacy was deeply felt. Most of the terraces had become slums before they were pulled down and she was sure he knew that.

'You must still have friends here, someone from school . . .?'

'No one,' Blake said sadly. 'I went to school, of course, but we didn't stay. You don't keep in touch at that age, do you? We kept moving on, though I'm not sure many got quite as far away as I did. This is the first time I've been back to Bradfield for more than thirty years.'

'And your parents?' Laura persisted.

'There's only Mother, of course, and she's in a rest home out in Ilkley: a rather more healthy place than the old song might lead you to believe, I'm told. She used to come out to California to see me every year without fail until about eighteen months ago, but she can't manage the flight now. A little bit yonderly, the matron says, not quite remembering as clearly as she did. Do they still use that word?'

'Other relations, brothers, sisters?'

'I'm afraid not,' Blake said, shaking his head sadly and passing her the plate of sandwiches.

'So why come back to Yorkshire now, Mr Blake?' Laura asked sharply, ignoring his interest in the survival of Yorkshire dialect and not bothering to conceal her disappointment that his visit seemed to offer so few openings for her.

'The film, my dear,' Blake said. 'This is all about *Jane Eyre*. A wonderful story. You know it, of course. It's been my life's ambition to play Rochester and the chance has come just at the right time. Another four or five years and perhaps I would have been thought too old.' He patted his dark hair carefully, and Lorelie shook her head emphatically and heaved her disproportionate breasts in Blake's direction.

'Of course you're not too old,' she breathed.

'Come with me tomorrow, Laura,' Blake said, pouring himself another cup of Lapsang Souchong. 'We're going on a little recce up the dales to see if we can find a good site for the rectory where Jane discovers her cousins. You remember? She runs away and ends up in this remote village?'

'I remember,' Laura said. 'Do you have an actress in mind to play Jane? She's only supposed to be about eighteen, isn't she?'

Blake's irritation was momentary and silent but fierce, and Laura, taken aback by the rictus of anger which flashed across his face, realised that John Blake's emollient façade might be no more than skin-deep.

'No,' he said at length. 'We won't cast Jane just yet. I'd like a British actress but we've no one in mind. Do you have any suggestions?'

Laura shook her head and concentrated on her cucumber sandwich. Whoever took on the part of Jane Eyre to Blake's Rochester could not be too young, whatever the book suggested, or the contrast with Blake would be too absurd and might reawaken the ugly rumours which had blighted his career in the seventies. She sipped her tea slowly as she digested the difficulties ahead.

'I'd love to come on your recce,' she said eventually. Given a day with the man, she might catch him with the mask down. In any case Lorelie obviously knew him very well indeed, and might be less discreet than her master if she could get her on her own. Laura smiled faintly to herself. Master was the word Jane Eyre had always used to describe Rochester and it seemed eminently appropriate for Blake and Lorelie.

As for the other interviews she needed for her profile, with family and friends, she would just have to do a little detective work of her own. She did not believe that there was no one in Bradfield who could remember John Blake as a boy if he had been anything like as obnoxious as he was now.


Michael Thackeray had learned to love Laura's grandmother, even though he knew she regarded him with extreme suspicion as someone liable to trifle with Laura's affections. But he forgave her possessiveness. It was, after all, an emotion he shared.

He parked on the strip of cracked concrete provided outside the Laurels and looked up at the nursing home with a sharp intake of breath. The building was old, but old without any distinction. It was a between-the-wars, flat-fronted, metal window-framed construction that might once have been two substantial semi-detached residences. They were now linked by a series of slightly ramshackle glazed porches and annexes, all painted a flaking white. It could inspire neither affection nor confidence that it was anything more than a fairly spartan dump for the old and unwanted, he thought. Joyce Ackroyd, he could unerringly predict, must hate it.

A teenage girl in a green overall answered his ring at the door and led him to a huge ground-floor room, the walls lined with easy chairs in which elderly people were slumped in various attitudes of restless repose. A television fixed high on the wall in one corner blared obtrusively but some of the residents still succeeded in sleeping, snoring gently. Others stared at the TV screen as if transfixed, while some merely gazed into space, nodding occasionally or shaking their heads as if conducting silent conversations with people only they could see.

One old woman, held in her chair by a series of straps like a baby, twitched and muttered to herself, clutching at her neck again and again as if trying to tear off a scarf or something even more restrictive although there was nothing to be seen. Beneath her chair a tell-tale stain on the floor told its story and explained the strong smell of disinfectant in the room, which Thackeray suspected overlay worse smells.

'Michael. Welcome to the Grim Reaper's waiting room.'

Thackeray spun round at the sound of Joyce Ackroyd's voice. Laura had pushed her wheelchair silently into the sitting room through a door behind him. She was closely followed by the teenaged girl in the green overall who scowled at Joyce's greeting.

'Could we talk somewhere quieter?' Thackeray asked the girl, glancing at the television and the assembled audience, some of whom had turned bleary eyes in the visitors' direction.

'I suppose you could go in the conservatory,' the girl said sulkily. 'It's right parky in there, though. There's no heating.'

'It'll do,' Thackeray said firmly. 'We need some privacy.'

The girl glanced around at the other residents and shrugged.

'They won't take any notice, any road,' she said dismissively. 'Half of them are asleep and the rest are ga-ga.' But she waved them to double doors on the other side of the room, before turning on her heel and stomping off without another glance at the residents.

Thackeray followed the wheelchair through the doors into a dank and dusty area which boasted a few dried-up pot plants and three dilapidated wicker chairs. The chipped tiles were patchy with black mould and drifts of crisp brown fallen leaves. Green streaks of algal growth disfigured the tall windows, dimming the daylight from outside and adding to the over-whelming sense of cheerlessness and neglect.

'I'll get this placed closed down when I get out,' Joyce hissed with something like her normal spirit.

'It's not a council home then?' Thackeray asked.

'No, it's not. They're not running their own homes now, are they, the council? They've all been closed! This is some fly-by-night private place they're paying an arm and a leg for,' she said fiercely, and Thackeray realised why some older councillors and police officers in Bradfield still spoke of the legendary Joyce Ackroyd with as much fear as respect.

'It's disgusting,' Laura said furiously, and Thackeray could see the unshed tears in her eyes. 'I'll get you out of here as soon as I can arrange somewhere better, I promise.'

'You'll do nothing of the sort,' Joyce said, gripping the arms of her wheelchair as if she was about to rise up out of it, miracu-lously restored to full mobility by a paroxysm of righteous indignation. 'If this is what these poor souls have to put up with for the rest of their lives then I can put up with it till I get back on my feet. I'll not have any sort of special treatment. There's too much of that kind of hypocrisy in t'Party without me adding to it.'

'Nan,' Laura said, despairingly. Thackeray caught her eye and shook his head slightly. He shared Laura's distress at Joyce's situation but felt driven by other imperatives.

'Can we talk about Mariella Bonnetti?' he said quietly. He took a photocopy of the *Gazette*'s faded photograph of the Italian girl out of his wallet, an indistinct reproduction of an already indistinct original, and passed it to Joyce. She took it with trembling hands and was silent, gazing at the pale oval face and dark eyes which still offered a haunting glimpse of beauty across forty years, and she sighed.

'Aye, that was Mariella. I remember the picture in the *Gazette*. She was a lovely girl. Is the body you've found hers?'

'It's certainly a possibility, though we haven't traced her family yet. That's why I needed to talk to you so urgently. I want you to tell me everything you can remember about the girl, and her family, and everyone else who lived in Peter Street at the time she disappeared.'

In a low voice Joyce told him everything that she had told Laura about her short stay in the gaunt terrace with its broad views of the town in the valley below.

'You've got to remember there was still a housing crisis on,' she said. 'Another housing crisis, I mean. You'd think after forty-odd years . . .' But her indignation seemed to have been exhausted and she merely shrugged bitterly at the twists of political fate which evidently tormented her.

'It was mainly families who'd nowhere else to go,' she said. 'Some only stayed a few weeks. Others were stuck there for years. It was totally unsuitable for families with children. The kitchen and bathrooms were shared, the flats didn't have their own.'

'And of course the Italians weren't exactly overwhelmed by Yorkshire hospitality, apparently,' Laura added with a note of bitterness which made Thackeray glance at her sharply, although he did not pursue the point.

'What I'd like is the names of all the families you can remember,' he said, turning back to Joyce. 'Apart from you and the Bonnettis, that is.'

'Well now,' Joyce said, 'let's think. There was Mrs Parkinson, of course. Thought she was the cat's whiskers, she did, though they weren't there long. Always trying to give the impression she'd come down in the world, but I had my doubts. She had two children, a lad of about seventeen, Roy I think he was called, and a daughter quite a bit younger, nine or ten maybe. I'm not sure now what she was called. Pamela maybe. She didn't play with the lads much. Where Mr Parkinson had got to was a source of endless gossip around the landings, I do remember. There was no sign of him and she never actually claimed she was a widow. She just never mentioned a husband at all. That was a bit of a scandal in those days, of course. But whoever he was, she insisted she had to keep up appearances, which was just another way of putting the rest of us down.'

Thackeray had taken out a notebook and wrote down the names as Joyce mentioned them. It was an interesting story, but sounded too like ancient history for him to be convinced that he had any realistic chance of tracing these fading memories and discovering flesh and blood.

'Then there were the Smiths,' Joyce went on. 'Alice, she was called. Now she did have a husband, but he'd been in a Japanese camp and though he was there he wasn't, if you know what I mean. A pale skinny man, he was. Used to sit out at the front of the house on sunny days just staring into space. Never said much, but sometimes you'd hear him screaming in the night. He had nightmares, she said.'

Joyce stopped for a moment, as if transfixed by the sights and sounds she was dragging into the light of day after so many years.

'It's all a long time ago,' she said.

'The Smiths,' Thackeray prompted quietly.

'Aye, the Smiths. They had a lad too, Ken I think he was called. He must have been about the same age as Mariella. Just the one child like me. Mr Smith died eventually, I heard, killed by the war just like Laura's grandfather. It just took longer. Then there was little Danny O'Meara, of course. A little devil, he was, small for his age, dark, bright eyes, but always into mischief and getting clouted by his dad. And Bridget, she was about twelve or thirteen, much quieter, a pretty little lass, and there were other O'Meara children but they were younger, a couple of girls and a boy perhaps, but too young to join with the older ones' games. I didn't know the parents very well. He worked away a lot of the time, I think, and she was so busy looking after the children she never had time to chat. Deirdre, she was called, very Irish, must have been a beautiful girl once, but she was worn out with it all.'

'How old was Danny?' Thackeray asked.

'Oh, they were all about the same age, fifteen, sixteen, except for Roy Parkinson – Parky they called him, of course – who was a bit older. He'd left school and was waiting for his call-up papers. They had to do National Service in those days, you know. Laura's dad was somewhere in between the big lads and the younger children, trying hard to tag along with the older boys. They played endless cricket matches in the factory yard opposite.'

'That's four families, including the Bonnettis. Is that all?' Thackeray asked.

'I'm trying to remember, Michael,' Joyce said with a touch of asperity. 'Of course, there were others. There were a couple of young mothers with babies, but I'm not sure I can remember their names. And the end of the terrace had been split up between a couple of Polish families, but they spoke very little English and kept themselves to themselves. The ones I recall most clearly are the families with youngsters Jack was friendly with.'

'But the Bonnettis didn't keep themselves to themselves?'

'He'd been in England for most of the war, you see. His English was very good, though hers wasn't. And then Mariella and two of her little brothers used to join in the games, in spite of the teasing and the name-calling. When it came down to it, the lads thought she was the bee's knees, she was such a pretty lass. They taught her to play cricket. It wasn't that unusual for the lasses to make up the numbers if there weren't enough lads to make a team. Cricket was a religion round here then, you know. Len Hutton, the Compton brothers, Locke and Laker. It was like football is now.'

'Did Mariella have a particular boyfriend?' Thackeray asked, gently steering Joyce back to what interested him.

'I wouldn't know, Michael,' Joyce said sadly. 'Jack was too young for that sort of thing and I was never aware she favoured any of the others especially. You always saw them in a group, not in twos, and her parents were very particular about her not staying out late, I remember. Good Catholics, of course.'

'Of course,' Thackeray said drily, having been brought up by good Catholics himself. Not that it had made any difference in the end, he recalled. When the nervous fumbling became too much he and Aileen had lain in heathery hollows on the moors and tried to reconcile their natural inclinations and their Church's precepts, and failed. It was a miracle, he thought, though not perhaps one of the holy kind, that their son had not been conceived long before the marriage they had made in such haste and repented so bitterly at leisure.

'So no obvious suspects when she disappeared?' he asked wearily. 'The boyfriend is always top of the list.'

'Isn't it a bit late to be raking over old ashes?' Joyce said, not responding directly to his question. 'Surely it's too long ago.'

'There's no time limit to a murder investigation,' Thackeray said. 'If the body really is Mariella's we're bound to make some enquiries.'

'If murder's what it was,' Joyce said. 'They didn't treat it like a murder inquiry at the time, not for long anyway. In the end it just seemed to be assumed she'd run away.'

'Did she seem to be unhappy at home?' Thackeray asked.

'She seemed to me to be a much-loved daughter,' Joyce said firmly. 'And on the street she certainly had her admirers, my lad amongst them, in spite of the prattling about sending the Eyeties back where they came from. But I'm sure it was no more than that. When she disappeared we were all upset. It breaks my heart now to think she's been lying there all these years in an unmarked grave.' Joyce shivered and a tear trickled down her pale cheek. Laura flashed Thackeray a look of desperation.

'I think,' Joyce said, 'I'd best go back to bed.'

# 6

Mower pulled the car into the kerb outside the Bonnettis' substantial detached house in a leafy Harrogate avenue and took stock.

'They didn't do too badly for themselves then,' he said.

'He owns about six restaurants,' DCI Thackeray said. 'One here, one in Knaresborough, another in York and two or three in Leeds, one in Bradfield. A very successful company, being run now by two of his sons.'

'Pretty good for a prisoner of war.'

'He was in the right place at the right time, I suppose,' Thackeray said. 'He had the expertise when people were being tempted away from fish and chips and meat and two veg into more exotic foods. He started up in Bradfield, of course, but apparently it didn't really take off until he moved on to places where people might be a bit more adventurous, not too nervous to try osso bucco and linguine and the rest. You know I think I might have been in his restaurant here in Harrogate years ago. I used to come to listen to jazz in a pub here and we went on for a meal once or twice to some little Italian place.'

Mower wondered who the 'we' might have been but knew better than to ask. Thackeray was a man with whom he had learned not to go beyond a certain point and that point, in time at least, was very firmly established as the moment when he had left his home town of Arnedale, on the edge of the Dales, some ten or eleven years before.

Thackeray, he knew, had lost a baby son and a wife, but assiduous probing amongst colleagues in Bradfield and Arnedale had not entirely clarified in Mower's mind what had happened then. But Mower knew a man who had been through hell when he met one, and he treated his boss with greater respect than came naturally because he recognised the well-tempered core beneath the somewhat remote and always controlled exterior.

'Right,' Thackeray said, not concealing the note of reluctance in his tone. 'Let's take these folks the bad news, shall we?'

'Couldn't it be a relief?' Mower ventured. 'Isn't it better to know the worst than to always be wondering?'

'After forty years of hoping she might be alive somewhere? I doubt it,' Thackeray said.

The gleaming oak door of the elegant stuccoed house was opened promptly by a well-built man in his late forties, his grey hair almost silver at the temples above a prominent nose and jowls which probably always looked as though they needed a shave. His deep set, slightly hooded brown eyes were opaque, evidently reserving judgement on the visitors, who were expected.

'Giuseppe Bonnetti,' he said, the voice low and precise. 'My mother and father are waiting for you, Chief Inspector. But I thought if I could just have a quiet word before we go in . . .?'

'Of course,' Thackeray said. The two police officers followed Bonnetti to one side of the broad sunlit hallway, with an intricately tiled floor which called to mind a villa in a sunnier climate. He led them into a small sitting room which was obviously used for watching television.

'They know that you've come to discuss the possibility that you have found the body of my sister Mariella,' Bonnetti said. He had taken the phone call from the police in Bradfield and arranged the meeting on behalf of his family. 'Naturally they're upset about that. But what I didn't tell you on the telephone, because my mother was listening, is that my father is not well. He's getting on for eighty, as you must realise, and he had a minor stroke six months ago. He denies that it's made any difference to him. He's a very determined man. But in fact he's not strong, he's partly paralysed down one side and his speech is sometimes difficult. When he does speak it's more likely to be in Italian than in English. It's odd really, because his English was always much better than Mama's. He's been offered treatment but he's not a good patient. He's a very difficult man to help. I just wanted you to bear all that in mind when you meet him.'

'Of course,' Thackeray said again, non-committally. 'You understand that at this stage I'm simply trying to identify a body which has been buried for a very long time? There are one or two indicators which only your parents can comment on.'

'Yes, of course, I understand,' Bonnetti said. 'And the whole family would be relieved, I think, if this turns out to be Mariella and she can be given a Christian burial, even after all these years. But you can imagine how distressing this is likely to be for the old people? And distress is not good for my father.'

'Do you remember your sister at all clearly yourself?' Thackeray asked. He knew Bonnetti was considerably younger than the daughter who had been brought to England by her mother when the war ended.

Bonnetti hesitated and then shrugged.

'Of course, though I was only seven when she disappeared,' he said. 'I was born in this country after my mother joined my father in Bradfield, so there was a big gap between me and Mariella. But naturally I can remember her being there when I was small. I had two smaller brothers and a sister and she used to look after me, in particular, when my mother was busy with the younger ones. I loved her very much.'

'What were you told when she disappeared?'

'I've been thinking about that,' Bonnetti said carefully. 'At first, I think, I was told that she had got lost and everyone was searching for her. Then later, though I don't remember how much later, that maybe she had run away and left us. It's all very vague in my mind. At that age you're aware that something is very wrong though you don't always understand exactly what. I can remember my mother crying a great deal, but in a big family there is always so much going on, so much noise and coming and going, that it can be confusing to a child. But I remember missing her very much. Suddenly a light had gone out of my life.'

Bonnetti ran a hand over his thick, grey hair and sighed, but the pain which they glimpsed momentarily in his eyes was quickly replaced by the expression of guarded caution with which he had greeted them.

'We've come a long way from Peter Street,' he said. 'You probably can't remember what it was like after the war with rationing and so on. My father used to grow tomatoes so that there was something to have with the pasta. I remember going to the allotment with him to pick them and him complaining bitterly that they wouldn't ripen properly in those cold English summers. I can remember my mama trying to cook Italian dishes without the ingredients ... I always think that's why Papa eventually went into the restaurant business. He wanted to give people what he had missed so much in those early days. And suddenly, from being the ex-enemy living in poverty, everyone wanted to know Paolo Bonnetti, they were flocking in to eat his delicious Italian food. It was quite a transformation.'

'Could we speak to your parents now?' Thackeray asked.

'Of course,' Bonnetti said and waved them back into the hall and then into a large sunny room at the rear of the house. Here the tiled floor was warmed by several Persian rugs and the white walls hung with what Thackeray assumed were only copies of some of the Italian masters. Between the sitting room and the flawless lawns of the garden, french windows opened on to a Victorian conservatory vibrant with early geraniums and a bougainvillaea just hinting at its full magenta glory. It was, as Mower had said, a long way from the overcrowded terraced houses of Peter Street to this approximation of the Mediterranean in a Yorkshire suburb.

A heavily built elderly woman with iron-grey hair swept back from her face, a tightly fitting black dress and gold-rimmed spectacles was sitting by the fire with an unfinished piece of tapestry work on the settee beside her. Opposite an equally substantial man sat bolt upright in his chair, one hand holding a newspaper awkwardly and the other resting lifelessly on his lap. He let the paper fall to the floor and Giuseppe hurried to pick it up and place it on the coffee table between his parents.

'My father, Paolo, and my mother, Signora Maria Bonnetti,' he said formally. 'Papa, these are the policemen from Bradfield I told you about.'

The older Bonnetti stared at Thackeray fiercely with eyes as dark as his son's but infinitely more unforgiving, while his wife fiddled nervously with a handkerchief on her lap. It was evident from her reddened eyes that she had been crying. The two old people listened in silence as Thackeray explained to them exactly what had been discovered on the muddy building site at Peter Hill.

'With remains of this age identification is extremely difficult,' he said. 'But there are two things which might help us make a positive identification. Firstly, can you tell me whether Mariella ever broke her arm?'

Paolo Bonnetti shook his head at that, and it was obvious that the movement was difficult. But the question had a different effect on his wife. Her eyes widened in a sallow, creased face and she opened her mouth as if to speak, though nothing came out but a faint moan.

'Mama?' Giuseppe said putting his arm around her.

'She did,' the old woman said. 'Before we came to England, while we were alone in Napoli, she fell on the stairs one day and broke her left arm.'

Bonnetti the elder was looking at her now with burning intensity as if this was the first he had ever heard of the accident.

'I don't know,' Maria said. 'Perhaps I never told Paolo, I don't remember. We were alone there with my mama for four years. It was a long time. Many things happened. But, *si*, Mariella did break her arm.'

Knowing the answer now, Thackeray slowly took a clear plastic evidence bag out of his inside pocket and passed it to Maria Bonnetti.

'We found this close to the body,' he said. 'Did it belong to Mariella?'

Maria stared at the tiny gold cross as if transfixed and then crossed herself as tears began to course down her creased cheeks.

'Her papa bought it for her for her first Communion,' she said. 'Oh, Paolo, they have found our Mariella after all this time. I told you she did not run away, not my Mariella. After all these years they have found her, thanks be to God. Now justice can be done.'

Rigid in his chair at the opposite side of the fire the old man gave a grunt and slumped back into the cushions. Suddenly anxious, his son moved to him and took his hand.

'It's all right, Papa,' he said. The old man looked at his son with eyes like bottomless pools and seemed to make a supreme effort to speak. What he said was not comprehensible to Thackeray or to Mower though his son seemed to understand. He nodded and squeezed his father's good hand in reassurance.

'He says, do you know how she died?'

Thackeray shook his head. 'I'm sorry,' he said. 'There's no indication of that.'

'So you don't know whether it was murder?' Giuseppe persisted.

'It's a very long time ago,' Thackeray said. 'We will try to trace the other people who lived in the street that summer, but that may be very difficult after all this time. I think the chances of finding out what happened are very remote.'

Behind him Mrs Bonnetti made a noise halfway between a scream and a groan and Thackeray turned sharply to catch the flash of fierce hatred which filled her eyes and distorted her heavy features.

'Of course it was murder,' she said. 'Those people, they hated us, they hated all of us. The boys, they chased after Mariella, but they still hated us. We were the wops, the Eye-ties, she was the Eye-tie whore, I heard them say it. They thought I couldn't understand, the *ragazzi*. They whispered about us all the time, teased the *bambini*, broke down Paolo's *pomodori* – the tomato plants. Of course they murdered her, and then they – how do you say it? – covered up for each other that day when she didn't come home. She had been playing with them, those boys. We told the police then. They killed her, all of them, and now you see how they buried her. I have known all the time, all these years, that she would not run away and leave us. I have known that she was dead.'

With the tears now streaming down her face she turned to her husband, still slumped awkwardly back against his cushions, his face suffused with colour, and her son, standing transfixed beside his father's chair.

'I told you I wanted to go back to Napoli, to go home before we die. And you would not have it. And now there is this to spoil our old age, to break our hearts all over again. My poor daughter, my beautiful daughter, *mia figlia, mia Mariella . . .*'

*

56

'*Mama mia!*' Kevin Mower exclaimed as he pulled away from the Bonnettis' house and carefully negotiated the speed humps which kept traffic to a respectful crawl the length of the tree-lined avenue. 'What did you make of that, Guv?'

Thackeray sat in the passenger seat, his face impassive.

'I think she has probably been bottling that up for years,' he said. 'But the rancour has probably deepened with time. Giuseppe said he didn't remember being teased particularly for being Italian, no more than kids always get teased, he said. But whichever of them is remembering most accurately – the seven-year-old who wasn't even sure what was going on or the mother who was no doubt distraught then and has brooded on the injustice of it all for more than forty years – it doesn't take us the smallest step further forward unless we can trace some of the other people who lived there at the time.'

'And Papa either can't or won't say anything,' Mower added.

'Put your foot down, Kevin,' Thackeray said as the Sergeant swung the car on to the main road to the west.

'Well, at least we've got an ID, which is more than we expected,' Mower said cheerfully, obediently pushing the car up to the speed limit. 'That will put a few other families with missing daughters out of their misery.'

'I doubt that,' Thackeray said.

Mower glanced at his passenger's rigid jaw and cursed himself roundly under his breath.

Joyce Ackroyd was slowly and reluctantly coming to terms with her new home. Her room was on the ground floor on a corridor devoted to patients in need of nursing care, most of them convalescents who had been moved out of the infirmary into 'the community'. Having made a nodding acquaintance with some of her immediate neighbours, few of whom seemed ever to move from their beds, Joyce rather doubted that any of them would journey much further than the cemetery when they left the Laurels.

She herself was determined to go home. She had been given her wheelchair at the hospital and had learned to manoeuvre herself slowly around the orthopaedic ward there. She saw no reason why she should not continue to become more mobile in her new environment and on her first morning had demanded to be helped out of bed and into the chair as soon as her breakfast tray had been cleared away. The nurse who had arrived to wash her and attend to her toilet looked doubtful.

'The physiotherapist at the hospital said there was no reason why I shouldn't walk again,' Joyce had said firmly. 'It'll take a bit of time and effort but then I'll be going home, don't you fret.'

'I'll talk to matron,' the nurse promised.

'You do that, dear,' Joyce said in her most forceful chair-of-the-housing-committee voice. Her persistence seemed to have been acknowledged, if not welcomed, when after lunch a sulky young assistant helped her into the chair, tucked a blanket around her legs and steered her out of the room and down the corridor towards the day room where the ostensibly more mobile residents spent most of their time in front of the television.

'When do I get my physiotherapy? Do you know?' Joyce demanded before she was parked next to a comatose old man whose head had fallen on to his chest. His mouth was open and a thin trickle of saliva dribbled on to his Fair Isle sweater as he snored gently.

'I don't know owt about that,' the care assistant had said huffily before stomping off to attend to an old woman who was demanding the toilet at the far end of the room.

'Three times a week they said I needed,' Joyce insisted, fighting down the faint and increasingly familiar feeling of panic which clutched at her chest. She had lain awake for hours the previous night trying to convince herself that she would be able to leave the Laurels and resume an independent life. She had failed, and not even the comforting daylight had fully restored her confidence. The longer she remained here, the more clearly she could see the trap of dependency closing its jaws around her, every ineffective protest making her weaker rather than stronger and sapping her will to escape. She nudged her neighbour, in the hope that he might hear, but he simply slumped down into his chair, snoring more noisily.

'My grand-daughter knows all about it,' Joyce persisted but

she knew she was talking to herself by this time and her voice faded as she glanced around for support from the other residents. None of them could or would meet her gaze, and fighting back a treacherous tear she began to wheel herself jerkily across to the door leading into the conservatory.

'Does this open?' she asked loudly.

'It's freezing cold out there, dear,' the assistant said. As far as Joyce could see she was the only member of staff on duty that afternoon.

'I'm well wrapped up,' Joyce said huffily, reaching out awkwardly to try to open the door and wrenching her hip painfully in the process.

'Mrs Ackroyd!' the assistant said, hurrying over to help her. 'You're being a naughty girl, aren't you?'

'It would be offensive if I called you a girl, young woman,' Joyce said, her eyes alight now. 'It's a good sixty years since I could claim the epithet. Now, I want to go outside for a bit of fresh air. Is there any reason why not?'

'I s'pose not,' the assistant said reluctantly, and opened the door for her, allowing her to manoeuvre the chair with difficulty into the dingy conservatory, and closing the door behind her again with a clatter. Joyce sighed. She had only demanded entrance to establish the fact that because she was elderly and temporarily incapacitated – very temporarily, she told herself firmly again – she would not be treated like a backward child. Now she had got her way, and was sitting in triumph amongst the desiccated geraniums, she wondered why she had bothered.

After a few minutes' depressed contemplation of her fate, she was surprised to hear the door from the day room open quietly behind her. There was no easy way to spin her chair round to see who had come in so she waited while shuffling footfalls worked their way slowly around her and she found herself face-to-face with a wizened figure in a long drooping maroon skirt, carpet slippers and several layers of cardigans. She recognised one of the women who had been sitting gazing at the television a few minutes before and she smiled uncertainly at her, surprised to meet eyes of piercing blue in the lined and wrinkled face, eyes which were as alert and intelligent as her own.

'It's Joyce, isn't it?' the woman said, her voice still firm even if the rest of her was not. 'I thought I recognised you. Joyce Ackroyd, little Jackie's mother.'

'It's been a long time if all you can remember is little Jackie,' Joyce said wryly. 'He's well over fifty and has had his first heart attack, has Jack. Getting his comeuppance for a misspent capitalist youth, you might say, is my Jack.'

'You don't remember me, love, do you?' the woman said, lowering herself heavily into one of the cane conservatory chairs which creaked ominously under her weight. 'But I knew you straight off, as soon as I saw you yesterday. You've not changed, you know, apart from you've lost that lovely red hair. Oh, I know we're all on our last legs in here, but I'd have known that voice anywhere. And you're still right bossy. I can remember you laying the law down all them years ago in Peter Street, always on about what the government were doing wrong that week.'

'Alice?' Joyce said uncertainly. 'Alice Smith?'

'Right. Your lad used to run after our Keith the year we lived up there. Don't you remember?'

'I remember, though I thought your lad was Ken, not Keith,' Joyce said quietly. She recalled Alice's husband, too, haunted and haunting, sitting in the sunshine on the stone steps in front of the house, gazing out with unseeing eyes over the town which was half obscured in a haze of smoke from the mills in the valley below. Not that the view had mattered a scrap, she thought. Whatever Fred Smith had been gazing at, she doubted that it was as close as the blackened roofs and tall chimneys of Bradfield.

'You moved out before I did,' Joyce said softly as the memories came flooding back.

'Aye, we got a place out Eckersley way,' Mrs Smith said. 'My husband were a priority case, they said, but he only lasted six months after we moved. They found him in t'lock on t'canal. Probably fell in, the coroner said. Probably got dizzy and fell in. But I knew he'd jumped. He couldn't escape, you see. He couldn't escape when he were out there on that railway in Burma, and he couldn't escape when he came back.'

'I remember,' Joyce said, suddenly overwhelmed by the long, suffocating shadows of the past. 'My man never came back at all,' she said.

'We'd have been better off if Fred hadn't come back neither,' Alice said fiercely. 'He were no use to me and he frightened our Keith half to death. Years and years we had of it, with him slowly getting worse instead of better. I think that's why those lads spent so much time together that summer. Keith didn't want to be at home with his dad. He'd do owt to get out o't'house.'

'We were all overcrowded in those flats,' Joyce said. 'I do remember.' Did Alice, she wondered, know about the body which had been so recently found on Peter Hill and, if not, should she tell her? Perhaps that would be better left to the police, she decided.

'How's your Keith?' she asked instead.

'Oh, he's done really well,' his mother said, pride lighting up her eyes again. 'He comes to see me every week without fail, you know. Always brings me flowers. He's a lovely boy, is Keith. Lives out at Broadley now, with his wife and two children. Well, not children, really. Almost grown up my grand-daughter is, getting married soon, and the lad's just gone off to university . . .'

Alice Smith's family history was interrupted abruptly by the door behind them crashing open.

'Mrs Ackroyd!' Joyce recognised the voice of Betty Johns, matron of the Laurels, whose regime she had already concluded was more suited to a gaol than a nursing home.

'Mrs Johns?' Joyce responded as firmly as she could while she struggled to turn her chair to face the new arrival. Alice Smith, she noticed, was looking distinctly uncomfortable, almost cowering back in her frail wicker chair in the face of the matron's evident displeasure.

'You ladies are going to get pneumonia sitting out here in this freezing cold,' Betty Johns went on, taking hold of the handles of Joyce's chair and pushing her none too gently back into the day room. She was a tall, well-built woman with a luxuriant head of dark hair, who favoured tight, navy blue dresses which emphasised her substantial bust, not quite a formal uniform but allowing ample space for her nurse's watch which swung from the pin in her cleavage like a badge of office.

'Come along, Alice dear. You should know better,' she threw over her shoulder. Alice Smith pulled herself painfully to her feet and did as she was told.

Without any further discussion Joyce found herself being pushed smartly to her room, spun round beside the bed and helped back beneath the sheets by ungentle hands.

'I wanted to talk to you about my physiotherapy,' she said, with as much dignity as she could scrape together after this unprovoked assault was complete. Mrs Johns looked at her coldly.

'I'll have to make enquiries about that,' she said. 'I don't recall physiotherapy in the contract with the local authority.'

'But the hospital said . . .' Joyce began.

'But the hospital's not paying the bill, are they, dear?'

'I need to learn to walk properly again,' Joyce said faintly, realising with agonising clarity for the first time that she was no longer in control of her fate and loathing the weakness which had brought her to this pass, and the feeling of utter helplessness which threatened to overwhelm her.

'I want to go home as soon as I can,' she said, her voice faltering slightly. She bit her lip in annoyance and attempted the glare which had curdled Tory blood in its time but now, she realised, seemed to have lost most of its power.

'Well, we'll have to see about that, won't we, dear?' Mrs Johns said. 'We'll just have to see whether you can cope with that again. It may not be as easy as you think. Now have you had any painkillers today?'

Joyce shook her head and Mrs Johns reached into her pocket and took out a bottle of pills from which she shook two into Joyce's hand.

'These aren't what I usually have,' Joyce said doubtfully.

Betty Johns handed her a glass of water from the bedside table.

'Don't you worry about that, dear,' she said. 'I think you'll find these are even better.'

And the matron closed the door behind her with ominous finality.

# 7

The Mercedes purred sweetly as it climbed out of the valley of the Maze into the high Pennines beyond Arnedale and gradually Laura Ackroyd began to relax and enjoy the views of rolling moorland which opened up on each side of the winding road. There had been a time when she had walked up here with her grandmother but the hills were shadowed now with darker memories.

'That's High Clough,' she said, nodding towards a village obliquely above them in the lee of the highest fells. 'There was a nasty murder there last winter. A grim place, one way and another.'

'Do you write about crime?' Blake asked.

'Not really,' Laura said. 'That business was more personal. I was working in Arnedale and got to know the woman who was killed.'

'So you do get involved with your subject matter,' Blake said with a knowing smile.

'Not in the way you mean,' Laura said sharply but she could see from her companion's expression that he did not believe her.

Irritated, she stared out of the window in silence as the road twisted to the top of a long incline and opened up a sudden view of a valley, its fields dotted with sheep and a village nestling far below in a fold in the hills. John Blake glanced at his companion with a faint smile revealing his gleaming white teeth.

'There's a pleasant pub down in the village,' he said. 'We can have lunch there and then go on up to the old farm, which I think will make a very convincing Moor House, where Jane Eyre meets her cousins.'

'It's certainly bleak enough up here,' Laura said, as they slowed to let a pair of shaggy sheep, gaze fixed on some grassy titbit indiscernible to the mere human eye, amble across the road in front of them. The road was unfenced and on the other side of the valley the moors rose steadily in undulating folds, yellow, green, bronze, finally fading to purple on the far horizon.

'Bog and mountain and bitterly cold in winter,' Blake said, following Laura's gaze. 'But Charlotte Brontë and her sisters seemed to like it.'

'I shouldn't think your film crew will. And Lorelie will have to buy herself a pair of wellies if you come up here in winter. She won't like that,' Laura said bitchily.

Laura had been slightly thrown when Blake had turned up alone to collect her that morning. She had expected to have to disentangle the actor from the American woman's protective embrace and was not sure how to interpret his decision to face her questions without assistance. Was it an indication that he did not rate her forensic skills highly enough to need support? Or that he preferred a *tête-à-tête* for other reasons? He was certainly arrogant enough to try charming her off her perch, she thought, and could hardly be aware that she was not for charming.

'Lorelie,' Blake said pensively. 'She's having a bad hair day, she says. You know, I'm not at all sure Lorelie and I will still be together when we get around to making this film.'

Laura raised an eyebrow at that, recognising a chilly finality in his voice which she suspected indicated that Lorelie had served her purpose, and that her purpose was not by any means only a professional one. But Blake turned his attention back to the twisting downhill road, leaving her his classic profile to study, and did not expand any further on his future plans for Lorelie.

'We'll need to shoot some of this moorland scenery, of course,' he continued at length. 'Jane's passage over the moors until she finds herself starving and destitute on the Rivers' doorstep is the nadir of the film for her, the point at which she almost despairs, don't you think?'

Laura, who had not read the book since she was at school, shrugged slightly, not wanting to admit her ignorance.

'Jane's not a droopy Victorian heroine,' she said, sure of her ground here, at least.

'She's a tough cookie,' Blake agreed. 'Like the Jane Austen heroines. She's a survivor with a firm line on morality.'

'Did you come up here when you were a boy?' Laura asked, much more interested in discussing Blake's line on morality and more.

'I think so,' Blake said vaguely. 'My mother used to take me up on the moors near Broadley, and over to Ilkley sometimes. She liked to take tea at Betty's Cafe. But I heard about this place, amazingly, from a Yorkshireman I met in LA. I was talking quite casually about the prospect of doing *Jane Eyre* and he said he knew exactly the place to film the country scenes.'

'So it's not a boyhood haunt?'

'Oh, no, I was never a great one for traipsing round in the mud. I was a town boy at heart. I still love cities, you know? People moan about LA, but to be honest I love it, traffic, smog, race riots and all. At least it's alive and full of zip. Exhausting of course, and unforgiving, but alive. Not like this God-forsaken country.'

'Can I quote you on that?' Laura asked quickly.

'I think not,' Blake said wryly. 'I'd like the Brits to flock to see my *Jane Eyre*, I guess.'

'So can we talk in a little more detail now about your time in Bradfield?' she persisted. 'That's what I really need for the piece for the *Gazette* when the museum opens. Can you get me a preview, by the way? I'd like to have a look round tomorrow, if that's possible.'

'I'm sure we can arrange that,' Blake said smoothly. 'I'll talk to Keith Spencer-Smith when we get back this afternoon. He'll lay on a visit for you.'

'Was he a boyhood friend, then?'

'Good grief, no. I told you. I was only here for a year or so and there's no one I kept in touch with. There's no mileage in my childhood for you, I'm afraid. I'd met Keith when he was in the States and then he wrote to me out of the blue about his new museum, said he'd read about the Brontë project and remembered I'd lived in Yorkshire and was I interested in opening it for him? I wouldn't have considered it except that I was going to be over here anyway.' Blake hesitated as the road took a steep turn down into a cleft in the moors just above the low stone-roofed houses which huddled amongst scrubby trees.

65

'This is the village,' he said. 'We'll have lunch here.'

'You don't have any particularly warm feelings about Bradfield, from the sound of it,' Laura hazarded.

Blake looked at her for a moment, his eyes blank. 'Don't get the wrong impression,' he said carefully. 'But I had a rootless childhood. I'm not a native of Yorkshire. I was born in Manchester, then when war broke out I was evacuated and lived with a family in Wales for three years. I hated that. They were Welsh speakers and it was like being in a foreign country. When I went back to my mother, my father was away in the Forces and she had moved to Yorkshire to be near her family.'

'So you came here when you were, what, about eight?'

'Eight years old, with a Welsh accent – can you imagine how that went down with the little tykes in a Bradfield council school? It took me about three weeks to learn to speak broad Yorkshire and kick anyone who didn't instead of being kicked myself. I think that's when I first realised that you didn't have to be yourself, you could be anyone you liked. It taught me to act – fast.'

And he had probably not stopped acting since, Laura thought to herself, as Blake parked the car outside a surprisingly well-kept pub to one side of the green at the centre of the huddle of cottages. The village consisted of little more than a single street which wound its way steeply down the hillside to a narrow stone bridge across a rushing stream. He got out of the car and opened the passenger door for her, waiting as the seat-belt slid automatically back to allow her out and offering a hand to help her.

They settled at a corner table in the low-ceilinged lounge bar and Blake fussed about to get Laura a drink and the homemade pie and salad which, according to the blackboard on the wall, was the dish of the day. It was a more homely setting than Laura had imagined him choosing, but several heads turned to look at the tall actor and he seemed to swell in the warm glow of people's attention before settling down opposite Laura and opening his hands expansively.

'So what more can I tell you, my dear?' he asked.

Laura placed her small tape-recorder on the table between them.

'Tell me about your family,' she said. 'What did your father do?'

'He left us,' Blake said flatly, and unexpectedly, the perfectly modulated voice suddenly dropping and becoming almost harsh. 'He came back from the Air Force and stayed with us for a while, I can't remember exactly how long. And then he went. And we moved on – again. I can remember there being rows, but I was never told exactly why he went, whether there was another woman. My mother simply wouldn't talk about it.'

'You were an only child?'

'That's right. My mother's pride and joy, I suppose.'

'Were you a spoilt child?'

'Inevitably,' Blake said drily. 'What son of an abandoned mother isn't spoilt? She was very ambitious for me. Pushed me to pass the grammar school entrance exam, paid for elocution lessons for me because she hated the accent I'd picked up, sent me to dancing and drama lessons when my English teacher told her I had talent, scrimped and saved . . . She was a remarkable woman, though of course I didn't know that at the time. Who does?'

'And she's still alive, you said?'

'Yes, I'll be going to see her before the museum opening. They say she's developing Alzheimer's, so I don't even know if she'll recognise me . . .'

'You were very close?'

'Yes, we were.' Blake pushed his plate away as if to indicate that he had spoken as much as he intended about his mother. Laura took the hint. There would be other opportunities to discover more about the relationship, she was sure.

'So you went to grammar school and then to RADA? Tell me about your education,' she said.

'Grammar schools – Leeds, Millford, Sheffield – it was an education,' Blake said without much enthusiasm. 'The usual stuff – Latin and French if you weren't keen on science. I wasn't keen on science. We moved around too much for me to do well.

I got my School Certificate and stayed on into the sixth form. But the thing that really turned me on was drama.'

For a moment those flat dark blue eyes lit up and Laura felt the layers of circumspection begin to peel away a fraction.

'I played Juliet when I was thirteen – a boys' school had to do it the way Shakespeare would have done it, of course – Julius Caesar when I was seventeen, and I joined an amateur theatre club. I couldn't get enough of it. Though I don't suppose anyone will remember my efforts now. I learned to smoke a cigarette in a long holder in some romantic comedy when I was about sixteen – totally incongruous, it must have been. I don't think I'd even started shaving and I was playing the romantic lead. Crazy.'

'But you haven't kept in touch with anyone from that time?'

Blake gave her another long cool look, the momentary enthusiasm for his own boyish passions fading as quickly as it had arrived. Laura could almost feel him closing down, and could not understand why.

'I've been away so long. We moved around too much. Off the record, I think I blotted Yorkshire from my mind when I left. I never liked the place, never felt at home. I think my mother felt the same. She moved away for a while at about the same time, so there was never any reason to come back. Nor opportunity, once I went to the States.'

'No girlfriends to visit?'

'Nothing like that,' Blake said flatly. 'And the street in Bradfield where we lived was pulled down long ago. It's not very fruitful territory for your article, I'm afraid.'

He leaned across and switched off the tape-recorder.

'Let's leave all that and talk about you for a bit, shall we?' he said with a look which she found hard to interpret.

'I don't think that will take us very far,' Laura said equally firmly.

'You're not married, are you?'

She shook her head.

'Have you ever been to the States?' he asked. She shook her head again, puzzled.

He put his hand momentarily over hers. 'We'll have to see

what we can do about that,' he said. 'You'd enjoy it. I could show you a lot in LA. Introduce you to a lot of people.'

'Show me a good time?' Laura asked innocently, raising an eyebrow just enough to let him know she was not fooled. To his credit, he threw back his head and laughed, running a hand histrionically through his hair and again attracting every eye in the room as he did so. But his amusement was not feigned. Nor was it unattractive.

'You'd give Jane Eyre a run for her money in the outraged innocence department, miss,' he said. 'OK, OK, let's keep this purely professional. But if you felt like working in La-La Land for a bit, you know where to come.'

'I'll give it some thought,' Laura said drily.


Laura got home late. Blake had driven her back to Bradfield after showing her round an empty and almost ruined old farmhouse which he insisted was perfect for his purposes. He had then insisted on buying her a meal at Ahmet's, the small curry restaurant on the Manchester road with a big reputation. He had heard about it in LA, he said, and knew that Lorelie Baum was not a fan of Asian cuisine. He would not allow Laura to refuse his invitation, he said, so she didn't argue, and she could see that he was putting himself out to please her, encouraging her to select her favourite dishes for him and amusing her with an apparently endless supply of anecdotes about life around the pools of white mansions in Beverly Hills.

He had a theory, he said, about the frantic pace at which life was lived there, with working breakfast followed by working lunch and working dinner followed by pool parties and beach parties and long scented nights under the palms, with Bourbon followed by coke and finished off with a soothing puff of dope, the smoke drifting towards the stars. If you live perched on top of hair-trigger tectonic plates which could swallow you up at any time, he said, it gave an edge to life, a certain brittleness, a determination to enjoy today what might in a very real sense not be there tomorrow.

'It's all a fantasy,' she said as she finished her lassi and wiped her hands with the hot rose-scented towel that the waiter had left them.

'I guess you may be right,' he said, and she caught the momentary sadness in his eyes, quickly veiled as he lifted an imperious finger for the waiter.

'And hence the desire to see on film a reflection of a more certain age?' she had asked.

He had looked at her soberly before signing the bill with the flourish of a platinum card. Everything he did was considered, rehearsed even, she thought with irritation. Even the chat-up lines. But just sometimes she thought he took her seriously.

'Maybe,' he said. 'Or I just yearn to play the tragic hero one more time.'


Laura opened the front door of her flat to be met by the strains of Billie Holiday and a faint smell of burnt toast. Thackeray was sitting with his feet up on the coffee table and his eyes closed, but something told her he was not asleep. She hung up her coat and went into the bedroom to unpin her hair, which she let cascade down in a copper stream around her face before she began to brush it. She felt rather than heard Thackeray come in behind her before she saw his reflection in the mirror.

'Hi,' she said softly. 'I didn't mean to wake you.'

He slid his arms around her and she leaned back on her stool, feeling the solidity of his body which filled her always with a sense of exultation.

'Sorry I'm late,' she said. 'He wanted to go to Ahmet's for a curry and I thought it was too good an opportunity to miss out on. The better I can get to know him the better I can write about him.'

'Within reason, I hope,' Thackeray said. 'If I find you're being pursued by some randy Hollywood cowboy I might have to find some excuse to run him out of town.'

'That's not part of the job description, Sheriff,' Laura said. 'You know good reporters always make an excuse and leave.'

He ran his hands under her hair, down her neck and shoulders until he reached her breasts and left them there, massaging them gently until she could not stand it any longer.

'If that's all you've got to offer, maybe I should have stayed with Blake,' she said. She turned towards him, unbuttoning her shirt, and he picked her up and carried her to the bed. They threw off their clothes and made love hungrily with the bedroom door open and the plaintive heartbreak of Billie Holiday in their ears.

Some time later she woke to find herself lying with her head on his chest and his arms still tightly wrapped around her.

'Michael,' she said quietly, lifting her head slightly to see his face. He was awake, watching her intently. 'What's the matter?' she asked.

'You're lying on my arm,' he said. 'It's gone completely numb.' She shifted her position and he stretched his left arm tentatively, wincing as the blood rushed back.

'That wasn't it, was it?' she asked.

He stroked her hair gently. 'Laura, my Laura,' he said. 'Can't you just take it a day at a time? Please?'

'Michael . . .' she began again, but he had already rolled over and slipped back into sleep.


# 8


The next day, a couple of paragraphs of a crime reporter's speculative prose dropped into the deep waters of Bradfield's collective memory and sent long slow ripples around the town. At police headquarters Superintendent Jack Longley noted the item on the front page with distaste.

'Who bloody leaked that, then?' he snapped at Thackeray, when the DCI arrived in his office. 'This place is like a bloody sieve. Pillow talk, was it?'

'No, sir,' Thackeray said flatly, knowing his vulnerability in this area and hating it. 'It was just a sharp bit of journalism on the crime reporter's part. After all, we did send Mower to look at their archives. It's a pity we hadn't done a better job in keeping the files ourselves. After all, a murder file is never supposed to be closed.'

'It went down as a missing person in the end,' Longley said. 'As far as I know there was never any evidence then that Mariella Bonnetti was killed. And there's no one left in the Force to ask different, as far as I can discover.'

'Well, we know they were wrong now,' Thackeray said. 'Just like the *Gazette* says, Mrs Bonnetti had no doubt that it was her daughter's crucifix we found. And if this was just a missing girl, she must be the first one in history who succeeded in burying herself under six feet of Bradfield clay.'

'So that lass of yours had nowt to do with this story?' Longley said, disbelief oozing from every pore.

'I never even told her I'd been to see the Bonnettis,' Thackeray answered angrily. 'Let alone what they told us.'

'Aye, well, you'd best cast your mind over how we set up a murder inquiry forty-four years on,' Longley said. 'I dare say this lass is as entitled to justice as anyone else. And there's no time limit on murder as far as I know. So if the beggar's still alive, we'd better see if we can track him down, hadn't we? I don't want the overtime bill through the roof, mind.'

'Low key, then?' Thackeray said sceptically. 'The whole thing sounds more like a bit of archeology than a murder inquiry to me.'

'Make it look respectable, without giving yourself a hernia, lad,' Longley said. 'Make haste slowly. I'm sure a well-educated copper like you can get your mind round that.'

'It's a pity the bones weren't left to rest in peace for all the good we're going to do Mariella,' Thackeray said quietly.

'How can you say that? Her mother'll get her Requiem Mass, won't she? Doesn't that count for owt any more?'

Thackeray looked at the Superintendent for a long moment, his eyes blank.

'It can't close an account that's been left open,' Thackeray said at length. 'And I doubt very much I'll be able to close it.'

*

At the *Gazette,* Laura found herself with that same crime reporter breathing heavily down her neck as she tried to put together the opening paragraph of her feature on John Blake's visit to Bradfield and the Yorkshire dales.

'Why didn't you tell me about this Italian girl they've found?' Bob Baker asked. He was a recent recruit to the reporting staff and eager as a puppy to make his mark. His attitude to Laura Ackroyd had veered from over-friendly to deeply suspicious within a week, after he discovered that her live-in lover was a detective.

'Ted knew the police were going through the archives,' Laura said irritably. 'I thought he would have told you. Anyway, I didn't know anything definite. It was just speculation.'

'Yes, well, Ted didn't tell me,' Baker said, with a note of petulance in his voice which grated on Laura's nerves. He ran a hand over his thickly gelled hair as if a strand might have wandered out of place and sighed dramatically. 'And then he has the cheek to give me a bollocking for not getting the story yesterday when the cops went out to see the family in Harrogate.'

'So who did tell you?' Laura asked, her curiosity roused in spite of herself now.

'Ah, wouldn't you like to know?' Baker sneered. 'But if I can't trust you to tell me what's going on when you pick up a good story, I'm bloody sure I can't trust you not to go sneaking back to your boyfriends in the Force when there's a leak, can I? I'll keep my sources to myself, if you don't mind.'

'Suit yourself,' Laura said dismissively. 'You seem very sure of your facts, though.'

'Yes, well, there's no secret about that, is there? The girl's mother has identified the body, hasn't she? There wasn't much doubt in her mind when I spoke to her, even if her son did butt in and try to take the phone off her. I'm off to Harrogate now to talk to her for a bit more detail. So your boyfriend can lump it. And that smart-arse Cockney sergeant.'

'Kevin Mower? What's he done to annoy you?'

'It's what he's not done, more like. I bumped into him in the Woolpack and simply asked him how the identification of the body was going and he got on his high horse and told me to talk to the Press Office. As if Press Offices ever came up with any useful information. When I was in Rochdale I had a really good relationship going with CID. Here they don't seem to want to know.'

'It's not long since an officer was suspended for talking to the tabloids,' Laura said.

Baker shrugged non-committally at that. 'Mower was the one you rescued when he got stabbed, wasn't he? You should have saved your energy on that one, love.'

Just for a moment a red mist swirled between Laura and the computer screen on which she determinedly kept her eyes and she felt her fingers sticky again with the blood which it had seemed would never stop pumping out of Mower's limp body.

'Bastard,' she whispered from between dry lips, but when she turned round her tormentor was already on the other side of the office putting on his coat.

She leaned her head against the cold screen for a moment and closed her eyes.

'Bastard,' she said again.


At the Laurels, Joyce Ackroyd had wheeled her chair into the main hallway ready to pounce on the copy of the *Gazette* which she knew was delivered every afternoon at about four. When she had asked the previous day for a morning paper the care assistant had sniffed her disapproval and said that she would have to ask the matron. The subject had not been mentioned again.

But Joyce's sharp eyes had already registered the fact that the evening paper arrived courtesy of a cheerful boy on a bike who threw it into the outer hallway without dismounting, and that it usually lay there for anything up to half an hour before anyone bothered to pick it up off the floor.

She manoeuvred her chair awkwardly so that she could open the glass door into the small outer hall and leaned over precariously to pick the paper up. Her arthritic hip and her plastered leg jangled with pain and made her gasp as her fingers scrabbled for a purchase on the precious newsprint. She had not taken the unfamiliar pills which had been handed out to her again that morning and was suffering for her suspicion.

The newspaper securely on her lap, Bob Baker's small contribution to the front page caught her eye immediately and she sighed to see her fears confirmed so promptly. So Signora Bonnetti was still alive after all this time, she thought sadly. Fate might have been kinder if it had not expected her to live to experience the brutal exhumation of her long-dead daughter's bones.

Joyce had to concentrate hard to summon up a mental picture of the lively, laughing Italian girl after all these years. It was easier to recall the mother, a heavy woman made heavier by apparently continuous pregnancies as Mariella's younger brothers and sisters arrived in quick succession. Once or twice the possibility of mentioning contraception had crossed Joyce's practical Bradfield mind, only to be dismissed not on the grounds of embarrassment as much as an irritated acceptance that she would be wasting her time. The only thing more regular than Signora Bonnetti's pregnancies, Joyce had thought angrily, was her clockwork departure for Mass, chivvying her brood before her up Peter Hill to the little Catholic Church half a mile away every Sunday morning.

She was an anxious woman, Joyce recalled, made more anxious by her husband's inability to keep work and by the niggling daily pinpricks of insults and disdain directed at her and her children by neighbours who resented strangers of any sort and former enemies most of all.

Communication with Signora Bonnetti had been difficult, and Joyce could remember Mariella, whose English improved rapidly, translating for her as she had tried to explain the latest intricacies of the post-war rationing system to the bewildered Italian. A pretty girl, dark, vivacious, a bobby-dazzler the lads had said – but the exact shape of her face, the map of eyes and nose and mouth, beyond that fuzzy newspaper picture Michael Thackeray had showed her, the sound of her voice, the way she walked and ran brown-limbed through the sunshine, had vanished into the mists of memory and try as she might Joyce could not recall them.

She was wrenched sharply back to the present by the voice of Betty Johns.

'Mrs Ackroyd! You are a naughty girl,' the matron said, spinning Joyce's wheelchair round so sharply that it tilted dangerously and Joyce only prevented herself from falling sideways by grabbing the armrests tightly. Again the pain stabbed angrily the length of her thigh but she gritted her teeth rather than cry out.

'You'll catch your death of cold out there in the porch. And my evening paper, too.' Mrs Johns took the *Gazette* off Joyce's lap without ceremony and began to push her at speed along the hall towards the day room.

Joyce bit her lip in vexation, but she did not want a confrontation which would inevitably end in her being wheeled back to her bedroom. There, she knew by now, she might languish for the rest of the day if no one remembered to fetch her back for the frugal final meal which would be served at six o'clock and cleared away at six-fifteen, whether the frailer residents had succeeded in consuming anything or not.

Joyce was becoming very angry, but it was an anger which she was content to let burn deep within herself for the moment. She did not want to leave the Laurels just yet, although she was as determined as ever to get back to her own home eventually. In the meantime she was keeping a mental note of every indignity that Betty Johns and her handful of staff heaped upon her personally but also, more crucially, on some of her companions who were much less able to look out for themselves.

Amongst those was Alice Smith. Parked unceremoniously in a corner of the day room by the matron, Joyce turned her chair with difficulty and looked around at the semi-comatose residents sitting in rows along the walls. She spotted Alice slumped in an uncomfortable-looking chair right under the noisy television set, her eyes half closed.

Determinedly Joyce wheeled herself across the room and took hold of her arm. Alice's eyes opened but her look was vacant and her smile vague.

'Hello, dear,' she said faintly. 'Have you come to watch *Corrie*?'

Joyce glanced up at the television set which was blasting out canned laughter to accompany one of the almost identical quiz shows which seemed to fill acres of time. She very much doubted whether any of the residents who sat with their eyes fixed on the flickering images actually took in much of what was happening on the screen.

'It's not time for *Coronation Street*,' she said. 'That's later. After tea. Would you like to come out in the conservatory for a little chat, Alice? There's a few things I want to ask you.'

'Oh, no, dear,' Alice said. 'I've got to watch *Corrie*. I always watch *Corrie* after we've had our tea.' Her eyes flickered up to the television set again but Joyce did not believe that she could see, let alone comprehend, what it offered. Joyce drew a sharp breath, on the point of trying to put Alice right on the time of day but she thought better of it. Alice Smith was out to lunch, as Laura would put it, and she would very much like to know why.


At the Clarendon, John Blake disentangled himself from Lorelie's somewhat spiky embrace and picked up the telephone beside his bed. She rolled away and wiped her face where she could feel the mascara had been smudged by her tears. The *Bradfield Gazette* lay scattered on the floor where he had flung it after glancing briefly at the front page.

She had been working at the desk on the other side of the room when she became aware of his dissatisfaction, her antennae finely tuned to his body language.

'Hon?' she'd said. 'Is something wrong, hon? We don't have anything adverse in that rag, do we, angel? I can't imagine . . .'

'No, nothing adverse,' Blake had come back perhaps a little too promptly. 'You're doing absolutely fine on the press front, Lorelie. Absolutely fine. Now find me the local phone book, will you? I need to look someone up.'

Unconvinced, she had crossed the room, sat down on the soft edge of the Clarendon's most extensive king-sized bed and attempted to smooth the all too permanent creases out of Blake's brow.

Perversely irritated by her approach he had pulled her on to the bed and stripped off her skirt and panties without ceremony.

His attentions were brutal and she could not contain a gasp of pain, which she knew would provoke him to further excesses.

'Jeez, you're hurting me, angel,' she said.

'Great,' John Blake said, the veins at his temples throbbing as his excitement increased. 'I'll make my phone call later.'

# 9

Sergeant Kevin Mower leaned back in his canteen chair and winced. Cautiously he slid a hand under his shirt and felt the small angry scar just below his shoulder where a knife had come perilously close to killing him just months before. They said your life flashed in front of your eyes as you died, he thought, but he knew it was not true. He had felt nothing but an overwhelming sense of panic as he realised the fatal extent of his miscalculation in the couple of seconds between the two blows which had come unseen from behind and the oblivion which quickly followed.

It was now, in the quiet aftermath, when he could see that his colleagues were beginning to forget and to treat him as casually as normal, that the enormity of his brush with death bothered him. For them the memory might be fading already, but for him it was not. He woke occasionally in the night, sweating and gasping for breath as he fought off unknown assailants in the dark. But it was after that, as he lay in bed waiting for his heart to stop pounding, that he wondered what of value he would have left behind if Laura Ackroyd had not been there that day to staunch the bleeding and save his life.

He noticed WDC Val Ridley watching him from the queue at the canteen counter and straightened his chair. She would not have shed many tears at his funeral, he thought bitterly as he watched her cross the room towards him, neat, blonde, collected and with pale blue eyes which always harboured deep suspicion when she was in his vicinity.

'What have I done to deserve this?' he asked lightly as she pulled up a chair and sat down beside him.

'Not a lot, Sarge,' she said.

'You'd go down well with the lads in the Met, Val,' Mower said. 'They work on the basis that most people are guilty until they're proved innocent.'

'That's why you left, is it?' she asked.

'Well, it wasn't for the talent "oop north".'

'What about this Italian girl?' she said. 'I get the feeling no one's falling over themselves about her.'

'It was a long time ago,' Mower said mildly. 'The chances of getting a result must be pretty slim. But you're wrong, as it happens. I've just persuaded the Guv'nor to let me go and see the only O'Meara in the phone book. One of the lads who used to hang out with Mariella was a Danny O'Meara. There's just a chance he's still around. Do you want to come with me to check it out?'

The pursuit of Danny O'Meara took the edgy team of Sergeant Mower and Val Ridley further than they had expected. Late that afternoon they found themselves driving up the winding drive of Long Moor Psychiatric Hospital, a sprawling Victorian pile now largely derelict and abandoned as patients had been moved out into the community, which for many meant on to the streets.

The drive out from Bradfield had been largely silent. Val had stared resolutely out of the window as Mower drove fast up the narrow roads to the hamlet of Long Moor where the hospital had been built a century ago on the edge of the sweeping Pennine moors. After trying and failing to penetrate Ridley's icy disapproval, Mower had shrugged and decided to get the trip over as quickly as possible. She remained impassive as he swung recklessly round the road's sharp corners before squealing to a halt at the hospital gates to explain their mission to the uniformed porter.

Their visit to O'Meara's home had been brief and emotional. The door had been opened by a young woman, smartly dressed in a grey business suit, dark stockings and heels, who had nodded briefly when they had explained why they were there.

'My mother's inside,' she said, indicating the front room of the terraced house. Her mother turned out to be a crumpled woman who must, Mower guessed, be in her mid-fifties but looked ten years older, grey straggly hair falling into her eyes and masking an unhealthy-looking puffy face. She was sitting close to the gas fire in her dressing gown in a room which looked as if it had been unused and undusted for a considerable length of time. She looked up only briefly when her daughter told her who the visitors were and Mower explained what they wanted.

'She gets very depressed herself when my father's bad,' the younger woman explained. 'This time he's had to go into hospital. It's been going on for years. It's not been easy for her.'

Mower had let Val Ridley coax the dispiriting story of Daniel O'Meara's life from the two women. He was indeed the boy who had played with Mariella Bonnetti in Peter Street all those years ago. Grown up, he had married Margaret, the woman who now sat hunched over the blue flames. He had fathered four children, who had somehow scrambled up and out of Bradfield's impoverished terraces to make something of themselves in spite of their father's recurrent illness which had made it almost impossible for him to hold down a job.

'I'd have left him years ago,' his daughter had said dismissively. She had glanced at her mother. 'But of course she listens to the priest, doesn't she?'

The older woman had turned at that and given her daughter a look of pure dislike.

'He can't help it,' she said. 'He's not responsible, is he? For being sick, I mean. She's like all of them. Thinks he can just pull himself together. Isn't that what you say, Kay? You're always telling him to pull himself together?'

'You make excuses for him,' Kay retorted, turning away. Mower felt Ridley's disapproving eyes follow his as he appraised the shapely legs beneath the short tight skirt.

'When did he go to hospital?' Val Ridley asked with an edge to her voice which was not entirely justified by the fact that she recognised the two women were rehearsing old arguments that could go on indefinitely. 'Where has he gone?'

It emerged that O'Meara had taken a turn for the worse three days ago, refusing to get out of bed, neglecting to wash or dress, and threatening suicide before lapsing into a state of paranoia and hiding under the bedclothes whenever anyone entered his room.

'Did anything spark this attack off?' Mower had asked, but neither woman could think of any reason why Danny O'Meara had slipped so suddenly back into the depression which had dogged him for years.

'Did he ever talk about living in Peter Street when he was a lad?' Val Ridley had asked casually but both women had shaken their heads, evidently making no connection with the discovery there of the Italian girl's body which had been reported in the *Gazette*.

'Our Bridget might know,' Kay said. 'She was the one who was always close to Dad. He used to tell her stories, daft things, all nonsense I used to think.' They had taken down Bridget O'Meara's address in Leeds in case it was needed.

As they had left the dispirited and dispiriting O'Meara household to pursue their quarry to Long Moor they heard the front door open and close again behind them. Kay O'Meara, car keys in her hand, caught them up as Mower opened his car door.

'I didn't want to say in front of my mother,' she said. 'But I think Dad was being dunned for money. I saw him talking to a bloke at the end of the street the other evening as I drove past. There was definitely an argument going on.'

'No one you knew?' Val Ridley asked and the young woman had shaken her head.

'I only got a glimpse of him,' she said. 'He was tall, well dressed, grey haired, I think. Not enough to recognise. He's a terrible gambler, my dad. It was probably someone from the bookies.'

'We'll ask him about it,' Mower had said, not neglecting to watch appreciatively as Kay O'Meara swung her long legs into her car and slammed the door almost as hard as Val Ridley slammed hers. But it looked, Mower thought as he pulled up outside the small section of the hospital which still showed signs of life, like very long odds that they would get anything useful out of the man they had come to see.

They were met by a casually dressed nurse, his hair tied back in a pony-tail and an identity badge pinned to his sweatshirt which told them his name was Gary. When they explained their mission he looked vague.

'He's got a visitor already. If he's still here,' he said. 'I'll check for you.'

He wandered off into the further regions of the hospital and disappeared from view, leaving the two officers standing in what had obviously been the hall of the original house around which the hospital had been built. The place had a curiously temporary air about it, the once elegant curving staircase hemmed in by partitions, the original doors replaced by flimsy modern affairs with panels of safety glass at the top, the paintwork chipped, the floor of maroon and white Italianate tiles cracked and stained.

'I should think this place would *give* you depression rather than cure it,' Mower said sourly.

'I think they've given up on cures, haven't they?' Val Ridley offered. 'Dump them in the community and leave us to scrape 'em up when they get out of hand or the cardboard boxes spring a leak. Isn't that the prescription?'

Mower glanced at her reflectively.

'I didn't know you felt so strongly,' he said.

'Well, there's a lot you don't know,' Val Ridley replied. 'And a lot you won't find out if all you're interested in is getting a hand inside every pair of knickers that comes within range.'

'Ouch,' Mower said with a grin. It was not knickers he seemed to be getting under as much as someone's skin. But before he could make any capital out of that conclusion, Gary strolled back from wherever he had been making enquiries.

'He's gone for a walk in the grounds with his visitor, apparently,' he said.

'He's fit for that, is he?' Mower said sharply. 'I thought he was suicidal.'

The nurse gave Mower a faintly supercilious smile.

'Oh, he's fine now he's on medication,' he said. 'He'll be going home in a day or two. This episode was just a slight setback.'

'They can wander in and out of here, then?' Val Ridley asked dubiously.

'Some can, if they're not sectioned. Danny's a voluntary

patient. We do have a couple of secure wards. But there's not much call for that these days,' Gary said complacently. 'They don't rave, you know, like they used to. There's medication for most conditions. We've moved on a bit since *One Flew Over the Cuckoo's Nest.*'

'We might debate that some time,' Val Ridley said with some asperity, heading briskly for the door.

'You've come up from Bradfield, have you?' Gary asked Mower inconsequentially. 'CID? You must work with Mr Thackeray.'

Mower drew a sharp breath at that, a question springing to mind which he hardly dared ask. But there was no need. Gary was a gossip who did not need encouragement.

'He still comes up now and again to see his wife. She doesn't know him of course, but I suppose he feels he must. Poor beggar.'

'Any idea where Mr O'Meara might have gone?' Val asked over her shoulder from the doorstep where she had been surveying the extensive grounds. She had evidently not been listening and appeared to be unaware that what the nurse had just said had rendered the Sergeant speechless as its implications sank in.

Gary shrugged. 'There's quite a few acres out there. Great on a nice day like today but a waste of space most of the year. If you follow the paths round the back of the house you get a good view right down to the railway at the bottom. You should be able to see Danny and his friend from there. They won't have left the grounds. He's not cleared for outside trips just yet.'

'Who was the visitor?' Mower asked, trying to gather his scattered thoughts.

'I'm not sure,' Gary said as he ushered them back to the door. He hesitated as he reached for the security lock. 'Just a friend. Tall, well-dressed bloke. Oldish. Grey hair. Nice for him. The family doesn't visit, you know. Funny how different people's reactions are to mental illness, isn't it?'

Mower and Ridley stood in the weak sunshine on the overgrown terrace at the back of the house for a moment scanning the hospital grounds. There were wooden benches here and there

83

on the rough-cut grass and a few people sitting huddled up in coats against the unseasonably cool wind. They made their way down the slope, enquiring for Danny O'Meara of everyone they met but without gaining any coherent information. At the bottom of the hill, where a rusting wire fence separated a bedraggled shrubbery from the steep slope of the railway embankment, the view of the Maze valley, with Bradfield a smudge of grey on the horizon, stretched for miles. Mower glanced along the cutting to where the shining rails disappeared around a curve, and something caught his eye.

'Oh, Jesus,' he said, his stomach clenching in a shockwave to which his scars reacted with angry jabs of pain.

Val Ridley followed his eyes and saw the body lying like a discarded toy between the rails and the head, face up, where it had rolled into the grass at the edge of the cutting a yard away. Even from a distance they could see the crimson blood splashed and streaked across the gravel of the track.

'O'Meara,' she whispered through dry lips.

'A dead cert, I'd say,' Mower said. 'So much for Gary's medication. And if that's O'Meara, where the hell's his friend?'

'You mean it may not be suicide?' Val asked. Mower glanced at her, taking in the pallor of her face and her tightly clenched fists which she quickly shoved into the pockets of her jacket. He knew better than to ask if she was all right.

'Well, if it's murder that'll stir the boss up, won't it? You'll get your full inquiry into the Italian girl's death.'

'About bloody time,' WDC Ridley said. But what filled Kevin Mower with foreboding was the knowledge that he must call Michael Thackeray and ask him to come to Long Moor Hospital, and that he must do it now.

'Oh, God,' he said to himself as he pulled out his mobile phone. 'Haven't you punished me enough recently, you old bastard? What did I do to deserve this?'


Fosters' Mills dominated the steepest of Bradfield's seven hills, its great stone slab of a classical façade and tapering chimney visible for tens of miles around. It was years now since the buildings had reverberated to the roar of the looms which had brought a century of prosperity to the narrow terraces of back-to-back cottages that once lined the steep streets between the mill and the town. The terraces were long gone, replaced by squat blocks of 1960s maisonettes, but the mill had remained, a vast sandstone monument to past glories and a standing rebuke to a generation of Bradfielders who could find no use for it.

Until, that is, Keith Spencer-Smith erupted on to the scene, appointed by the town council to take its rudimentary tourist industry by the scruff of the neck and shake it into life. A new Branson, one enthusiastic councillor had said, though the *Gazette* reckoned this had more to do with his beard than his acumen.

John Blake's Mercedes slid smoothly up the hill towards the Mill, which had become the jewel in Spencer-Smith's heavily self-promoted crown. His enemies, and he had more than a few, reckoned that if Spencer-Smith could find a technology which could bottle the smells of outside privies and smoke-polluted air that had made nineteenth-century Bradfield unique he would certainly try. If it moved, local lore had it, then Keith Spencer-Smith would sell it.

Lorelie Baum had relinquished her seat beside John Blake in the front of the Mercedes to Laura when they met outside the *Gazette*. She had slammed the rear door so hard that it gave a most unGermanic crash and the big car trembled slightly.

'Temper,' Blake had said, turning to give Lorelie the benefit of one of his most toothsome smiles. 'Laura, honey, you will have lunch with us after Keith has shown us round, won't you?'

'I doubt if there'll be time,' Laura said. 'I'll have to write something for tomorrow's first edition when I get back.' As far as she was concerned, lunch with Lorelie in attendance would be so much wasted time. She could not be bothered enduring Blake's increasingly unrestrained attentions without hope of reward.

To get his museum off the ground, on the slightly suspect pretext that an early cinematographer, Les Crossley, who had made his mark in Hollywood had been born in Broadley just six miles away, Spencer-Smith had twisted every arm of every millionaire with even the remotest connection with the textile industry. That and a windfall from the National Lottery had realised his dream, to the astonishment of a town council who were left wondering where the tourists who might be attracted to such a superficially unpromising destination could be housed. Spencer-Smith, it was rumoured, was now using the same strong-arm tactics on hotel chains who might provide the cineasts with beds and breakfasts and club owners who might drag the town's night-life out of the lager and vindaloo time-warp in which it was fixed.

John Blake parked in a cobbled yard at the side of the tall mill wall beneath the hoists where bales of wool had once been lifted into the building. Keith Spencer-Smith was waiting for them on the steps leading to what had been the loading doors, attended by two young women in very short skirts with clipboards and dazzling smiles at the ready. He was taller than John Blake, as fair as the actor was dark, with a silky beard closely trimmed to the line of his jaw. Wearing a silver-grey suit and a red and white polka-dot tie he looked every inch the successful entrepreneur.

With an expression of some disdain Lorelie picked her way in high heels over dustsheets and trailing cables where workmen were putting the finishing touches to the main reception area inside the enormous double doors.

'If I'd known this was still a construction lot I'd have worn denims,' she said petulantly. Laura, in a black trouser suit, aubergine shirt and her favourite laced boots could not suppress the smallest smile of triumph.

Introductions over, the women followed the men into the bowels of the huge building, where the floors which had once housed the machinery had been transformed into closed galleries to tell the history of the film industry from flickering start to virtual reality finish. There was a full-sized television studio where children could put themselves on to videotape, a viewing theatre which could handle everything from black and white silent movies to the latest wide-screen extravaganzas, and every kind of gadget and gizmo which had turned museum visiting from a silent pilgrimage into a high-tech adventure.

'This must have cost a fortune,' Laura said to Keith Spencer-Smith, impressed.

'It's taken some time to raise the money,' he admitted.

'Something Keith's always been good at,' Blake said.

'You've known each other a long time, then?' Laura asked, not, she was well aware, for the first time.

'We bumped into each other again in the States . . .'

'I can tell you something about John's time in the military if you like,' Lorelie broke in. 'He could have gone to Korea, you know. Some of his best friends got sent to Korea.'

'But he didn't?' Laura countered.

'Well, no, but that was a real scary time for those young men, isn't that right, John?'

'Right,' Blake said shortly. 'But you're here to talk about the museum today, Laura, aren't you? Let's not waste time on me.'

Keith Spencer-Smith took her arm and steered her in the direction of the top-floor windows which offered a panoramic view of the town in the valley and the hills beyond.

'If you look here you can just see Broadley where Les Crossley was born, see there, beyond the church spire?'

'I have to confess I've never heard of him,' Laura said. 'How did you come across him?'

'I've always been interested in cinema,' Spencer-Smith said. 'He's in the history books. Developing something like this has been a dream of mine for years.'

'There's nothing else like it north of London,' Blake said proprietorially.

'There'll be big media interest for the opening,' Lorelie put in. 'Now can I please see where the photo opportunities are going to be? We can't have John up against those dark gallery back-drops. Too grim. And he favours his left profile, you know.'

She stalked away with Spencer-Smith's assistants to seek a suitably lit frame to set off her employer's fading charms to best advantage. Laura sensed a tension between the two men that she could not fully understand.

'Did you stay in Yorkshire, then?' she asked Spencer-Smith.

'Oh, no, I've been around,' he said. 'Devon, Scotland, abroad.

You know the tourist business. But when this came up . . .' He shrugged. 'It seemed like a challenge I couldn't turn down.'

Selling Bradfield as a tourist destination seemed to Laura like a career move from hell for any semi-successful promoter, but she contrived to look suitably impressed. With her mind only half on the job, she dutifully followed their host around the rest of the museum, a ghostly, echoing place without its complement of bright lights and flickering technology that would not be switched on until the opening.

As they worked their way back to reception Lorelie caught up with them again, her heels clattering like machine-gun fire down the cast-iron staircase painted in black and red.

'Tom Cruise's people never get treated like this,' she exclaimed angrily to Blake. 'These kids don't know shit from Shinola!'

'Take it easy,' Blake said. 'It'll be all right on the night.'

'You gotta be joking,' Lorelie said ominously, stalking out of the main entrance and back to the car.

'Time of the month?' Spencer-Smith asked, but Blake shrugged.

'Far be it from me . . .' Blake said, glancing at Laura for sympathy but finding none. 'She'll be fine. And you, Laura? Have you got enough for your feature?'

'I think so,' Laura said. 'If I need to check anything I'll give you or Keith a call.' Though she was sure by now that the things which needed checking about John Blake would need a more wily approach than she had so far brought to bear.

# 10

DCI Michael Thackeray walked from the central police station to the side entrance of Bradfield Infirmary with his mind in a turmoil that he knew was both extreme and dangerous. It was eight-thirty on the sort of chilly morning which brought gusts of sleety rain slanting down from the hills surrounding the town. The weather was an apt reflection of the icy lump which seemed to have congealed inside him ever since Kevin Mower's call from Long Moor Hospital the previous afternoon.

He had instructed the Sergeant to set in motion the procedures which surround a suspicious death. By the time Thackeray himself had driven with deep reluctance up the familiar winding lane and walked to the railway embankment, the mutilated body had been removed to the mortuary and Mower was standing on the track, the wind ballooning his jacket and rippling his short dark hair. He was deep in conversation with a couple of uniformed officers. Looking back, Thackeray still could not decide whether the glance Mower had flashed in his direction was simply one of acknowledgement or of a sympathy he had never sought and bitterly resented.

Thackeray had been shown the place where the body had lain between the tracks, the smear of blood on the rail where the passing train had severed not only Danny O'Meara's head but also one of his hands, the place where the head had come to rest, the chain-link fence, rusted and sagging, where even a child could have climbed on to the embankment from the hospital grounds.

It was a quiet, secret place. Trees and shrubs overhung the little-used, neglected track with a curtain of green and the air was damp and heavy with the smell of vegetation and wild flowers. The gables and clock tower of the hospital, Thackeray realised with a sense of relief, were out of sight above them.

Thackeray had instructed Mower to go back to the hospital and take statements from the nurses who had dealt with O'Meara as a patient. He had accepted the uniformed sergeant's offer to interview the train driver who had felt it best for the sake of his passengers not to stop his train to investigate the body he had been unable to avoid as he drove his two-carriage diesel round the tight Long Moor curve on the way to Arnedale. He had never been in any doubt that the huddled figure on the track, which he had glimpsed briefly before it disappeared under his wheels, could not have survived. He had reported the incident when he had reached the next station and was now at his home in a state of shock waiting to be interviewed.

Thackeray had driven immediately back to Bradfield with a

sense of relief that he had been so easily able to avoid the clamber up the embankment towards the hospital. But he knew by then that Mower's sardonically raised eyebrow certainly meant that he had learned what Thackeray had intended that no one should ever know, that his wife Aileen existed at Long Moor in a state of permanent unknowing.

He had sat in his office until midnight, fighting down the craving for a drink which he had successfully resisted for so long that its newly sharpened claws threw him off-balance. He had gone back to Laura's flat tired, morose and unable to talk, thrown himself into bed and turned his back on her.

Next morning he woke before it was light, unrefreshed. When Laura had turned over and asked sleepily what was wrong he claimed an early appointment and left quickly to shave in the police station washroom, where his gaunt reflection in the mirror shocked him. He had taken a solitary breakfast in the canteen. By eight-forty he was putting on the overall which Amos Atherton's lab assistant handed him and gazing with well-controlled disgust at the remains of Danny O'Meara on the pathologist's table.

'A messy little beggar, this one,' Atherton said cheerfully as he began his examination. 'You'd think if he was already in Long Moor he could have found enough pills to finish himself off without all this gore.'

'Suicide then?' Thackeray asked.

Atherton gave him a flash of slightly bleary blue eyes. 'Got summat else in mind, have you?' he asked.

'Straws in the wind, no more,' Thackeray said. 'A missing visitor, a nurse who says he was well on the mend.'

'Well then, we'll take it right steady, shall we?'

Atherton turned back to his table, his concentration intense as he continued his external examination of the corpse, tape-recording his comments as he went along.

'If he were pushed on to t'track, you'd expect to find some sign of a struggle,' he said, turning to Thackeray at length. 'But there's nowt I can see on the trunk or the arms. Surprisingly unmarked, considering, but that's because of the way he was lying between the rails.'

Thackeray looked away as Atherton turned his attention to the severed head, the neck and hair still dark with blood, the features washed for identification but disfigured by massive lacerations across the nose and cheeks.

'From the position of the body he was face down when the train hit him,' Atherton said. 'Which is what you'd expect if he put himself on the track. It'd be a brave man who watched the train coming round the bend.'

'The hospital says that the medication might have made him woozy but euphoric, certainly not suicidal,' Thackeray said.

'Aye, well, we'll check the level of drugs in his blood,' Atherton said abstractedly as he turned the head and began to peer amongst the matted grey hair. A sharp whistle of breath between his teeth was all the indication he gave that he had found something significant as he examined the scalp minutely.

'This may be what you're looking for,' he said at last, glancing at his impassive audience. 'Happen you'll need to examine the train for traces of blood and hair but I can't see myself how it could have severed his head like this and caught him a blow on the top of the skull which has fractured it an' all.'

'You mean he was hit by something else?' Thackeray asked quietly.

'Looks to me as if he was hit by a round object, your proverbial blunt instrument, either attached to the train, or on the track – though I can't imagine the head rolling with sufficient force to pick up an injury like this on the ground.'

Thackeray leaned forward reluctantly to gaze at an indentation in Danny O'Meara's skull which appeared to him like nothing so much as a blow with a golf-ball.

'A weapon?' Thackeray said.

'It'd make sense, wouldn't it?' Atherton said. 'Knock him cold then lay him out on t'track and ninety-nine to one the train'll obliterate any evidence of the previous injury. That would explain the nice clean cut across the neck, too. Suicide is generally even more messy. Folk might think they can lay their head on the line and wait but generally they panic at the last minute and get made into mincemeat. Lots of bits.'

'Thanks, Amos,' Thackeray said in protest.

'Seriously, lad, you need to get your forensic folk on to this sharpish, especially as it's raining. Whatever caused this injury, whether it was part of the train, or summat on the track or your blunt instrument, whatever, it will carry the evidence for a while. The indentation's deep and it looks as if it bled, which would indicate that it was done before the poor beggar caught his last train. There'll be traces of blood and hair somewhere, you can bank on it.'

'Did it kill him?'

'Possibly,' Atherton said. 'But it's academic if it was caused by the train, isn't it? A blow on the head seconds before it's severed is neither here nor there. But if it was minutes before . . .'

Thackeray nodded and forced himself to take a last look at what was left of Danny O'Meara before he moved away to take off his overall. Even before the train had done its brutal work, there had not been much left of the boy who had played with the Italian girl all those years before: a skinny, almost emaciated body, a face seamed and lined beyond its years, a straggle of overlong grey hair. If this was Mariella's killer, Thackeray thought, he looked as if he had already served a life sentence, as perhaps, in a sense, he had.

But he was increasingly convinced that his execution was not self-inflicted. He knew now that he would have to follow the trail of Mariella's killer more determinedly than either he or Jack Longley had anticipated. He more than half hoped to pin the blame here, on a dead man, where it could do least harm after the passage of so many years. He had seldom felt so unprepared, intellectually and emotionally, to launch a murder inquiry.


Laura flung herself into the corner of Vicky Mendelson's seductively deep sofa and allowed her friend's two small sons to cuddle up beside her. As she read them their story she glanced occasionally over the boys' curly dark heads to where Vicky was shovelling apricot and rice into her baby daughter's ever-open mouth. It was a domestic scene which Laura found soothing although she was sharply aware that envy was never far away when she visited this comfortably untidy home. She had met

Michael Thackeray for the first time at Vicky and David Mendelson's dinner table and was still unsure whether this was the best
or the worst thing that had ever happened to her.

She gave Daniel and Nathan a hug and closed their book.

'Do you want me to bath you?' she asked, but Daniel shook
his head gravely.

'We're allowed to go by ourselves now so long as I test the
water with my fingers before we get in.'

'You're growing up, Daniel,' Laura said. Nathan, the younger
brother, chubbier and more devil-may-care, was already strug-
gling out of his T-shirt, his eyes sparkling in anticipation.

'Come on, Danny,' he commanded. 'Hurry up.'

When the boys had gone upstairs, Laura stretched out with a
groan.

'Bad day?' Vicky asked, wiping Naomi Laura's sticky mouth
and settling her in a baby-chair on the floor before pouring two
generous vodka and tonics.

'One way and another,' Laura said, taking her glass circumspectly, aware that tears were not far away.

'What is it?' Vicky asked softly, sitting down on the floor close
to her daughter, who was burbling sleepily. 'Is Michael giving
you a hard time? I thought when he moved in you might be able
to pin him down at last.'

'Michael? No, he's just very busy,' Laura said. 'In late and out
again very early this morning. Par for the course.'

'So?' Vicky pressed. 'Come on, Laura. Something's wrong. You
can't fool me.'

'It's Joyce,' Laura said, her voice breaking dangerously. 'I went
to see her at lunchtime and she seemed quite poorly. She hates it
in that place and usually she's full of it, how awful the matron
is, how badly the more helpless residents are being treated, how
she'll have their guts for garters before she has the place closed
down. But today she seemed just apathetic, somehow. As if she
didn't care any more. And then she fell asleep in her chair,
looking so old and worn out that I couldn't bear it.'

'It doesn't sound like the Joyce we all know and love,' Vicky
said.

'I spoke to the matron and she just said it was old age. They

93

all went like that in the end. But not Joyce! I've got to get her out of there, Vicky. It's doing her no good. It's killing her.'

'What about a private home?'

'This is a private home, but the council pays for the places. Anyway, she'd hate to go private completely,' Laura said morosely. 'And I certainly can't afford it on my salary. I think I'll have to talk to my father.'

'It's his responsibility more than yours,' Vicky assured her.

'I don't think he quite sees it like that,' Laura said. 'She's always turned down his offers of help. He's just as pig-headed as she is.'

'Runs in the family,' Vicky said, laughing.

'Well, one of us is going to have to swallow our pride.'

'Stay to supper? David will be home soon.'

Laura shook her head regretfully. She seemed to find little time these days for Vicky and David, the friends with whom she had shared her student days.

'I'd better get back in case Michael comes in wanting something to eat,' she said.

'How very domestic,' Vicky mocked. 'It sounds as if the taming is coming on a treat to me.' Their eyes met for a moment and neither of them was smiling. Laura stood up quickly, picked up her namesake and gave the sleepy child a fleeting kiss, knowing that anything more would betray her completely.

'I should be so lucky,' she said with a lightness she did not feel. 'I must go, though. Love to David, and you take care of your mummy, Naomi Laura. You're both precious.'

Vicky took back her daughter and stood at the front door with the child in her arms, watching Laura as she drove away.

'Bloody men,' she said into the baby's silky red hair. 'Why do even the best of them end up behaving badly?'


It was after midnight again when Michael Thackeray returned to Laura's flat, but this time he found her sitting in front of the television watching a late film, wearing the silky pyjamas of soft gold which they both knew he liked to the point of distraction. She turned slightly in her chair and watched him as he hung up his coat and saw at once that her preparations might have been in vain. He looked grey with fatigue and avoided her eyes as he went into the kitchen and came back with a glass of milk.

'You're up late,' he said, flinging himself into an armchair. 'Are you not working tomorrow?'

'As ever,' she said. 'There's the grand opening of the movie museum coming up and I haven't nearly finished my profile of John Blake. But I didn't think I'd sleep if I went to bed.' She flicked the TV off.

'I need to talk to you,' she said, unaware of the effect her words had on his heart-rate in spite of the resolute distance he was keeping.

'Can it wait till tomorrow?' he asked. 'I'm shattered. There's been a death which could be linked to the murder of the Italian girl. But it's the devil's own job to know where to start with an inquiry that's over forty years old.'

'Then indirectly we're into the same problem,' she said, and his sense of panic subsided slightly. 'Joyce can help you with that one, I'm sure she can, but I've got to get her out of that place she's in. The matron, superintendent or whatever she calls herself, must have done her training in Holloway, by the look of her. I swear I'll do a major piece on granny-bashing, but not till I've got Joyce well out of her clutches.'

'Come on, Laura, it can't be as bad as all that,' Thackeray said wearily, knowing as soon as he had uttered the words they were a serious mistake. Laura's cheeks flushed pink and her eyes sparkled.

'It can be and it bloody well is,' she said with conviction. 'It might even be police business. I think they're doing something to keep them quiet. Tranquillisers, probably. Joyce just wasn't herself today. I've never known her so quiet and depressed.'

'If she – or you – are going to make allegations like that you need some concrete evidence,' Thackeray said. 'She may still be suffering from shock after her fall. It can take people a long time to get over an accident at that age.'

'It's more than that. I'm going to call my father tomorrow,' Laura said flatly. 'I want him to come over and help me sort this out.'

'I'll not say no to that, though it might cost me a trip to Portugal,' Thackeray said quietly. 'I want to talk to him myself. It looks as if I'll have to talk to everyone who knew the Italian girl after all, and that includes your father.'

'He was only a child,' Laura said. 'I can't imagine he'll remember much.'

'Everyone remembers where they were on the day of the Coronation, I'm told,' Thackeray said. 'It's like the day Diana died or Maggie Thatcher resigned.'

Laura grinned. 'I got so drunk that night,' she said pensively. 'We had a celebration party after work. David Mendelson always said he'd dance in the streets the day she went, so we made him do it – not something you often see an august member of the legal profession do. It's just a pity things didn't improve. Still, we live in hope with the new lot.'

'Your father will remember Coronation Day,' Thackeray said. He did not share Laura's intermittent faith in the political process, a legacy of her childhood hero-worship of her combative grandmother.

'Joyce will remember more,' Laura said. 'But you'd better catch her while she can remember anything at all.' Her face reflected the return of the anxiety which had gnawed her all day. She looked bereft, Thackeray thought, and the fear that he could only offer her more pain twisted like a knife in his stomach.

'Do you want me to go?' Thackeray asked, not looking at her.

'Go? What do you mean? Go where?'

'Leave. So that you can bring Joyce to stay here.'

Laura looked at him with such a mixture of shock and disbelief that it hit him like a physical blow.

'You know I never want you to leave,' she said, her voice choked with emotion. 'Joyce can't live here, three floors up. We've talked about that. You know it's not an option.' She moved to sit beside him and he responded to her embrace in spite of himself.

'Are you trying to seduce me?' he said eventually.

'Do I need to?' she asked, unbuttoning his shirt and running her hands possessively down his naked back. Just for a moment he hesitated before accepting that there was nothing he could do

96

to resist. But as his mouth closed over hers and he wrapped her in his arms a small, chilly voice at the back of his mind reminded him of all that he had intended to say that night, which would now remain unsaid, and of how much he despised himself.

# 11

Laura drove up to the Laurels at lunchtime the next day and went in, leaving her car engine running and the passenger door open. She found her grandmother in the hallway in her wheel-chair and her heart contracted in pain as she saw how shrunken and frail Joyce looked.

'Are you ready?' she asked, glancing around for help to get Joyce out of the building and into the car. 'Is there no one here? Are you warm enough in that jacket?'

'It's never warm in this place,' Joyce said with surprising asperity, and Laura realised that although she appeared to be lolling wearily in her chair her eyes were bright.

'You sound just like my mother, and that's going back a bit,' Joyce whispered. 'Now you listen to me. Pick up those crutches by the door so we don't have to take this dratted chair . . .'

'I think there's room for it in the car . . .'

'Not with Alice in as well there isn't,' Joyce said. 'Alice is coming with us, but we'll have to pick her up round the back. I don't want anyone to see us.'

'Alice?' Laura said.

'Alice Smith. She used to live near me. They've put her on these pills that they tried to get me to take. But I flushed mine down the lav this morning. Shut-up pills, I call them. Keep folk quiet when they've no business being quiet.'

'We can't take her out without telling anyone,' Laura protested weakly, not needing much of a push to let her outrage at what her grandmother was saying overcome her scruples about deceiving the staff of the Laurels.

'Why not?' Joyce administered the push sharply. 'We're over

twenty-one. This isn't a prison, as far as I'm aware. Why the heck shouldn't we go out if we want to?'

'Pensioners' lib, is it?' Laura's delight at seeing her grandmother apparently restored to something like normality finally overcame her qualms. 'Where do you want me to take you then?'

'Up to my place,' Joyce said firmly. 'I can cope up there on the level. I know you've got to go back to work, pet, but we can wait there till you've finished and then you can come and fetch us.'

'I'd take the afternoon off but I have to go to a do at the town hall about tourism and the cinema museum. I simply can't miss that.'

'Don't you fret. We'll be fine,' Joyce said. 'Just you get that man of yours up to Peter Hill an' all. He wants to know about Peter Street on Coronation Day, doesn't he? Well, Alice and I'll tell him, don't you worry. I reckon there's not a lot we can't remember about what was going on in those flats if we put our minds to it. You'll see. I got her to promise not to take her pills either, so she'll be in her right mind, all being well.'

Laura pushed Joyce out into the car park and helped her, with difficulty, into the back seat of the Beetle. She noticed how Joyce winced with pain as she tried to arrange her limbs comfortably to accommodate the plastered leg.

'Have you not had your painkillers?' she asked.

Joyce shook her head, her lips compressed.

'Chucked them away too,' she said. 'I'll take nothing in there. They're different from the ones my doctor prescribed and I won't have my head interfered with by that woman.'

Laura glanced back at the blank windows of the nursing home but did not comment. She would, she determined, make an opportunity soon to find out just what was going on at the Laurels. For now it would have to be enough to get Joyce and her friend away for a while. Joyce might joke about her sounding like her mother, but she suspected that she was as aware as she was herself that their relationship was inexorably changing as time went by. Joyce might hope she could still lead where Laura would follow, but increasingly Laura knew that she was taking the decisions for Joyce.

'Where's Alice?' she asked.

'She's waiting at the back by the kitchen door,' Joyce said. 'You can drive round. There'll be no one about now. We've had our dinner and the kitchen staff go home after. They only give us cold tea and the care assistants dish that up, what there is of it. Bread and scrape usually, but most of them are too far gone to complain. There's not one of those girls in a union, you know? Thirty bob an hour and not one of them in a union.'

Joyce shook her head in incomprehension at the careless ways of the younger generation as Laura slipped the car into gear and drove slowly round to the back of the building. Sure enough a slight figure in a droopy purple cardigan and a long skirt of a colour grown indeterminate through too much washing was standing in the porch giving on to the back door.

Laura got out of the car again and wrinkled her nose in disgust as she passed three enormous dust-bins overflowing with garbage. Her curiosity aroused, she looked through the doorway into the kitchens, which even at a cursory glance she could see were littered with unwashed dishes and looked distinctly greasy. Alice Smith followed the direction of her horrified gaze, a malicious smile lighting up her face for a moment.

'I've seen worse,' Alice said. 'But not much. Old Mrs Brook found a cockroach in her salad the other day, and she's doolally enough to have eaten it if the care lass hadn't spotted it in time. A bit crunchy, that would've been.'

'Are they all on pills?' Laura asked faintly, as she absorbed the full extent of dirt and grime in the kitchen.

'Most on'em,' Alice said. 'Those that aren't genuinely ga-ga, any road. And I expect they're on summat to stop them roaming. Here, look, I kept mine this morning and I feel a sight better for it, an' all.' She held out her hand to reveal two damp and slightly sticky white pills adhering to her palm.

Laura took them off her, wrapped them in a paper tissue and stowed it away in her handbag. She would find out somehow just what it was Betty Johns was dosing her patients with, she thought to herself as she took Alice's arm and steered her towards the car.

'Come on, Alice,' Joyce called, leaning out of the car door perilously. 'If you don't get a move on Dracula's daughter'll notice we're both AWOL and put us to bed without our supper.'

Alice walked slowly over to the car and with some difficulty slotted stiff limbs into the passenger seat. She pulled at her cardigan fretfully as Laura fastened the seat-belt around her.

'You know I never did have a purple cardy,' she said. 'Horrible colour. I always hated it. This belongs to that poor Mrs Ellis who died.'

'So where are your own clothes?' Laura asked, crashing the car into gear and accelerating out of the home's driveway at a speed which pushed her two passengers back into their seats.

'Steady on, love,' Joyce said. 'There's nowt to be gained by rescuing us from Morticia and putting us straight into hospital with multiple injuries.'

'Sorry,' Laura said, flashing her grandmother a grin over her shoulder. She swung more circumspectly into the main road to begin the climb up to the council estate, known universally in the town as Wuthering Heights, where her grandmother lived in a bungalow in the shadow of three dilapidated tower blocks. 'It's just the thought of them muddling your clothes up. You'll be getting the wrong specs and dentures next.'

'It's been known,' Joyce said drily.

'Jesus wept,' Laura said, anger welling up like a red tide. She glanced at her watch. 'I've got to be back at the office in fifteen minutes,' she said. 'But I should be able to get away after the town hall tea-party. I'll talk to Michael and see you back at your place about four. Is that OK?'

'She'll have missed Alice by then,' Joyce said. 'She'll be throwing a wobbly. And a damn good thing too.'


Laura had to admit that John Blake was a pro. Exhibiting all the actor's ability to blossom and glow under the lights, he had spent an hour glad-handing the middle-aged worthies of Bradfield's municipal and theatrical establishments, joshing with the men, from the mayor in his heavy worsted to the chairman of the local arts committee in his too-tight denim, and indiscriminately flattering the women, from those in high heels and unwisely permed hair to the ageing hippies in flowing florals and beads.

Keith Spencer-Smith and Lorelie Baum had hovered in the background as their protégé charmed his way around a reception at the town hall to promote the *Jane Eyre* project and the new museum. The cameras flashed encouragingly as Blake ended his charmingly modest speech with a self-deprecating anecdote about his near-miss at the Oscars all of twenty years ago. John Blake's fortuitous visit to Bradfield had been too good an opportunity to miss to promote tourism in Brontë country, Spencer-Smith confided. The *Jane Eyre* film and the new museum, to be opened in just two days, were a heaven-sent gift for Bradfield.

'It was quite a coup to get a Hollywood star here,' Laura said. 'You've known John Blake some time, then, have you?'

'Yes, yes, I've met him before,' Spencer-Smith said. 'In London. And I had a trip to Hollywood a few years ago.'

Laura was about to probe further but her attention was distracted as Blake himself approached, flushed with pleasure at his reception. Lorelie was a step behind him in a fuschia suit, cut low at the neck and short at the skirt above knee-high patent boots.

'Laura, darling, did I do all right, do you think?' Blake asked, catching up with her as she pulled open the heavy mahogany doors leading out to the town hall square.

'You were fine,' Laura said, trying to inject some enthusiasm into her voice. If the man needed stroking to this extent she supposed she would have to oblige.

'Have dinner with me tonight?' Blake said. Laura could see Lorelie's eyes darken with anger although her smile never faltered by so much as a millimetre. 'You said you wanted another chat. There's a new place Keith has been telling me about, out towards Harrogate . . .'

'Lakers? It's booked about six months in advance,' Laura said, laughing over her shoulder as she kept a step ahead of him on the flight of steps which led down to the square. Opposite she could see the rain-stained concrete bulk of police headquarters.

'Oh, Lorelie will get us in, won't you, honey?' Blake said. 'A table for two? No problem?'

'Sure, no problem,' Lorelie said through gritted teeth as Laura smiled at her sweetly.

'Not too early, though,' Laura said. 'I've some things to finish first.'

'I'll pick you up at eight-thirty,' Blake offered. 'Will that do? Give me your address.'

'Fine,' Laura said faintly, her attention distracted by a dark car driven by Michael Thackeray which had drawn up at the kerb a few yards away. He had offered to collect the old ladies and from the rear window her grandmother's face was also clearly visible. Embarrassed, and annoyed with herself for being embarrassed, she scribbled her address on a piece of paper and thrust it into Blake's outstretched hand, but before she could move away he took her by the shoulders and kissed her rapidly on both cheeks.

'*A bientôt*,' he said.

'Oh, shit,' Laura whispered under her breath as she spun on her heel and walked towards the car, aware that two pairs of eyes at least were watching her with the deepest suspicion.


Michael Thackeray half turned to look with a mixture of affection and exasperation at the two elderly women in the back seat of the unmarked police car in which he had collected Laura from the town hall. He had seemed unexpectedly enthusiastic on the phone when he had offered to collect Joyce and Alice and then Laura herself for the trip to Peter Hill. But he had said nothing as she slid into the seat beside him, meeting her raised eyebrows and helpless shrug with a look she could not easily interpret. For his part he had devoted himself exclusively to Joyce Ackroyd and Alice Smith as he drove to Peter Hill.

He parked the car on the muddy and littered road at Joyce's peremptory instruction, alongside the terrace of tall Victorian houses a hundred yards from the high wooden fence which concealed the building site where Mariella Bonnetti's body had been found. There was no sign of the construction workers today. They had been sent off to more profitable sites until the police had finished their routine work here.

There was little left of Peter Street's tall houses where Joyce and her son, Laura's father, had lived briefly when he was a boy. Windows, from semi-basement to attic, were boarded up. They must once have given the street's shifting population an extensive view over the town in the valley below, where the sun was catching the sheen of recent rain on slate roofs and the town hall tower, its gothic decoration picked out in gold, glittered in the late afternoon light.

'Right, ladies,' Thackeray said. 'Is this far enough? Can you see what you need to see from here?'

Laura got out and opened the car door at Alice Smith's side. 'You stay there, Nan,' she said to Joyce, but her grandmother shook her head.

'I can manage,' she said, opening the door at her own side of the car. Thackeray got out quickly and helped her to her feet on the uneven pavement while Laura hurried around the car with the crutches. She saw panic for a second in Joyce's eyes as she clung to Thackeray and fumbled with the arm grips before she was able to get her balance, wincing with pain as she put her plastered leg on the ground.

'We'll get you back on your feet, Nan, I promise. They can do marvellous things now. Tell her, Michael. They can do marvellous things.'

Thackeray looked helplessly at the two women, so alike, with the same oval face and fine hair, in Joyce's case faded now to snow-white from the vivid copper which was Laura's glory. He had thought that he could never be torn apart by anyone like this again.

'If Laura can't get you on your feet, no one can,' he said to Joyce.

'Do you remember how Fred used to sit on them steps there, Joyce?' Alice Smith said suddenly, pointing to the steep flight which led up to a front door where someone had painted a huge number six in fluorescent pink. 'Number six. That were our house. The whole of the ground floor we had, a bit more space than most, and Fred used to sit out there watching the kiddies playing.'

'Is that what he was watching?' Joyce asked.

There was a silence as Alice seemed to move back in time to consider the question, her eyes distant and her face creased as if in pain.

'Aye, I think it was,' she said. 'Though you could never be sure wi' Fred, when he came back. He said nowt.'

'Can you tell me about Fred and the children?' Thackeray asked gently.

'He hated them,' Alice said with unexpected vehemence. 'He hated them because they were young and had everything ahead of them and he was dying. He knew that. At night, sometimes, he . . .' She hesitated and her lip trembled slightly and she drew a deep breath to steady herself.

'At night?' Thackeray prompted, so quietly that Laura, standing a few feet away with a protective arm around Joyce, could barely hear him.

'At night he used to cuss them,' Alice said firmly. 'He cussed the noise they made running up and down t'stairs. There were no carpets on them stairs. You couldn't get carpet for love nor money. The whole place echoed as they banged about. And he cussed them when they played out late. They'd play till it got dark that summer, nine, ten o'clock at night you'd still hear them running, laughing . . . living! Shouted for our lad to come in, he did, shouted and cussed and hit him when he came, if he could get close enough. But Keith were quicker, by then, quicker and stronger an' all.'

'I thought he was called Ken,' Joyce said irritably to Thackeray. 'I got it wrong. It's all so long ago, I've forgotten half of them, you know.'

'He was a big lad, by that time, was Keith. Bigger than his dad. Fred'd shrunk when he came back from that place. Thin as a lath and shrunken somehow, by what them devils did to him. He didn't know the lad, of course, when he got home. I hardly knew I was pregnant after that last leave before he was sent out East.'

'And the Italian girl?' Thackeray murmured.

'He hated the Italians worst of all, all those children, all that noise, laughing, crying, jabbering – all that foreign noise. And they were Eye-ties, weren't they? What were them cowardly

Eye-ties doing in Bradfield? he asked. Over and over he asked that. He couldn't understand what they were doing here, in his country, when they'd fought on the other side. I think he thought that if they could come over here then it'd be the Japs next . . . It made him ill, that did, thinking about that. He was full o'hate, was Fred, full of it, till the day he died.'

Alice gazed up at the dilapidated terrace of houses in something like wonderment, as if she was unaware of the effect she was having on her audience.

'That were your place, Joyce, weren't it?' she asked, pointing at a first-floor window at the end of the block.

Joyce nodded. 'I never knew Fred felt like that,' she said. 'He was civil enough when I spoke to him. He wandered a bit in his mind, I thought, but he was civil enough.'

'Oh, he liked you, love,' Alice said unexpectedly. 'That red hair of yours. It reminded him of his sister, Edna, the one who lived in Cleethorpes. I've never seen her from the day of Fred's funeral to this. But he liked to talk about Edna, did Fred. She were his favourite.'

Thackeray ran a hand through his hair and caught Laura's eye. After years of interrogation he was at a loss to know how to ask this old woman the question to which he most urgently wanted an answer. Laura read his mind and guessed that the most direct route to what he wanted to know might be the most circuitous.

'How much can you remember of Coronation Day?' she asked Joyce, but including Alice in a sideways smile of encouragement.

'We were all indoors, pet,' Joyce said. 'We watched the television at Mrs Parkinson's and then we had our tea indoors because the weather was so bad.'

'Was Fred with you?' Thackeray asked.

'He was for his tea. Then we went home. He wasn't too good in company,' Alice said. 'The children had gone to play out, and I was the next to go. I took Fred home before he got too worked up.'

'And he stayed at home then, did he? Until you went to bed?'

Alice looked at Michael Thackeray, her eyes quite clear now and unafraid.

'He went out of doors later on. It had dried up a bit by then and it was warm inside. He went out and sat on t'step like he always did. He'd not enjoyed the excitement, hadn't Fred. It had all been a bit too much for him.'

'So let me get this straight, Mrs Smith,' Thackeray said. 'The kids were out playing. Fred was on the step. But you could see him there?'

'Not all the time,' Alice said. 'I couldn't see him all the time. He were still outside when our Keith came in from playing and I got the lad a bite of supper in t'kitchen. That were at the back of the house. I couldn't see Fred while I were in the kitchen.'

'Do you think Fred could have . . .?' Thackeray hesitated. 'Do you think Fred could have had anything to do with Mariella's disappearance?' he asked at last.

'I've thought for forty years he must have killed her,' Alice said simply. 'I don't know how, and I'd have said nowt while he was alive. He deserved to live what was left to him in peace after what he'd been through. And then there were Keith to think of, a life to make for himself. But I've thought for all these years that Fred must have done it. I don't know where or when or how he found the strength, so you're wasting your breath asking. But I've always thought he must have killed her.'


# 12


Laura lay rigid in the narrow single bed of her own spare bedroom, watching the grey light of dawn creep through the curtains and over the ceiling. She had gone to bed cursing her own stupidity, slept fitfully for a couple of hours, and woken again with a dry mouth and a thumping headache cursing herself even more roundly. Wide awake now as she heard a distant clock chime four, she tried to ignore the throbbing behind her eyes and review objectively the events which had led her to slam the spare-room door in Michael Thackeray's face and go to bed alone.

It had all begun to go wrong almost as soon as she had joined

Michael and the two elderly women in his car that afternoon. She had not expected him to come himself to interview Joyce again, had half expected him to delegate the job to Kevin Mower or to the blonde policewoman she knew only as Val, and she had been incautious enough to express her surprise. Thackeray had reacted with irritation which she guessed stemmed as much from the fleeting kiss he had seen Blake give her as from any serious belief that she was not pleased to see him.

She had never suspected him of possessiveness but there was no doubt of the anger in his eyes when she told him a little later that she would be having dinner with Blake again that evening, and at the only restaurant in Yorkshire to have gained two Michelin stars.

'Is there a quid pro quo?' he had asked, and had turned away when she tried to laugh the question off.

Then there had been the row with Betty Johns when she had delivered Joyce and Alice Smith back to the nursing home at six o'clock that evening. The matron had advanced down the hallway to the front door when they arrived, her face flushed and her bosom heaving, and had delivered a fierce tirade about irresponsible behaviour amounting to abduction.

Alice had cowered in the doorway while the Ackroyds, grandmother and daughter, gave as good as they got, but when in the end Joyce had been bundled unceremoniously into her wheelchair, gasping with pain, Laura was left in a frenzy of frustration as the front door was slammed shut. What filled her with torment more than her grandmother's vigorous protests was the look of stark fear in Alice Smith's eyes as she too had been pulled inside.

'I didn't realise that you hadn't told them you were taking Alice out,' Thackeray had observed mildly, putting his arm around her as she sat trembling in the front seat of his car again.

'I'll have Joyce out of that place tomorrow,' Laura vowed, shrugging him off. 'She can't stay. That woman is a monster.'

'You said you would call your father.'

'Yes, yes, I'll call my bloody father,' Laura said. 'He should *be* here, shouldn't he? I shouldn't have to sort all this out alone. But that's men for you, isn't it? Never there when you need them.' She knew she was being childish and unfair and that in lashing

107

out she risked hurting Thackeray more than anyone but she was too angry herself to notice the pain in his eyes.

'We'll see them both tomorrow to take formal statements about what they can remember of Mariella,' he said evenly. 'I'll get Val Ridley to cast an eye over the place at the same time. If there's something seriously wrong there she'll sniff it out.'

Back home, changing for her dinner date, she found a brown envelope which Joyce had given her earlier and she had pushed into her bag without thinking. She flicked through the contents quickly, in between putting up her hair and applying her make-up, and was surprised to see a collection of faded black and white snap-shots which must have been taken around the time when Joyce and her own father were living in Peter Street. She left them lying on the bed while she completed her toilet and, after glancing in her long mirror and pronouncing herself well satisfied with what she saw, she took the packet into Thackeray who was watching television.

'Joyce gave me these for you,' she said, dropping them into his lap.

Thackeray stubbed out his cigarette and glanced at the photographs and then at Laura. She was wearing a three-quarter-length black skirt, a cream silk shirt under a velvet jacket, discreet gold jewellery, and with her hair coiled in a copper crown on top of her head she took his breath away.

'Lucky man,' he had said quietly. 'Will you be late?'

'I shouldn't think so,' she said. 'Michael, it's work.'

'Yes,' he had said, and now looking back on what came later she knew he had been right to distrust her. It had been more than a pleasant professional chore from the moment John Blake arrived in the Merc to collect her and settled her into the ready-warmed leather seat with old-fashioned courtesy. She had enjoyed the food and the wine by several glasses too many, had allowed herself to be flattered by the attention of the man who, even at his age, still attracted more glances than most from fellow diners. And when he had pulled into a lay-by on the main road to Bradfield and put his arm around her, she had not objected. Looking back she knew she had been more drunk than perhaps she realised. But not that drunk. She had known very well what she was doing.

'You and I could get to know each other a lot better,' he had said, reaching out for a switch that let the seats gently recline and then leaning towards her. 'You have that English beauty I'm looking for in my Jane Eyre.' He leaned across her and pulled her hair back from her face. 'Very Victorian,' he murmured. 'Though I don't think little Jane was a red-head. Pity.'

She let him kiss her and told herself that there was nothing wrong with some uncomplicated sex for once, the sort of thing she would not have thought twice about before she shackled herself to the roller-coaster of a relationship with Michael Thackeray. As John Blake's tongue explored hers she knew that she wanted him as much as he seemed to want her and she did not demur when he began to unbutton her shirt.

It was only a sharp tap on the window which eventually led her to push him away and press her face against the cold glass of the car window in embarrassment. Blake lowered his window a fraction.

'Not here, sir, if you don't mind,' the policeman had said, flashing his torch into the interior of the car. Blake jerked his seat upright sharply with a muttered curse and started the engine.

'England never changes, does it?' he said. 'The same thing happened to me once in a Mini and a damn sight more inconvenient that was.' He sighed. 'I can't ask you back,' he said. 'Lorelie will be prowling round the suite with a stop-watch counting off the minutes. I can't tell you how sorry that makes me, Laura.'

He had driven her home and she had let herself into the flat feeling sick and miserable. Thackeray was still up, with her grandmother's snap-shots spread out on the coffee table in front of him. He glanced up as she came in, evidently preoccupied and oblivious to her dishevelled state.

'Look at this,' he said.

She bent over, careful not to get close enough to let him smell the alcohol on her breath, almost afraid he would be able to sense her disloyalty through her skin. He was looking at a faded photograph of half a dozen children and young people evidently taken on the steps outside Alice Smith's house in Peter Street.

'Who do you recognise?' he asked.

She studied the picture more closely. 'My father,' she said slowly, pointing to the youngest of the group, a freckled boy in short trousers whose red hair was evident even in black and white. 'And is that Mariella? It must be.' The Italian girl sat on the steps in the middle of the group, a mass of dark curly hair around a laughing face, a gold ornament at her neck catching the sunlight which was making most of the youngsters screw up their eyes. She was sitting between the two tallest, fair-haired boys, holding the hand of one and sharing a proprietorial grip on a cricket bat with the slightly younger of the two. The picture was faded and cracked with age but even after more than forty years it was obvious that Mariella was the centre of attention.

'No one else there you recognise?' Thackeray persisted, but Laura shook her head.

'I don't think so,' she said. 'Should I?' She turned the snapshot over and saw that her grandmother had pencilled in the names of the children on the back.

'Roy Parkinson,' she said. 'That's Roy Parkinson. And the blonde boy is Keith Smith. And who's the younger girl?'

'Bridget O'Meara,' Thackeray said. 'Next to her brother Danny.'

'The man who's just died?' Laura asked. 'Is there a connection? Seriously?'

'I don't know,' Thackeray said. 'It's all a long time ago so we may never know. But I think I might have a chat with your John Blake.'

'Blake?' Laura said, her mouth suddenly dry. 'Why would you want to talk to him?'

'He says he lived here as a child,' Thackeray said. 'You know he does. He might have been at school with some of these kids.'

'Do you think so?' Laura said, trying not to let too much scepticism creep into her voice while wanting to find any excuse to keep Thackeray as far away from Blake as it was possible to get.

'Why not? In any case, he's being very cagey about his past, isn't he? Have you found anything out about the man? Really? Or is he just stringing you along, buttering you up with treats like a trip to Lakers so he can get the sort of profile he wants?'

'That's ridiculous, Michael,' Laura said. 'He lived in the old part of town, towards Wuthering, where they pulled all the slum terraces down.'

'Which street, Laura?' Thackeray persisted. 'Exactly where? What's happened to investigative journalism here?'

The realisation that she had no answers to these questions hit Laura too hard for comfort. She flung the photograph on to the pile on the table.

'You're just annoyed because I went out to dinner with him again tonight,' she said. 'You're being very childish. What did you think I was going to do? Fall into bed with him?'

Thackeray leaned back in his chair and looked at her soberly.

'If I'd seriously thought that I might not have been here when you came home,' he said.

'But it crossed your mind,' she said with all the bitterness she could muster. She left him staring obsessively at the photograph of the children and shut herself in the spare bedroom, leaning her head against the door and letting the tears flow unchecked down her cheeks and on to her favourite silk shirt, which she had encouraged John Blake to unbutton.

Thackeray did not knock at the door and in the end she fell into bed and slept. Now as a chilly morning dawned, she knew with dreadful clarity what she had risked last night. She also knew that some of Thackeray's angry allegations were only too justified. She had allowed John Blake to charm her off her perch and she guessed that his passion last night was probably as contrived as any of his performances on the screen. She had allowed herself to be manipulated and what she did not know was how she could ever tell Michael Thackeray what a fool she had been.

Detective Sergeant Kevin Mower was surprised to find Michael Thackeray in the office before him the next morning. It had not been unusual for the DCI to appear early when Mower had first known him. In fact there had been many mornings when he had wondered whether his boss had bothered to go home at all. But since he had moved in with Laura Ackroyd his habits seemed to have become more regular and his morning demeanour a shade less forbidding than it used to be.

But not today, Mower realised, his antennae well tuned to the moods of superior officers. The atmosphere in the office was positively arctic, he felt, as he hung the jacket of his suit carefully over the back of his chair, loosened his Italian silk tie and the top button of his shirt and took stock of the pile of files and messages on his desk.

He could think of no particular reason that he could have provoked Thackeray's displeasure personally and with the wisdom of long experience immediately put it down to woman trouble. Had Laura Ackroyd, he wondered, also stumbled on the item of information which he was still concealing in the murkiest recesses of his mind, tentatively bringing it out now and again to assess its potential for advantage or harm.

'Coffee, Guv?' he asked, but was rewarded only by a dismissive shake of the head as Thackeray continued to pore over a thick file in front of him. Mower shrugged and settled to his own work until they were interrupted by a uniformed officer who handed a fresh file to Thackeray.

'The PM report from Mr Atherton, sir,' he said. Thackeray flicked through it almost impatiently.

'Right,' he said to Mower. 'Amos reckons that it's practically impossible for all O'Meara's injuries to have been self-inflicted. He thinks he was either already dead or unconscious when the train hit him. And as forensics can't find any evidence of anything except the wheels of the train touching him, nothing else which could have inflicted the blow on the back of the head, it looks as if it's definitely murder.'

'Well at least with this one there's a chance we're looking for a live suspect instead of some guy who's been dead and buried for forty-odd years,' Mower said. He had just been reading Thackeray's notes on his conversation with Alice Smith the previous day.

'Maybe,' Thackeray said non-committally.

'You don't go for Alice's story then?' Mower asked, surprised.

'I don't go for anything until I see some evidence,' Thackeray said. 'What Alice Smith suspected is neither here nor there. If you accept that, you have to accept that Danny O'Meara's suspicious death is just a coincidence and I don't go for coincidences either.'

Thackeray hesitated for a moment and then came to a decision.

'As far as that's concerned see what you can dig out on John Blake's background, will you?'

'John Blake? The film actor?' Mower could not disguise his surprise but Thackeray avoided his eye.

'The film actor,' he said. 'The one doing the returned prodigal performance. He's been all over the *Gazette*. But he seems to be remarkably reticent about his background. He must be around the same age as some of Danny O'Meara's friends in Peter Street. See if you can find out where he went to school, where he lived, when he went to RADA – I think that's where he trained.'

'So we carry on with that inquiry too, Guv? We assume they're connected?' Mower felt slightly bemused by the new tack Thackeray was taking but he kept his thoughts strictly to himself as his quick brain tried to make some connections between the film actor, his recent appearance in the *Gazette*, for which Mower knew he had been interviewed by Laura Ackroyd, and his boss's unexpected interest in his past.

'Like the Superintendent says, Kevin, we don't need to break our necks over it. But we'll bear it in mind when we go and see Mrs O'Meara, shall we?'

'Right, Guv,' Mower said.

'And while we're doing that, I want whoever saw O'Meara's visitor at Long Moor to help with a computer-generated portrait – the man on the gate, the nurse who saw them go into the grounds. They're saying he arrived at the gates on foot, which is unusual out there. But maybe he parked a car outside somewhere. Check that out. And I want everyone who was at the hospital on Monday afternoon interviewed. Someone must have seen something if O'Meara was taken down that railway embankment against his will.'

'Everyone, Guv?' Mower ventured.

'Everyone who is medically fit to give a statement,' Thackeray said very quietly, the sudden tension in his jaw warning Mower that he was treading on very thin ice indeed. The Sergeant got up quickly and put on his jacket.

'Consider it done, Guv,' he said.


A whole clan of O'Mearas had gathered at Danny's home by the time Thackeray and Mower arrived later that morning and were let in by Kay, the dead man's daughter, who offered no more than a nod of recognition as she waved them into the living room. The centre of attention was Margaret O'Meara, who was sitting close to the television with a heavy cardigan around her shoulders, her hair even more unkempt than the last time Mower had seen her, her face blotched and puffy and her eyes blood-shot with tears.

She was surrounded by a litter of empty tea-cups and glasses and used plates, which balanced precariously on top of piles of newspapers and magazines, on the corners of shelves and completely covered the coffee table in front of her. The room was awash with flowers in vases and jam jars, filling the air with a sickly sweetness, and sympathy cards were already beginning to fill the mantelshelf above the elaborate gas log-fire in the old-fashioned tiled grate.

Thackeray and Mower had to edge their way into the room through a crowd of middle-aged women who glanced at them curiously for only seconds before they resumed their animated conversation.

'Mum, it's the police again,' Kay said loudly enough to attract everyone's attention for a moment. Danny O'Meara's widow looked up briefly from the card she was reading and dug the hefty young woman who was sitting next to her in the ribs.

'Make a bit of space, then,' she said. 'Let the Sergeant through, can't you?'

'This is Chief Inspector Thackeray who's in charge of the investigation,' Mower said. The two men had the attention of the whole room now, and Thackeray glanced around at the audience of friends and neighbours and sighed.

'I'd like a private word with Mrs O'Meara and her daughter, if I may,' he said.

Very reluctantly the visitors edged their way out of the room into the crowded hall and kitchen and Mower closed the door behind them with rather more force than was strictly necessary. Mrs O'Meara put down the cards she was holding and turned pale eyes on Thackeray, but it was Kay who realised the significance of his arrival.

'What's happened?' she said sharply. 'You don't get the top brass investigating suicides. It's not as if he hadn't tried before.' Mower flashed her an appreciative look, again noting the short black skirt above not to be underestimated legs, and the firm breasts beneath her plain white shirt. And brains as well, he thought, before catching Thackeray's interrogative eye and realising that the Chief Inspector was waiting for him.

'How many times did your father try to kill himself?' he asked Kay.

'Oh, God, I don't know,' she said. 'How many times, Mother? Four? Five?'

Her mother evidently made an heroic effort to focus her mind but did not speak and the effort was more than she could cope with. Huge tears coursed down her flabby cheeks again and she buried her face in a paper tissue and blew her nose noisily.

Kay turned away in irritation and, perhaps, disgust.

'It was too many,' she said. 'Too many for any of us to put up with.'

'Has he ever tried to kill himself on the railway before?' Mower persisted, concentrating on the girl whose sharp blue eyes always seemed to take in more than was being put into words.

'No, not that way. Pills mainly, pills and Scotch together once. Never anything violent. I'd never have thought he'd have the bottle to do that.'

'Mrs O'Meara,' Thackeray broke in. 'I'm sorry to have to bring more bad news, but we have reason to believe that your husband's death was not self-inflicted at all.'

'An accident, you mean?' Mrs O'Meara said, animated enough at last to take notice of what was going on around her. 'You

115

mean it were an accident? I told Father Turner I didn't believe he'd kill himself . . .' She hesitated, aware that Thackeray had shaken his head at this outburst.

'You mean he was killed, don't you?' Kay said flatly. 'Someone pushed him under that train, didn't they? Who was it? One of the other patients? Another bloody nut-case? That's why you're here, isn't it, Inspector?'

'We don't know what happened, but the post-mortem indicates that he was dead or unconscious before the train hit him. He wouldn't have known anything about it, Mrs O'Meara, as far as the pathologist can tell.' Thackeray's voice was flat and expressionless and Mower knew that he was hating every minute of this interview.

'There are a few questions we'd like to ask you about your husband, Mrs O'Meara,' Mower said. 'If you feel up to answering them.'

'Kay, get Father Turner on t'phone and tell him what's happened,' Mrs O'Meara said to her daughter.

'In a moment, please,' Thackeray said sharply. 'A few questions first.'

'What can we tell you?' Kay O'Meara asked, taking her mother's hand in hers.

'Do you know anyone who hated your father enough to kill him?' Mower asked.

Both women shook their heads in astonishment at this. 'I don't think you understand what depression does to people,' Kay said impatiently. 'He hardly ever went anywhere. He never had a job to speak of. He had no friends, never mind enemies, just family and a lot of them got sick and tired of him in the end. He got into debt wi' the bookies sometimes, but we usually managed to pay them off, one way or another.'

'You had no more thoughts about the man you saw him talking to before he went into hospital?' Mower asked.

'I told you, I only caught a glimpse from the car. Not anyone I recognised, grey haired, well dressed but I didn't get a good look at his face,' Kay said. 'I just thought it was someone dunning him for money again. It wasn't unusual.'

'But it was after that he went down-hill again?'

'Yes, it was,' Kay said.

'Who needs enemies when he's stuck up there wi' a gang of loonies?' Mrs O'Meara broke in suddenly. 'If someone pushed him under a train it'll be one o'them, won't it, stands to reason.'

Mower glanced at Thackeray, who hardly seemed to be breathing, his face like stone.

'Did any of the family visit him at Long Moor?' Mower asked, quickly. 'Mrs O'Meara?'

'I can't get right out there to t'back of bloody beyond on t'bus,' she said. 'Any road, it doesn't do any good, visiting him. If he's bad he doesn't hardly know you and if he's getting better he'll be home in a couple of days so there's no point.'

'Miss O'Meara? Did you go to see your father?' Mower persisted, but Kay shook her head dismissively.

'I'm at work all day,' she said. 'And like Mum says, there's no point. He's never in there long, just a couple of days generally. They don't like keeping them in, you know. Haven't you heard of care in the community?'

'Your husband was one of quite a large family, I think,' Thackeray said suddenly, his voice strained. 'Where are his brothers and sisters now?'

Margaret O'Meara did not seem to think the question strange.

'There were six on'em,' she said. 'Danny were the oldest, his brother Paddy's in Australia and the other brother Dermot's in London. We haven't heard from them for years. His sister Mary lives out Arnedale way and Kitty stayed in Bradfield. She's here if you want to talk to her. And there was Bridget, of course. We named our Bridget after Danny's oldest sister. She died years ago.'

'Tell him everything, Mother,' Kay said sharply, but when her mother shook her head dumbly she evidently decided to complete the story herself. 'My Auntie Bridget she would have been, though she was dead long before I was born. She killed herself, didn't she? Or so my father always said. She must have been about twenty and my dad twenty-one or -two. Apparently they were at a party up at Wuthering, when them flats were new in

117

the sixties. And she got drunk and jumped off the balcony. They said it was an accident but my father always swore it was deliberate.'

'Deliberate?' Thackeray said sharply.

'Suicide, I mean.'

'He never got over that,' her mother said, stuffing a handkerchief against her mouth to smother the spasm of grief which overcame her. 'We were walking out, Danny and me, and I married him any road because I thought he'd get over it but he never did. He blamed himself, you see. He thought he should have saved her, though I don't think he even knew she were on t'balcony so I never saw the sense in that. He loved Bridget . . . more than any of the others. Always blamed himself that she went the way she did.'

'Did Bridget have a boyfriend?' Thackeray asked.

'Not that I remember,' Mrs O'Meara said. 'I don't think she thought much of lads, kept herself to herself, a miserable little thing she seemed to me. Danny used to say he dragged her to that party to try and cheer her up. So he reckoned it was his fault she fell.'

Thackeray stood up abruptly.

'We'll do our best to find out who killed your husband, Mrs O'Meara,' he said. 'And if you can think of any reason anyone might have had for attacking him, let us know. Anyone who might have had a grudge, recently or not.'

Thackeray led the way back to the car and sat for a moment in the passenger seat with his eyes closed.

'Almost forty years,' he said, so quietly that Mower could hardly hear him as he started the engine and pulled away from the kerb. 'He hadn't got over it after almost forty years.'

'Do you really think there's a connection, Guv?' Mower asked dubiously.

'I don't know, Kevin,' Thackeray said. 'But if O'Meara's family never visit him when he's in hospital and he doesn't have any friends to speak of, who did go up there to see him the day he died? And why? And why was his sister Bridget such a miserable little thing that she went to a party and jumped off a balcony? And who can tell us anyway after all this time?'

118

# 13

The bleakly tiled and deserted corridors of the Laurels echoed as Laura Ackroyd marched from the day room, where the usual residents slumped in their chairs either asleep or with glazed eyes focused on the television set which was blaring out the children's programme *Blue Peter*. She headed for the medical wing and her grandmother's bedroom. She opened the door unceremoniously to find Joyce asleep, her face an unhealthy grey against the pillow, one arm flung above her head almost as if to ward off a blow. Her fingers were curved into a gnarled claw and her other hand clutched the bedclothes like a life-line, the knuckles white as she stirred uneasily.

Laura drew a sharp breath and closed the door behind her, leaning against it for a moment before moving to the bed and putting a hand gently on Joyce's shoulder.

'Nan, wake up, darling,' she said.

Her grandmother rolled awkwardly on to her side with a groan and her eyelids flickered but did not open. Laura stroked the thin white hair away from her face, feeling the pulse at her temple beneath the papery skin. The old woman's fragility frightened her more than she dared admit.

'Nan, wake up,' she said, a little more loudly, but there was no response. Laura bit her lip in frustration and looked around the narrow room. There was a half-empty glass of water on the bedside table but no sign of any medication. Very gently she unclasped Joyce's hand from the sheets and drew the bedclothes up over her shoulders and tucked them in firmly, before going out into the corridor again in the grip of a blind fury.

The matron's office was at the end of the corridor and she knocked on the door peremptorily before walking in uninvited. Betty Johns was sitting at her desk with her phone in her hand.

'Excuse me, I seem to have an unexpected visitor here,' she said to her caller before hanging up. She stood up to meet Laura with an expression on her broad face which could only be described as a snarl.

'Miss Ackroyd,' she said. 'I'm surprised you have the gall to show your face here again after yesterday.'

'While my grandmother is here, I'll show my face whenever I choose, Mrs Johns,' Laura said. 'And right now I'd like you to tell me why she's in bed so soundly asleep that I can't wake her? What have you given her to knock her out like that? And why?'

'Well!' Mrs Johns said, smoothing her dress down over her buttocks and advancing around the desk with the determination of a battleship about to commence a bombardment.

'Do you really think all that excitement yesterday did either of those old ladies any good? They are patients, Miss Ackroyd, patients under my care, and if they are reduced to a state of nervous exhaustion by interfering young women like you then of course the doctor is likely to prescribe sedatives.'

'My grandmother enjoyed every minute of her outing yesterday,' Laura said. 'She's only broken her leg, for God's sake. She's not senile.'

'Well, that's what you say,' Betty Johns came back triumphantly. 'But you know, when you observe her closely – and I'm sure as a busy woman you won't have been able to do that yourself recently – when you have her under observation I'm not so sure about her mental condition.'

'What do you mean?' Laura asked sharply.

'She's increasingly vague, like so many of them are,' Betty Johns said, her voice softening into soothing professional tones. 'And so over-optimistic about going home and what she'll be able to do for herself in future. I keep trying to break it to her gently that I think she'll be with us for some considerable time, but she won't have it, you know. So sad. And so difficult for you to come to terms with, dear, I do understand that.'

Laura swallowed hard and met Betty Johns' eyes, like small hard diamonds in her bland pink and white face.

'I intend to take my grandmother away from here just as soon as I've made alternative arrangements for her,' she said coldly.

'Well, that's your privilege,' the matron said. 'It'll cost you, of course, and don't imagine you'll get a different diagnosis anywhere else, because you won't. In the meantime I think it would be better if you didn't visit. Mrs Smith's son is very angry indeed that you included her in your little jaunt yesterday. Very angry. And Alice is quite exhausted and confused, poor pet. Right out of it. It'll take her days to recover.'

'You mean you'll make sure it does,' Laura said.

'I don't know what you mean, Miss Ackroyd.'

Laura shrugged and turned away, her desperation threatening to overwhelm her self-control. She opened the office door. 'I'll let you know when I'm coming to pick Joyce up,' she said.

'Such a shame when these independent old ladies lose it,' Mrs Johns said, following close behind her to the front door and holding it open for her. 'The beginning of the end, of course, but not a nice way to go.'

'Bitch!' Laura said as she slammed her car into gear and swung it sharply out of the gate on to the road, unaware until it was far too late that another car was turning almost as sharply into the entrance. She hit the brakes hard and the two vehicles avoided each other by the thickness of a coat of paint, leaving her to pull over to the kerb trembling with fright and pent-up despair.

She glanced back at the Laurels where the front door was just closing behind an indistinguishable male figure who had left his offending silver BMW parked carelessly across the forecourt. She wondered if he was a doctor and whether she should go back at once and challenge Betty Johns' cruel prognosis for Joyce, but could not summon up the strength to renew the battle now.

Once home she raced up all three flights of stairs in an effort to dissipate the panic that had seized her. The flat was empty and there were no messages on the answer-machine. She poured herself a large vodka and tonic and picked up the phone. The ringing tone at the other end went on for a long time before eventually she heard a familiar voice respond.

'Dad,' she said. 'Can you come over? Nan's worse and I'm not happy with the place she's in and I can't get her out of there without some help.' The words poured out so quickly that she wondered if she had made any sort of sense when a lengthy silence followed.

For an agonising moment she thought her father would

121

prevaricate as he had always prevaricated on the rare occasions when she had asked for help during the years he and her mother had lived in Portugal. But this time the panic she felt must have communicated itself down the line clearly enough to gain a slight purchase on his self-centred soul.

'Book me a room at the Clarendon,' Jack Ackroyd said. 'A single'll do. Your mother'll not come. You know how she hates flying.'

'Tomorrow?' Laura said.

'Aye, if I can get on a flight,' Jack said. 'I'll let you know.'

Several vodka and tonics later, Laura woke to find the television flickering silently and no other light except for a faint glow from the street below. She got up and stretched stiff limbs before going to the window and looking out. There was no sign of Thackeray's car and her own was parked at a careless angle to the kerb where she had abandoned it in her hurry to get home. She wondered bleakly if he would come back or whether she had fatally destabilised his fragile hold on the life they were leading together. She drew the curtains with a sigh and put on the lights. Her head was muzzy and her stomach sick and empty. It seemed a lifetime since she had eaten a hurried lunch at her desk.

As she picked at some scrambled eggs and buttered some toast in the kitchen she heard the front door open and close quietly. She turned as Michael Thackeray came into the room behind her and saw the anxiety in his eyes.

'I'm sorry, I'm sorry,' she said wildly. 'I shouldn't have shut you out last night.'

'And I'm sorry. I shouldn't have gone out this morning without talking to you,' he said quietly. 'You look exhausted. What's wrong?'

'Oh, Michael, Joyce is so ill and frail and I've sent for my father and I'm so afraid of losing her,' Laura said. Everything that had happened at the Laurels came tumbling out in such a jumble of words that Thackeray could barely take it all in. As he listened and took in her distress his own anger grew.

'She admitted Joyce had been drugged?' he asked.

'For her own good,' Laura said contemptuously. 'And I didn't even get to see Alice Smith. She's probably in just the same situation. Do you think her son knows what's going on?'

'It figures,' Thackeray said slowly. 'I sent Val Ridley down there to take statements from them and the matron said that they were both unwell today. I wanted to ask Alice about her son. She talked a lot about Fred but very little about Keith when we had them up at Peter Hill yesterday.'

'Betty Johns told me that he was furious that we'd taken her out without permission,' Laura said thoughtfully.

'So he's around then?' Thackeray replied sharply. 'I got the impression from Alice that he'd moved away somewhere.'

'Alice can be a bit vague, even without her pills. Don't you believe her when she says that Fred probably killed Mariella?'

'Not without some corroboration,' Thackeray said. 'Which may simply not be there after all this time. But if her son is here, I want to talk to him. I'll go to the Laurels myself tomorrow if only to let your matron know that she's attracting some attention. Why have you taken the Italian girl to heart so? It was all a very long time ago.'

'Oh, I don't know,' Laura said dismissively, although she did know. She had dreamed about school the previous night, as she had tossed around alone in her narrow bed, reliving a time she had almost forgotten when small blonde savages with cut-glass accents and cold blue eyes had tormented a red-headed stranger whose vowels did not fit. How much worse had it been, she wondered, for the Italian girl dumped not only into a strange school but a strange country full of little xenophobes still obsessed with the hatreds of war? She shook herself back to her present discontents.

'Look in on Joyce,' Laura said. 'Please.'

'Of course,' Thackeray said readily enough. 'Though I don't think she approves of me, does she? She wants me to make an honest woman of you.'

'And you don't,' Laura said, knowing she was pushing her luck.

Thackeray looked away, as he always did, his eyes suddenly remote.

'Not yet, Laura,' he said.

'And perhaps not ever.' She finished the sentence for him silently. Damn you, she thought.

'Bed, then?' she asked cheerfully, knowing it was an invitation he could not refuse, especially after the previous night, and that there at least he was unequivocally hers. But deep inside the gnawing anxiety about Joyce, which had eased slightly with the knowledge that her father was reluctantly coming to her rescue, had only fuelled her more long-lasting fears about her own future. There's no certainty in life or death, she told herself firmly, but she knew that was what she craved all the same.

DCI Thackeray and Sergeant Mower caught up with Giuseppe Bonnetti the next day in the cramped office behind the second-floor dining room of the Santa Lucia restaurant in Leeds. This was no ordinary spaghetti house, that much was obvious as the two officers were shown upstairs. The walls were snow-white, the carpets thick, the tableware gleaming and the aroma of food enticing enough to remind Mower forcefully that it was long past his lunchtime and his boss had, as usual, shown no signs of suffering from the normal appetites which assailed the Sergeant with such regularity and force. But of raffia-wrapped Chianti bottles and the strains of *O Sole Mio* there was no hint at all at Santa Lucia, and the chance of a quick *spag bol* looked remote.

With hooded eyes Bonnetti peered slightly impatiently over gold-rimmed glasses as they were shown in. He closed his ledger and switched off his computer with a sigh.

'What can I do for you, gentlemen?' he asked. 'Have you made any progress on my sister's death?'

'I'm afraid not,' Thackeray said, taking the room's only available free chair, which had not been offered. Mower glanced around before perching himself against the window-sill which was cluttered with ledgers and files. Whatever the Bonnettis had been prepared to pay a designer for the public part of the restaurant had not been extended to this cluttered little back room.

'I tried to contact you in Harrogate . . .' Thackeray began only to be interrupted brusquely by the restaurateur.

'This is our newest venture,' he said dismissively, as if the police should have understood his priorities. 'I'm spending a great deal of my time here just now. Leeds is a very competitive environment, you know? There's money about again and they want good value and high quality.'

'I'm sure they would in Leeds,' Thackeray said drily.

Bonnetti stared at the Chief Inspector for long enough to make Mower feel uncomfortable. But he broke the silence first, raising his hands in the archetypal Italian gesture of interrogation.

'So how can I help you, Chief Inspector?'

'Do you remember the O'Meara family from when you were a child, Mr Bonnetti?' Thackeray asked. 'Bridget, Daniel and several younger children.'

Bonnetti shrugged expansively. 'Danny,' he said. 'I think I recall Danny with my sister Mariella. At Mass, maybe. We were all Catholics, of course. Do you think . . .?'

'We have absolutely no evidence to link Daniel O'Meara with your sister's death,' Thackeray said. 'What I was much more interested in was whether you had come across him later, as adults?'

'This is the man you have just found dead on a railway line?' Bonnetti said. 'I read it in the *Yorkshire Post*. I did wonder . . .'

'You recognised the name?'

'I recognised it,' Bonnetti said sombrely. 'And the photograph they published. I have seen him much more recently than when we were children. He worked for a little while as a kitchen porter in our Bradfield restaurant. He made himself known to me. I think he thought I could help him in some way with his problems.'

'And could you, Mr Bonnetti?' Thackeray asked quietly.

Bonnetti ran a hand across his thick, greying hair and shook his head firmly. 'It was a bad time for the family,' he said. 'My father had just had his stroke. And my manager in Bradfield was not satisfied with O'Meara's work. He sacked him quite quickly. My own impression when I saw him was that he was sick – you know, in the head? Very sick. Did he kill himself on this railway line? That would not surprise me.'

'I think it wouldn't surprise anyone who knew him, Mr Bonnetti,' Thackeray said. 'But we're still enquiring into the circumstances of his death. It's too early to tell exactly what happened.'

'So when would be the last time you saw Danny O'Meara?' Mower asked suddenly. 'Exactly?'

Bonnetti gave another of his extensive shrugs.

'It must be six months ago. We relaunched the Bradfield restaurant before Christmas. It was my father's first small trattoria, too small really for a top-class establishment of the nineties, but he hung on to it for sentimental reasons. We all got our training there, waiting on table, commis chef. Papa believed in us starting at the bottom. But last year the premises next door fell vacant so we decided to expand and refurbish. Danny O'Meara must have been there for a few weeks after that. He approached me one evening when I was visiting, reminded me who he was, told me his troubles. I could not truly say I remembered him in Peter Street. I was too young to go around with those older boys.'

'And what exactly were his troubles?' Thackeray asked.

'Oh, money mainly, as far as I can remember. As I said, I turned him away. I felt no obligation . . .'

'Of course, why should you?' Thackeray said. 'And you haven't seen him since?'

'No,' Bonnetti said flatly. 'I have to confess that he has not even crossed my mind from that day to this, until I saw the paragraph in the newspaper, that is.'

'It didn't cross your mind when you met him again that he might know something about your sister's disappearance?'

'Mariella died many years ago, Chief Inspector,' Bonnetti said. 'I was a small boy. I can't even remember her very clearly, as I've told you already. If you think I have had either time or inclination to harbour thoughts of finding her killer over all those years – if indeed I'd thought she had been killed – you can have no idea how all-absorbing it is to set up a successful business as my father and I have done. There was a sadness in the family about Mariella. Thoughts of vendetta, no. That is not the way anyone behaves these days. And, in any case, we thought she had run away.'

'Giuseppe might not have harboured thoughts of revenge,' Mower said thoughtfully. 'He's too much wedded to *la dolce vita*, maybe. But I wouldn't put it past the old boy. It'd be interesting to know where he got his capital to launch himself into the restaurant business so successfully. Who backed impoverished ex-PoWs in Bradfield in the nineteen fifties?'

Back in the CID offices, Mower was carefully positioning his jacket on the back of his chair. Thackeray allowed himself a faint smile.

'You watch too many films, Kevin,' he said. 'If there's one thing you can be sure about Danny O'Meara's death, it's the fact that he wasn't hit over the head by a half-paralysed elderly man who can hardly get out of his chair.'

'The Godfather doesn't do the deed himself, Guv,' Mower said scornfully.

'Well, check out what happened when Bonnetti met O'Meara in the restaurant kitchen if you like,' Thackeray said. 'But I don't think you'll get much joy. In the meantime, let's catch up on what's been happening while we've been in Leeds, shall we?'

Mower turned his attention to his desk where, buried beneath a pile of reports waiting to be read, he found a bulky envelope inside which was a plastic packet.

'Well, well,' he said, crossing the room and dropping the packet on to Thackeray's desk with a clatter. 'It looks as though we've got our weapon after all.'

Inside the packet was a heavy chrome spanner with a rounded head. And on the head were distinct traces of a brown substance which could only be dried blood. Thackeray picked up the package delicately and held it to the light while Mower read the note that had been attached.

'They found it under bushes close to the hospital gates,' he said. 'Presumably chucked from the car our lad drove up there in.'

'Get on to the security man on the gate,' Thackeray said. 'He must know what vehicles were around that afternoon. And give him a description of Bonnetti, just in case our friend was being economical with the truth. And find out what sort of car he drives.'

'Now you're talking,' Mower said happily. 'He's got a look of Al Pacino, has our Giuseppe . . .'

'I'm not sure Hollywood's my favourite place just at the moment,' Thackeray said dismissively. 'So let's keep our feet on the ground, shall we? Did you get anywhere with your enquiries on John Blake?'

'Nothing known, Guv,' Mower said quickly, his antennae picking up unexpectedly bad vibes. 'I've asked Val to dig around into his history – school, college, that sort of thing. Don't worry, I'll keep him in mind.'

With Thackeray this prickly, he thought, he would need to watch himself. When push came to shove, he thought, Thackeray could be as ruthless as anyone he knew and the unacknowledged secret they now shared sat like a lead weight on his chest.

'I'll get this straight to forensics, then?' he asked, holding out his hand for the package which Thackeray still held in a grip that was unaccountably white-knuckled. The Chief Inspector seemed to shake himself slightly before he replied.

'And see whether Amos Atherton's got the results of those blood tests yet, will you? I'd like to know just how much resistance Danny O'Meara could put up when someone took him down on to that railway track.'

Mower hefted the heavy spanner speculatively, his eyes as hard as Thackeray's now.

'I reckon it wouldn't make much difference, Guv, if this is what they hit him with. He wasn't a big man. He wouldn't stand a chance.'

# 14

Lorelie Baum sat in the foyer bar of the Clarendon Hotel, little black skirt hitched Wimbledon high, long thin legs twined above impossibly high-heeled shoes, almost but not quite oblivious to the admiring glances she was attracting. Her own gaze was fixed intently on the revolving door from the street. She had been waiting, propped on a tall bar stool facing the entrance, for a good half-hour, but she had not noticed the passing of time.

While the comings and goings of the busy foyer swirled around her, she had been reliving her recent encounter with John Blake, an encounter which had left her emotionally humiliated and physically bruised. It had started with a not unexpected but still devastating phone call from Los Angeles which she had taken while Blake had been out at lunch with Keith Spencer-Smith. With the suddenness of a tropical storm blown off course across the Atlantic, she had learned of major problems with the financial backing for *Jane Eyre*. Blake, riding back to the suite on a cloud of alcohol and euphoria, had not wanted to hear what she was telling him.

Plunged into one of the black rages for which he was notorious, he had blamed Lorelie for the threatened collapse of his plans, knocked her across the room and pushed her out of the door with instructions to boost his profile on this side of the Pond to encourage their British supporters, or look for another job.

Lorelie had called the *Bradfield Gazette* and arranged to meet Laura Ackroyd for a drink. While she waited she considered the choice which faced her. She was very tempted to throw Blake to as many wolves among her contacts in the press as she could tempt with a putrid morsel or two – and she reckoned she had a rank selection to choose from – before decamping for home. She opened her bag cautiously to check that she had her passport and tickets with her. Alternatively she might make one last effort to save him and his project from disaster.

She sat stroking the darkening bruise on her arm and it was not until she saw Laura Ackroyd whirl through the revolving doors, red hair flying, face flushed from running, her shocking-pink shirt coming adrift from her short black skirt, that she decided that she'd be damned if she would give John up at this stage to this unkempt Limey bitch.

'Laura, honey,' she cried, unravelling her long limbs from the stool and causing at least four elderly Bradfielders at the bar to choke into their Scotch as they took in the combined charms of two unequivocal bobby-dazzlers at once. She met Laura by the door and pecked her on both cheeks.

'What will you have, honey? The drinks are on me. I've got you just the greatest exclusive, a story to die for.' She put her arm around Laura, dug bony fingers into her shoulder until she flinched and whispered in her ear, 'I can tell you now who's going to play Jane. And I promise you, you will not believe it.'

Laura looked at Lorelie sceptically.

'I thought John wanted some unknown little English actress,' she said. 'It's not a part for some glamorous Hollywood star, is it?'

'We-e-ll,' Lorelie said seriously, 'I guess you might think that. But you know how these deals go? They need someone bankable. It's true, John was thinking English – one of your gorgeous young women, Helena, perhaps, or Imogen, you know? But the name in the frame over there is better than that.'

Laura racked her brains to think of a bankable Hollywood actress who might get away with playing a plain English governess in her late teens, and had to admit failure. The more she heard about the film the more dubious the whole enterprise sounded.

'Does this mean that your backers don't think John Blake is bankable enough?' she asked waspishly.

Lorelie's eyes glittered for a moment though Laura was not sure whether the emotion which briefly cracked her mask-like make-up was anger or distress. 'Why, sure he's bankable,' Lorelie said quickly, lowering her voice. 'But we've got a generation thing here, haven't we? Let's face it, my mother wet her knickers for John Blake, for God's sake. But we need to get the kids in to films these days, the late teens, early twenties. So how do you feel about Gwyneth?'

'Gwyneth?' Laura said slowly. *'Emma*? That Gwyneth? Well, it's certainly an interesting idea, though *Emma's* a bit different from *Jane Eyre*. Is it definite?'

'As good as, honey, as good as,' Lorelie reassured her. 'When does your piece appear in *Sunday Extra*?'

'In two weeks' time,' Laura said. 'I need to finalise it next weekend.'

'Right, you'll be the first to get the confirmation,' Lorelie said. 'And no one else hears about it until the magazine comes out. OK?'

'Fine,' Laura said, with more certainty than she felt. 'Let me buy you a drink. It's the least I can do.' But as they made their way to the bar through the crush of dark suits and admiring glances, she could not help wondering what Lorelie wanted in return for an exclusive which most of the show-business reporters on the national newspapers would give their expense accounts for. She had a nasty feeling that she had been bought and that she would not like the price.


Joyce Ackroyd woke from a deep refreshing sleep halfway through the afternoon, her head clearer than it had been for days. She allowed herself a small, grim smile and felt under the pillow where she had secreted the two pills which had been given to her after lunch. In the game of cat and mouse she had been playing with the care staff this was an unequivocal victory. But today her plans went much further.

Pushing herself painfully up against the pillows she sat motionless, listening. She knew she did not hear as well as she used to do but she was sure that the silence of the Laurels was real. The place was still deep in its drug-induced mid-afternoon slumber. If she was to get away with what she and Alice had planned, she knew she had to move quickly. And given the handicap of the heavy, itchy cast on her leg that was going to be difficult.

With infinite patience she eased her legs over the side of her

131

bed, using her hands to manoeuvre the plaster cast on to the floor. She had been helped – shoved, more like, she thought to herself angrily, fingering a bruise at the top of her arm – into bed unwillingly, in her underwear. Her skirt and blouse lay across a chair on the other side of the room and her crutches were propped up against the wall by the door. She looked at the five feet which separated her from her clothes and bit her lip in frustration. It took far longer than she had anticipated to make her way on one good leg from the bed, inch by inch around the wall, hanging grimly on to the furniture, and then back again even more precariously to the bed with her clothes in her hand.

By the time she had got her skirt awkwardly over her head and eased it down into something approaching its normal configuration, and slipped on and buttoned up her blouse, she felt exhausted and her leg was beginning to throb with pain.

'Damn and blast it,' she muttered under her breath as she began to edge her way carefully around the room again towards the door. With a crutch under her left arm it was easier to stand but as she eased the door of her room open the second crutch, held precariously under her elbow while she manipulated the door handle, fell to the floor with a clatter. For what seemed like minutes, although she knew it could be no more than seconds, the sound echoed down the cheerless corridor outside and she waited, heart thumping, to see whether it had disturbed anyone. If Betty Johns came storming from her office to investigate, Joyce knew all was lost. There was no way she could get back to her bed in time to pretend to be asleep.

But the silence was total.

'It's like the bloody *Marie Celeste*,' Joyce said to herself with a malicious smile of satisfaction. 'You could sneak in and cut everyone's throats and no one would be any the wiser.'

Even more cautiously she tucked her second crutch under her arm and swung her way slowly out into the corridor, closing the door of her room behind her. The air was cold and rank. She puckered her nose fastidiously. The pungent smell of disinfectant only just concealed the biting odour of incontinence with which she had reluctantly become familiar.

She turned left towards the end of the corridor furthest away

132

from the reception area and Betty Johns' office. Alice Smith's door was closed but the handle turned sweetly in Joyce's arthritic grip and she inched her way awkwardly into the dimly lit room and closed it behind her.

'Alice,' Joyce said in a sharp whisper. 'Alice, wake up. It's time to go.' There was no response from the huddled figure under the blankets. Joyce swung herself across to the bed and shook her friend's shoulder. Alice did not move and as Joyce let her hand rest lightly on the slight figure in the bed, her heart seemed to freeze and she drew a sharp breath in alarm. Gently she pulled the bedclothes back and touched Alice's grey and wizened face, half buried in the pillows. She lay there like a crumpled bird tossed aside by a cat. Her skin felt cool and Joyce could feel no pulse when she ran her hand lightly across her neck.

'Has Dracula's daughter got you, then, love?' she asked quietly, choking back fierce emotion. 'I'll have her for this, I promise you, Alice. She'll not get away with this.'

Slowly and painfully she turned away from the bed and swung herself back out into the corridor, closing the door behind her. To her right the fire door required only a firm push before it opened, letting in a gust of fresh air and a flood of sunshine. Taking a deep angry breath Joyce swung her crutches out through the door and made her way to the front of the Laurels and out into the street.

A couple of hundred yards down the road towards the centre of Bradfield she stopped for a moment. Her arms were aching and her breath was coming in painful gasps. She watched the traffic speed past her, oblivious to her distress as she looked in both directions for the familiar red of a telephone box. Cursing the wayward telephone company which had made its facilities too hard for elderly eyes to distinguish at a distance she suddenly saw salvation in the form of a cruising taxi. She waved a crutch urgently and the lavender Vauxhall bounced to a halt at the kerb. The young Asian driver leaned across and looked at Joyce dubiously.

'I'm private hire, luv. I'm not supposed to ply for trade on t'street . . .'

'Never mind that. Take me to the police station,' Joyce said sharply, pulling open the car door and half falling into the back seat with a huge sense of relief, dragging her crutches behind her.

'What's up, gran'ma?' asked the driver with a grin, half turning in his seat. 'You look like tha'st seen a ghost.'

'I have, lad, I have,' Joyce said. 'And someone'll swing for it, an' all.'


The first message on her answer-phone had Laura cursing her father, who had again failed to get on a flight to London. The second sent her running in a panic from the flat before she had even had time to slip off her jacket. She had got home early and refreshed, her hair still damp from an after-work swim at the pool she used as regularly as she could find the time. She had tossed a bag of shopping on to the kitchen work-bench and casually switched on her messages only to be riveted by Thackeray's voice, her heart missing a beat when she heard what he had to say.

'I missed you at work,' he had said, no trace of emotion to take the edge off the cool, almost official tone. 'Your grandmother's been taken to the infirmary. She's unwell. I'm not sure how seriously. Can you get there?' There was a long interval of hissing tape before the machine spluttered into life again and Laura realised she had been holding her breath as various nightmare scenarios flashed in front of her eyes.

'Laura, I'm sorry,' Thackeray said. 'All hell's broken loose here. I'll get to you as soon as I can.'

Laura could not remember later how she had driven the Beetle through the rush-hour traffic or where she had parked. Sick with anxiety, she forced her way to the reception desk in casualty through groups of anxious and dishevelled people clutching unhappy children or injured limbs. She was directed to a cubicle where a nurse looked round in surprise when Laura flung back the curtains. She found Joyce lying on the high bed, looking deathly pale and infinitely fragile against the pillows, though sufficiently aware to greet her grand-daughter with a smile which still had something of her indomitable spirit in it.

'Nan, what have you been doing to yourself?' Laura asked, her voice sounding unreal.

'Don't you fret, pet,' Joyce said. 'They say it's nobbut a twinge, nothing to worry about.'

The nurse looked up from the chart she was filling in, hardly needing to be told that the visitor with her red hair and anguished green eyes was a relative.

'You must be Laura,' she said. 'Mrs Ackroyd's been telling me about you.'

'What happened?' Laura asked hoarsely.

'Your grandmother's been overdoing it a bit this afternoon,' the nurse said drily. 'Some chest pains, nothing too serious, but the doctor would like her to stay in overnight as a precaution.'

'You're sure . . .?'

'A touch of indigestion,' Joyce said firmly, but the nurse shook her head with just as much determination.

'A bit more worrying than that,' she said. 'She needs some tests.'

'Nan, what have you been doing?' Laura said, bewildered but the nurse did not allow time for a response.

'The doctor wants her to rest,' she insisted.

'Can I see him? The doctor?' Laura demanded.

'He's very busy. He's with another case just now,' the nurse said. 'But he's admitted her and we've a bed waiting upstairs. I've no doubt your grandmother'll be able to tell you all about it tomorrow. But I think it would be better if you left her to rest now.'

Laura put her arms around Joyce and kissed her.

'It was Alice,' Joyce said in a voice so faint that Laura had to lean close to catch the words. 'Poor dear old Alice.'

'Tell me tomorrow, darling,' she said. 'And do what the doctor tells you.'

'Aye, well, it'll keep, I dare say,' Joyce muttered almost to herself. 'I did what I could.'

Reluctantly Laura allowed herself to be ushered out of the cubicle as two porters came in and began to wheel Joyce's bed out after her and push it towards the lifts at the end of the corridor. Feeling dazed, Laura made her way back towards reception, where she was surprised to see Kevin Mower heading purposefully towards her.

'Laura,' he said, evidently as surprised as she was. 'I was coming to see how your grandmother was. We'll be wanting a statement.'

'A statement?' Laura repeated, feeling stupid and close to tears. 'Why on earth do you want a statement? Anyway you can't see her. They want her to rest. They won't even let me stay with her.'

Mower took in Laura's still damp hair, which was hanging loose in ringlets around a face drained of colour and eyes clouded with bewilderment, and recognised a case of shock when he saw one. Tentatively he put an arm around her shoulders and guided her towards the cafeteria on the other end of the reception area, sat her in a chair and bought her a cup of hot, sweet tea.

'She's going to be OK, you know,' he said. 'Michael was on the phone to check her out before he sent me down here. They think it's a touch of angina brought on by stress. Nothing that can't be treated.'

'What stress?' Laura said. 'She's supposed to be convalescing in a nursing home, for God's sake. She shouldn't be under any stress. And why are you and Michael involved? I don't understand what's going on.'

So Mower told her how Joyce Ackroyd had hobbled into the central police station two hours earlier demanding money to pay the young taxi driver, who had ushered her solicitously up the steps and in through the swing doors, to report a murder at the Laurels.

'Alice Smith,' Laura said dully. 'Is that who she meant?'

'She's in intensive care,' Mower said. 'We told social services and they and uniformed went down there mob-handed. Alice wasn't dead but she's in a coma. It looks like an overdose of whatever sedative it is they've been using. Your grandmother brought a couple of pills in with her so it shouldn't be difficult to prove. Betty Johns has been arrested and social services are moving all the residents into temporary accommodation while they clean the place up. And just to add to the excitement, it turns out that Alice's son is Keith Spencer-Smith, your head honcho at the tourist board.'

'Of course,' Laura said softly. 'It was him I saw rushing in to the Laurels that day. I only got a glimpse of him but he looked familiar and I couldn't place him. Drives a BMW?'

'I think he does, yes,' Mower said.

'With that beard of his he doesn't look anything like the photographs my grandmother has, does he? But why didn't he come forward when you found Mariella's body? What's he got to hide, the devious bastard?'

Mower sipped his tea reflectively, knowing that these were the precise questions Michael Thackeray would be asking Smith at this very moment. He was intensely aware of Laura's closeness, which had always disturbed him, and now it stirred a deep anger at the deviousness of other people of their acquaintance. The sense of power his knowledge gave him was intoxicating but the temptation to use it faded as he watched Laura struggle to come to terms with what had just happened. He was filled with sadness at the idea that some day she could, indeed almost inevitably would, be hurt by what he knew. But he also realised, with a certainty that took his cynical soul by surprise, that he was not capable of striking that particular blow.

'Michael,' she said suddenly and he thought for one terrible moment that she had read his thoughts. 'Michael left a message on my answer-phone.'

'We tried to contact you at work and at home as soon as your grandmother turned up at the nick,' Mower said.

'I left the office early and went shopping and then for a swim,' Laura explained.

'He's interviewing Spencer-Smith,' Kevin said. 'He couldn't get away. That man has some questions to answer.'

'Right.' Laura did not need to put her disappointment into words and Mower stared resolutely into his tea as he fought off a treacherous desire to put his arm around her again. But he knew it would not be interpreted as a brotherly gesture a second time. He sighed at the unfairness of life and glanced at his watch.

'I need to get back,' he said. 'If Alice doesn't recover we may be looking at a manslaughter charge for buxom Betty and I've no doubt Spencer-Smith is going to have lots to tell us about the Italian girl.'

'Poor Mariella,' Laura said angrily. 'Those boys bullied her and used her, didn't they?'

'I suppose they did,' Mower said, startled by the passion in her voice. 'Can I run you home?'

'No, I'll be OK now,' Laura said, getting to her feet. 'There's something I want to check before I go home. Tell Michael I'll see him later, will you?'

'Of course,' Mower said. He stayed at the table watching as she dodged her way through the crowds to the exit. 'Jammy bastard,' he said under his breath. And there was more than a little venom in the phrase.

## 15

DCI Michael Thackeray faced Keith Spencer-Smith across an interview room table and the frost in the air between them made WDC Val Ridley shiver. The atmosphere was so chilly she almost imagined she could see her breath in front of her face. She had witnessed Thackeray's cold anger before, an emotion as controlled as the man himself but still offering an almost tangible threat to anyone who came within its range.

She could not imagine why the tall, bearded, middle-aged man, impeccably dressed in a silver-grey business suit and blue and gold tie, who sat across the table from them, had incurred this degree of dislike. But there was no doubt that he, too, arriving accompanied by his solicitor who sat watching the proceedings uneasily, was taking the interview very seriously indeed.

'Did you ask Betty Johns to use the means she did to keep your mother quiet after she had spoken to me on Wednesday?' Thackeray asked, almost before the formalities had been completed.

'Of course not,' Spencer-Smith came back quickly. 'Why on earth would I do that?'

'That's the question I've been asking myself ever since I heard what had happened to Alice,' Thackeray said. 'And I can think of several reasons. So let's start at the beginning, shall we? Tell me first of all why you changed your name?'

Spencer-Smith shrugged easily. 'I didn't,' he said. 'Spencer was my mother's name. There are too many plain Smiths around so I decided to use both names, that's all. It's not illegal. In fact in some countries it's standard practice. It was a marketing ploy, if you like. No more than that.'

'Do you know why your mother never mentioned that you were her son when I discussed the Bonnetti girl's disappearance with her?' Thackeray thought of Alice Smith's sad-eyed confession regarding her husband and wondered why he had been so obtuse about the fact that she had barely mentioned what had happened to her son, then or later. Had he really been led up the garden path by the frail old woman now fighting for her life in intensive care?

'I've no idea,' Spencer-Smith said. 'Was there any particular reason why she should have mentioned me?'

'I really don't see that you can hold my client responsible for what his mother did or did not say, Chief Inspector,' the solicitor intervened.

'Just so long as I can be sure that he hadn't asked her not to mention this rather salient fact,' Thackeray said. 'And of course we're not going to be able to ask her about that, are we? Someone has made sure of that.'

'When she recovers—' Spencer-Smith began but Thackeray did not let him finish.

'*If* she recovers,' he said sharply. 'And let me remind you both that if she doesn't recover, we will be discussing very serious charges with Betty Johns, and perhaps others as well.'

'I think my client should reserve his position on that,' the solicitor said. 'I'd be surprised if you had any evidence to adduce that what has happened was anything other than an unfortunate accident.'

Thackeray looked at the lawyer coldly.

'I shouldn't bank on it,' he said. 'But let's move on to the question which your client can certainly answer.' He turned from the lawyer back to Spencer-Smith, his broad shoulders hunched over the papers on the table in front of him.

'Why, when Mariella Bonnetti's body was identified, did you not come forward to tell me what you can remember of the time when, by all accounts, you and your friends were in daily touch with the girl – right up to the day she disappeared?'

Spencer-Smith shrugged again. 'I had no idea, Chief Inspector,' he said. 'I've been working eighteen-hour days getting this museum project off the ground. I didn't know you'd found a body or identified it. Of course, if I had known . . .'

'You don't read the local papers?' Thackeray broke in sharply. 'You work with the local council and you don't read the papers?'

'I've been too busy.'

'You don't even read the local papers when they are covering your own projects?' Thackeray stuck out a hand to Val Ridley, who hurriedly passed him a folded copy of the *Bradfield Gazette* from the file in front of her. He spread it out carefully on the table. On the front page, the description of the identification of the body from the building site was accompanied by a blown-up version of the photograph of Mariella which had been rescued from the archives. Right next to it, a single-column story carried the news that John Blake had arrived in Bradfield to open the cinema museum in a few days' time. Spencer-Smith and his lawyer examined the page briefly.

'My secretary looks after the press clippings,' Spencer-Smith said dismissively. 'I saw the clipping about the museum, of course, but I'd no idea what else was on that page. I never saw the *Gazette* that day.'

'So, you didn't ask your mother to mislead me, you had no idea that Betty Johns was pumping her dangerously full of tranquillisers, you didn't know Mariella's body had been found? So what do you know, Mr Smith?' Thackeray said.

'What do you mean?'

'I mean, now we've established just who you are and that you knew Mariella all those years ago, what can you tell me about what was going on between her and the lads she used to hang around with?'

'Mariella, Mariella,' Spencer-Smith said irritably. 'No one paid much attention, you know, when she went missing. She was just the Eye-tie girl who'd run away. They weren't very popular, you know, so soon after the war. They weren't the only Italians in Bradfield and they were not welcome. I can't even remember seeing a policeman at the time, never mind having to answer any questions. How do you know she was murdered anyway?'

'Girls who just run away don't end up under six foot of Bradfield muck, Mr Smith,' Val Ridley said sharply. 'Someone put her there, and the chances are whoever put her there killed her.'

'Well it wasn't me,' Spencer-Smith said flatly.

'You were out with her that day,' Thackeray said.

'A whole lot of us were out with her, as you put it,' Spencer-Smith snapped dismissively. 'And we came back with her and we all went home.'

'Did you see Mariella go home? Her parents say she never arrived.'

Spencer-Smith had the grace to hesitate for a moment, as if trying to visualise that damp and miserable summer day.

'I don't think I actually saw her go into the house,' he said at last. 'We left her with some of the other kids in the factory yard, I think.'

'We?' Thackeray pounced.

'Me and Roy Parkinson,' Spencer-Smith said. 'We went off on our own to his place. To finish off the cakes and things, as far as I can remember. It's all a long time ago.'

'Do you know that your mother thinks it was your father who killed Mariella?' Thackeray said. 'She says she's always believed he did it. Could that be true, do you think?'

'My father was half crippled, Chief Inspector,' Spencer-Smith came back quickly. 'He could barely get himself up the stairs to bed at night. He'd have had trouble digging a hole deep enough to plant a pansy let alone a girl's body.'

'He could have had help,' Thackeray suggested.

'Chief Inspector, this is verging on the fantastical,' Spencer-Smith's lawyer objected.

Thackeray nodded briefly though Val Ridley could see that his eyes had not lost their chill.

'So if not you, and not your father, who?' Thackeray went on, but this time Spencer-Smith did not reply. He sat looking at his hands on the table, as if trying to will himself back to the hazy days of his adolescence.

'Did you have sex with Mariella?' Val Ridley demanded suddenly.

Spencer-Smith smiled faintly at that.

'Chance would have been a fine thing,' he said. 'We'd all have liked to have sex with Mariella. She was a pretty girl, and well developed with it. But teaching her to bowl with my arm round her middle was as close as I got. No one got a look in but Parky, as far as I can remember. He was the oldest, always letting us know how experienced he was about that sort of thing. A load of bullshit, I expect, but you know what boys are like.'

'Parky again? Whatever happened to Roy Parkinson?' Thackeray asked.

'I really don't know,' Spencer-Smith said. 'He went off to do his National Service and his mother moved away. I never saw him again.'

'You see one of my problems with this investigation is how few of you it's been possible to talk to,' Thackeray said more thoughtfully. He took Joyce Ackroyd's photograph of the teenagers out of Val Ridley's file and put it on the table in front of Spencer-Smith. 'You are here – unwillingly and very late in the day, it has to be said. But where are the rest of your friends? Jack Ackroyd is in Portugal, Roy Parkinson has vanished, the O'Meara girl committed suicide years ago, and now her brother is dead in suspicious circumstances.'

Spencer-Smith pulled the photograph closer.

'Bridget O'Meara. God. I'd almost forgotten about Bridie. Another of Parky's conquests.'

'Conquests?' Val Ridley said quickly. 'She can't be more than twelve.'

'Thirteen, I think she was. But the age never bothered Parky.

Of course, I don't know how far he went. Only how far he said he went. The same with Mariella. Who knows what to believe? It was a long summer. We were all aching for it. But who got it with whom I can't tell you. I only know I went back to school in September just as frustrated as I'd been in July.'

'Have you seen Danny O'Meara since?' Thackeray asked.

'No, I haven't. Not since I left school, anyway.'

'This is all more than forty years ago, Chief Inspector,' Spencer-Smith's solicitor said wearily. 'Is this really getting any of us anywhere at all?'

'If it wasn't for the remarkable coincidence of Danny O'Meara's death so soon after Mariella's body was found, I'd be inclined to share your scepticism,' Thackeray said. 'Tell me just two more things, Mr Spencer-Smith. First, where were you on Monday afternoon?'

Spencer-Smith looked startled, gave the question a moment's thought and then said firmly, 'I was at the museum with John Blake and his dreadful PR woman, the stick insect – what's her name? – Lorelie. All afternoon. I'm sure they'll vouch for me. Lorelie hardly let me out of her sight. And the second question, Chief Inspector?'

'Who do you think killed Mariella Bonnetti?'

Spencer-Smith thought a little longer about this question and when he spoke again his tone was just as firm.

'You have to remember that we didn't know she was dead, so it's not a question I thought about at the time. But, looking back, the most likely person has to be Parky. For most of us that summer was just games of cricket in the factory yard, an occasional snog if we were lucky in the garden of the derelict house at the back of Peter Street. But Parky was like a young goat. Perhaps he got carried away.'


'It's too bloody convenient,' Thackeray said angrily. He was sitting in shirt-sleeves in Superintendent Jack Longley's office, which faced west and was still filled with early evening sunshine. His boss, forehead shining with sweat, leaned back in his chair, his pale blue eyes acute but not unfriendly.

'You don't believe the elusive Keith Smith, then?'

'There's no one left to contradict him, is there?' Thackeray said. 'Suspects and witnesses who are either dead or disappeared are very useful to those still around, aren't they? They can't answer back. Perhaps Jack Ackroyd will be able to throw more light on what was going on. When he eventually turns up.'

'He's definitely coming over here, is he? If not, you'd better go to see him.'

'Laura says he's trying to get a flight,' Thackeray said shortly. 'It's the worst time of year.'

'You're taking this personally, Michael,' Longley said, not unsympathetically. But it was a muted warning as much as a statement of fact and Thackeray glanced away to the window where a gang of starlings squabbled in the cherry trees outside.

'Yes, well, there's a personal element in it, isn't there?' he said quietly. 'Apart from anything else, I feel responsible for the old ladies. I'd put money on Alice Smith's overdose being a direct result of the talk I had with her a couple of days before. Someone wanted her to shut up. And I could have handled it better.' What he could not admit to Longley was that Laura had rushed him into that meeting with Alice and her grandmother.

'How is she?' Longley asked.

'Still in intensive care, still unconscious. I don't think she's going to make it,' Thackeray said sombrely.

'And the matron?'

'We've let her go on police bail. We know where to find her when we want her. But even if Alice Smith dies it will be very difficult to prove she actively meant to harm her. She's been dishing pills out so long, apparently, with such abandon, that she could claim it was an accident. But social services and the health trust are on to her case. One way or another I don't think she'll have charge of vulnerable old people again.'

'And Mrs Ackroyd?' Longley asked, knowing that her condition would be even closer to Thackeray's heart.

'She's resting, according to Kevin Mower, who's just got back from the hospital. It's nothing too serious, apparently. She just knocked herself out getting down here on her blasted crutches.

144

Why the hell she didn't phone . . .' Thackeray shrugged, with a mixture of exasperation and admiration.

'She's a tough old bird is Joyce Ackroyd,' Longley said. 'She'll not let a mere matron get her down.'

'If she hadn't broken her leg and ended up in the Laurels, Betty Johns might have got away with her reign of terror indefinitely, I suppose. But I think on the whole I'd rather have the whistle-blowing done by informants a bit less frail than Joyce.'

'We're none of us getting any younger,' Longley said lugubriously. The phone at his elbow shrilled suddenly and he picked it up, listened for a moment and glanced in Thackeray's direction.

'Aye, he's here,' he said. 'I'll send him down.' He hung up thoughtfully. 'It's Kevin Mower. Wants to speak to you urgently, he says. Knocked a bit of sense into him, didn't it, that lucky escape he had wi' the knife woman?'

'I hope so, sir,' Thackeray said with feeling. 'But I wouldn't bank on it.'


All eager anticipation, Mower took the stairs two at a time ahead of his boss as they entered the reception area where a pale, dark-haired young woman in a crumpled summer dress and cotton jacket was waiting for them.

'You wanted to see me in connection with the death of Daniel O'Meara?' Thackeray asked.

'I'm Bridget, his daughter. Bridget Tate now, my married name,' the young woman said. 'My sister Kay said you think my dad's death wasn't suicide. That he was killed . . .'

'It's a possibility, Mrs Tate,' Thackeray said.

They took her into an interview room and sat her down. Thackeray told her why Daniel O'Meara's injuries were unlikely to have been self-inflicted but when they pressed her to imagine who could have hated her father enough to leave him unconscious in the path of a train, she shook her head in bewilderment.

'He was a gentle man, my dad,' she said. 'I don't think he had an enemy in the world. I've not seen as much of him or my mam as I should these last few years, with young kids of my own, living on the other side of Leeds. You know how it is? You need three different buses to get up to their place, and with two kids and a push-chair . . .' She shrugged wearily. 'But I can't imagine anyone wanting to kill him. Surely you must suspect the patients at the hospital. Some of them must be violent—'

'We'll be looking at all the possibilities, of course,' Thackeray said quickly. Too quickly, Mower thought, knowing full well that Thackeray had shown little interest in the series of painstaking interviews with O'Meara's fellow patients that had been dutifully filed by uniformed officers.

'Kay said that you were asking about my aunt, Dad's sister Bridget, an' all,' Bridget said, evidently puzzled by their interest.

'It's a line of enquiry,' Thackeray said. 'Did your father tell you how she died?'

Bridget Tate took her time to tell them very slowly, and at second-hand, how her aunt had plunged from a balcony almost forty years before and why her father had never recovered from the shock.

'Dad used to talk to me when I was a kid,' she said, her voice breaking. 'I was his favourite. He hardly ever had a job and we used to go for long walks in the park and down by the canal while my mam was at work. He talked a lot about his sister Bridie. Said I wasn't to tell Mam because she didn't like it. He said Bridie had killed herself years ago and it was his fault. He cried once or twice, sitting on a seat by the bandstand. That really upset me, that did. I'd never seen a grown man cry before.'

Bridget Tate hesitated, not far from tears herself.

'Why did he think it was his fault?' Thackeray asked quietly. 'Did he say?'

'It was nothing to do with him actually,' Bridget said angrily. 'It was the usual story. Some beggar got her pregnant. And in those days that was all hushed up, especially in a good Catholic family like ours. He said she went away to one of those mother-and-baby homes the nuns had and the baby was adopted. She never saw it again. I suppose Dad thought he should have protected her better. He was the oldest and he seems to have been right soppy about her.'

'When was this? Do you know? What year?' Thackeray asked.

'She was thirteen, he said. Only bloody thirteen. Can you believe it? In those days, an' all. My mam'll know which year it was.'

'Nineteen fifty-three at a guess,' Thackeray said quietly. 'Did your father say who was responsible?'

'I don't think anyone knew for sure. But he thought it was an older lad who went away soon after.'

'Roy Parkinson?'

'Yes, I think that was the name. But no one bothered about him, apparently. He wasn't a Catholic and anyway she was too young to marry. They just got her out o't'way as quick as they could and hushed everything up.' Bridget Tate shook her head angrily. 'Priests,' she said.

'And your father believed this was why your aunt died?'

'He said she grieved for that baby. And she never would look at another lad. The night she died he'd seen her earlier at the party a bit sozzled and crying in a corner and he'd not taken any notice. The next thing he knows there's all this shouting and screaming and she's gone over the balcony.'

'Did she jump or was she pushed? Did he say?' Thackeray pressed.

'She jumped,' Bridget said flatly. 'I think the inquest decided it was an accident, but then the family would want that, any road. They'd push for that. But my dad was always sure she jumped. All because they couldn't bear to let her keep her baby. Poor kid. I can imagine how she felt, can't you?'

'I can imagine,' Thackeray agreed so quietly that Kevin Mower could barely hear him.

'There was another tragedy around that time,' Mower said quickly. 'Did your father ever talk to you about the Italian girl who disappeared? They were neighbours in Peter Street.'

'Mariella,' Bridget said, with a shudder. 'That's the body you've just found, isn't it? After all those years, it hardly seems possible she could turn up like that.'

147

'Did he mention Mariella?' Mower asked.

'Just in passing, like,' Bridget said. 'When he was talking about Bridie, and how they used to all play together wi' the lad who got her into trouble. I think he fancied Mariella, but he'd be too young to do owt about it. With the older lads around, I don't think my dad got a look-in.'

'Keith Smith and Roy Parkinson?' Thackeray said.

'Yes, summat like that. They used to play cricket. And sometimes, he said, on days when it was too hot to run around, they used to go into the garden of this big empty house on the hill behind Peter Street. It was all overgrown and shady and my dad and Bridie used to pick flowers, he said. Columbines and roses. And she was frightened of the bees buzzing about. Bridie would take them home and put them in a jam jar for her mam. He reckoned that was where Roy took her when . . . you know.'

'Did your father ever say what happened to Roy Parkinson?' Thackeray asked, but Bridget shook her head.

'He said he'd gone away by the time they found out about the baby. I dare say she waited as long as she could before she let on. And as I say, no one wanted a fuss. They just wanted rid of it.'

'He never mentioned Coronation Day?'

'Not that I remember, not 'specially,' Bridget said. 'Was that the day Mariella disappeared?'

'They all got bored watching the television and went off together,' Thackeray said. 'Roy and Keith, your father and his sister, Mariella, and Jack Ackroyd. Now three of them are dead, one we can't trace and the other two have not been much help so far.'

'It's like a judgement, isn't it, the body coming back to haunt them after all this time? Do you believe in fate, Inspector? I do.'

Thackeray shook his head dismissively.

'If you think of anything else that might help us, Mrs Tate, you will let us know,' he said.

She looked at him, her eyes sad. 'They must have been very alike, Bridget and my dad,' she said. 'Given to depression, you know? The rest of us must take after my mam, I suppose. We don't seem to get so down.'


By the time he got back to Laura's flat, Thackeray had to admit that he felt pretty down himself. Bridget Tate's retelling of a familiar old story had touched chords which he had rather it had not. He parked under the trees outside the house, immediately aware that Laura's car was not in its usual place and, glancing upwards, he could see that none of the lights were on in the flat. It was after eleven but was still very early for Laura to have gone to bed.

The disappointment at knowing she was not there to welcome him was as sharp as a knife between his ribs. It brought all the tensions of the last few days rushing back into his tired mind and he knew that if he and Laura did not resolve the strains in their relationship soon it would disintegrate. He did not think it could last much longer on the sexual chemistry which gave them both so much pleasure.

He could not be certain that either truth or lies would save him, but he knew with absolute conviction that he would not be able to bear a return to his previous solitary state. The prisoner who had been given a glimpse of freedom, he thought, could be driven quickly mad when the cell door clanged shut again. After ten years of virtual exile from the human race he had taken a chance on Laura he did not think he was still capable of taking. If he lost her, he lost everything again, and he did not know how he would survive.

He climbed the stairs quickly and let himself in, switched on the lights and looked around in vain for any indication that she had left him a note to say where she had gone. The ingredients for their meal still lay in their supermarket carrier bag on the kitchen work-bench, a damp towel and swim-suit close by ready to go into the washing machine.

The flat had an abandoned air and he began to grow anxious. He listened in growing alarm to his own message to her on the answer-phone but there was nothing else except a hissing silence

149

although he played the tape to its end. She had obviously not been home since she had left hurriedly to go to the hospital to see Joyce.

'Why the hell doesn't that blasted paper get her a mobile phone?' he asked himself fruitlessly. Ted Grant's penny-pinching rationale was that reporters needed mobiles, feature writers didn't. For half an hour Thackeray sat smoking, lighting cigarette after cigarette and stubbing them out before they were half finished. He tried to put Laura out of his mind as he went over the two deaths he was investigating, separated by so many years but increasingly linked, it seemed to him, by skeins of powerful emotion.

He and Mower had sent Bridget Tate home to her husband and children in a taxi, both of them subdued by what they had learned about events in Coronation Year. Thackeray knew only too well how long grief could last but if Mower understood how painfully he had been reminded of that by Bridget, he was circumspect enough to keep his thoughts to himself.

But as the clock moved inexorably past midnight, Thackeray could sit it out no longer. He rang first Ted Grant and then Vicky Mendelson to see if either of them knew where Laura might be. Ted blustered and Vicky complained sleepily but they knew nothing. Then he rang Mower.

It took the Sergeant ten minutes to arrive at the flat, slim in jeans and a black designer polo shirt, his hair dishevelled and a hint of anxiety in his eyes. He found Thackeray in shirt-sleeves, a well-filled ashtray on the coffee table, his face haggard and as close to panic as Mower had ever seen him.

'Guv?' he said.

'Get on to John Blake,' Thackeray said. 'She's been spending a lot of time with him for this profile she's writing.'

'If you say so,' Mower said doubtfully. 'All she said when she left me at the hospital was that she had something to check out. Nothing about Blake.'

'Do it, Kevin,' Thackeray said. 'If I speak to that bastard I'll say something I regret.'

Mower shrugged, picked up the phone and made a brief call.

'John Blake and Lorelie Baum are both in their suite, according to reception at the Clarendon,' he said. 'I'll check casualty.' He felt Thackeray's eyes boring into the back of his neck as he checked the accident reports at the hospital and the control room at police headquarters, without result.

'Nothing,' he said. 'Do you want me to put out a call for her car?'

'I don't know,' Thackeray said. 'D'you think I'm being a fool?'

Mower hesitated, knowing he was moving into uncharted territory. 'You know her better than I do, Guv. If it's really out of character . . .' He shrugged.

'You spoke to her at the hospital,' Thackeray said. 'Did she seem OK then? Or did you give her any reason . . .?' He stopped, although Mower had no doubt what he was asking and that on his answer hung his own future as well as Thackeray's. He ran his hand lightly over the still sensitive scar tissue on his shoulder, avoiding the accusation in Thackeray's eyes.

'I didn't . . . wouldn't do anything to hurt Laura,' he said slowly. 'You should know that. Even though I know – you know I know, for fuck's sake – she's going to get hurt one day.'

'And you don't like that,' Thackeray said bitterly.

'No, I bloody well don't like that,' Mower came back quickly. 'She saved my life, remember?'

'But you didn't show her the cause and just impediment? Like blasted *Jane Eyre*?'

'Never read it, Guv,' Mower said lightly. 'Just as well, maybe.'

Thackeray slumped back into his chair and closed his eyes, looking utterly defeated.

'So where the hell is she?' he said.

# 16

Laura wriggled her back in what must have been her twentieth attempt to adjust her spine to the sharp contours of a wall made of unyielding lumps of millstone grit. And for the twentieth time she knew she had not succeeded and she cursed the impetuosity which had led her into her current plight. She was cold, damp, tired, lost and had twisted her ankle when the heel on her shoe, designed for city streets not rough moorland, had tipped her from a tussock of grass into a boggy pool.

Laura realised she had made a serious mistake when John Blake had pulled the Mercedes off the high and winding moorland road on the way back from Ilkley. When he switched off the headlights and the engine, the darkness enfolded the car like a thick blanket. It was a narrow, little used road and tonight it seemed to be deserted. Tiny points of light on the far horizon gave the only hint that there was anyone but the two of them on the planet.

She could see Blake's face dimly in the fluorescent lights he had left on behind the dashboard. In profile he looked forbidding enough but when he turned towards her his eyes glittered in the darkness and she knew she would need all her wits to deny him what he had obviously stopped the car for.

'You and I have some unfinished business,' he said, switching on a cassette tape of Sinatra and reaching an arm out towards her.

'My generation,' he said, nodding at the radio. 'Do you like him?'

'I've no strong feelings,' she said dismissively. 'And there's nothing unfinished I can think of, John.' She leaned away from his embrace. 'It was good of you to take me out to see your mother's place, but I need to get back now. Anyway, Lorelie will be worried about you.' She deliberately tried to keep her tone light but Blake snorted angrily at the mention of Lorelie Baum's name.

'I thought I told you,' he said. 'Lorelie is definitely on the way out, finito-ed. She is one unattractive young woman in bed.'

'Well, I'm sorry,' Laura said. 'But I'm afraid I'm not seeking to take her place – professionally or in bed.'

Blake leaned across and put a hand on her knee, and held her a little too tightly for comfort. She took hold of his hand equally firmly and replaced it on his own side of the car.

'I'd like to go home now, please,' Laura said. 'I'm late and people will be wondering where I am.'

'You're not married, are you?' Blake asked suddenly. 'You didn't tell me that.'

'I'm not married,' Laura said. 'I did tell you that. But I live with someone. I told you that, too.'

'We all live with someone, so what's the problem, honey? You were eager enough the other night.'

'Not really,' Laura said.

'Oh, yes, really,' Blake said. 'D'you think I can't tell? I've spent most of my life fending off women who've got the hots for me.'

'Well, that's great for you, but I'm afraid this one hasn't, so you're not going to need to do any fending,' Laura said, cursing herself for imagining that John Blake might have provided her or any other woman with a night's guilt-free amusement.

'You are a sharp little cookie, aren't you?' Blake said. 'You could run rings round Lorelie, you know that?' And this time when he reached across the car to put an arm around her his grip was like iron. His other hand clamped itself just as tightly across her legs where she felt his thumb insinuate itself between her thighs.

'Come on, Laura, relax,' he said as his mouth closed over hers and his tongue met the resistance of her clenched teeth.

'I said no, damn you,' she insisted, trying desperately to squirm out of his grip.

'We're a long way from home, honey,' Blake said. 'You'll not find any friendly policemen up here at this time of night.'

'The last time someone tried something like this on with me it *was* a bloody policeman,' she said bitterly. 'And he got away with it.'

The urgency of the situation seemed suddenly to throw her mind into top gear.

'But you won't. You are an arrogant bastard, and a bully, and vain with it.' And it was his vanity which would defeat him, she thought grimly as with her left hand she reached for the door handle and with her right she grabbed hold of John Blake's hair, much of which, as she expected, came away in her hand. As she flung open the door on her side of the car she threw the hair-piece as far as she could into the darkness outside.

'What have you done, you stupid bitch!' Blake screamed. As

she rolled out of the car he caught her a furious blow on her arm. She hit the ground running and she did not stop until she had scaled the stone wall, which she could dimly make out at one side of the road, and put a hundred yards of tussocky moorland between herself and the car, scattering sleepy sheep as she went.

Blake did not follow. As she stood in the darkness trying to get her breath back, she could see him in the faint light from inside the car searching for his lost property in the long grass. More circumspectly she set off again, wishing that she had stopped off at home to change out of her tight short skirt into trousers before embarking on her impetuous trip with Blake. She hardly seemed to have made any distance when Blake switched on the Mercedes' powerful headlights and swung them in an arc like a searchlight across the treeless moor, catching her for an instant in the full beam. Cursing and feeling as if she had been stripped naked by the light, she headed for a slight rise in the ground which she guessed would shield her from the road.

As she breasted the rise, she heard Blake shout out behind her, and glancing back she saw that he was out of the car now, and had clambered on top of the dry-stone wall, evidently to get a better view of where she was heading. Dodging out of the beam of the headlights, she forced her legs up the steep slope to the top of the rise and plunged over the far side and out of sight into total darkness. Where was the moon when you needed it? she thought frantically.

Her arm was numb and her breath was coming in painful gasps by the time her city shoes gave up the unequal struggle with rocks and slippery marram grass. The heel gave way and pitched her sideways into a patch of semi-bog, where she lay for a moment, with all the breath knocked out of her and aware of the muddy water soaking her through to her panties. She gazed at a single star mocking her from the dark sky above and she wished she had been born with Jane Eyre's calm and reflective temperament.

As she got her breath back she looked around her and realised with a faint feeling of alarm that she had lost her bearings as well as her right shoe, which seemed to have been sucked into the boggy ground where she had fallen. She could still see those tantalising pinpricks of light on the horizon, signs of civilisation far too far away to reach, but there was no longer any indication in which direction the road lay. She knew she could not be more than three or four miles from the commuter village of Broadley, which itself lay on the edge of the Maze Valley where villages seamlessly ran into the towns and suburbs around Bradfield.

But for all the good that knowledge could do her, she might as well have been on the dark side of the moon. Because she also knew that the moor she was now lying on was riddled with ancient mine workings and abandoned quarries, whose craggy faces presented unwary walkers with unexpected hazards even in broad daylight. In the dark the moor was a death-trap.

Feeling gingerly in front of her with her single shod foot, in case another unseen bog or hole should catch her unawares, she found her way to a nearby stone wall and slumped down on a patch of warm and relatively dry grass vacated by a ewe, which was as startled by their midnight encounter as she was. She settled herself to sit it out until dawn.

It had all seemed such a good idea at the time, she thought sardonically, as the incongruity of her situation hit her – bruised, wet and bitterly cold in the middle of England in early summer and just a couple of miles from human habitation. She had left the hospital full of the urgency which had seized her as she had watched her grandmother being wheeled away.

She had remembered John Blake saying that his mother was in an excellent home for the elderly, and suddenly her one priority became not only locating that home but inspecting it before the NHS turned Joyce back out into the careless clutches of the 'community' again. What she really needed, she thought, was a solution to Joyce's problems to present to her father when he eventually turned up.

When she had called at the Clarendon, Blake had come down from his room and agreed readily enough to drive her there, taking the main road to Ilkley where the rest home he had selected for his mother was housed in a solid four-square Victorian building of blackened stone which, he said, had formerly been an hotel. The contrast with the Laurels could not have been greater, she thought as the door was opened by a neatly uniformed nurse and they were ushered into a comfortable sitting room with a bay window overlooking well-kept lawns with a view of open moorland beyond. Several elderly women were sitting about drinking tea and chatting. A foursome played bridge at a card-table in the window.

They had waited only a few minutes until the nurse ushered in a grey-haired woman, smartly dressed in a floral cotton suit but with that vague look in her eyes which Laura had begun to recognise.

'Your mother was very tired. I was just about to settle her down for the night, but I dare say she can manage a little while longer. She's always much more cheerful after you've been, you know,' the nurse said to Blake. She sat her down in a fireside chair with a rug over her knees.

'Would you like tea?' she asked and, when Blake refused, left them to talk. Blake took his mother's hand.

'She doesn't really know me any more,' he said. Mrs Blake smiled enthusiastically at them both. 'I had such a nice trip to Scarborough,' she said.

'It must be thirty years since she went to Scarborough,' Blake said impatiently. 'I've had her out in California half a dozen times since then, but she seems to have forgotten all that.'

'It's an awful thing, forgetfulness,' Laura said. 'My grandmother's mind is still as clear as a bell.'

'You're lucky then,' Blake muttered irritably.

'You shouldn't spoil me like this, George,' Mrs Blake said earnestly to her son, who dropped her hand as if he had been scalded and turned away.

'George was my father,' he said to Laura. 'He left us when I was a kid and she never had a good word to say for him. Now she doesn't know the difference.' He looked around the room impatiently and waved at the nurse, who could be seen in conversation just outside the sitting-room door. When she did not come he headed towards the door.

'I'll fetch someone,' he said. 'If we get her put to bed we can have a look round.'

The old woman watched Blake go and then leaned forward and patted Laura's hand.

'Never mind, Pam,' she said confidentially. 'We'll go to Scarborough again one of these days. We had such good times, didn't we, dear? And in California?'

'Now then, Mrs B, time for bed, is it?' the nurse said, bustling back into the room and helping her charge out of her chair with a firm but not ungentle hand.

'She's well away with the fairies today, isn't she, dear?' she said to Blake as she guided his mother towards the door. 'She has her good days and her bad days.'

Blake shrugged and watched his mother's departure without emotion.

'I'm sorry,' Laura said, meaning it. 'It's a cruel disease that leaves a body without the person you knew seeming to inhabit it any more. She seemed to think I was someone else. Who's Pam?'

Blake looked nonplussed for a moment, then smiled. 'My auntie Pam,' he said. 'Christ, she's been dead for years. Look, I don't want you writing about my mother. You do understand that, don't you?'

'Yes, of course. It wasn't because of the profile I wanted to come over here. I explained that.'

'Yes well, she's perfectly satisfactorily looked after here,' Blake said dismissively. 'And as you can see, if they've got all their marbles they can really have quite a pleasant time. It's not cheap though. Could your grandmother afford it?'

'No, but my father can,' Laura said.

Blake had shown her round the ground-floor rooms civilly enough and a nurse had taken them upstairs to look at some of the bedrooms. It was getting dark when they left and as they began the long climb out of the town on the road to Broadley, the scenic route back to Bradfield, the cluster of rocks on the summit of the cliffs to the west were silhouetted like the monstrous beasts they were named for against a sky of dove-grey streaked with lavender and pink.

Laura relaxed as Blake steered the big car expertly round the sharp bends on to the open moors as darkness fell. It was not until they had left the last signs of human habitation well behind them and he had suddenly stopped the car that she had realised her mistake.

She must have dozed off eventually, with her back to the hard dry-stone wall, because the next thing she knew there was a streak of pale grey in the sky to the east and her nostrils were full of the greasy smell of unwashed wool. A shaggy ewe and her lamb had settled themselves in the lee of the wall beside her and were protecting her from the full force of the sharp dawn breeze.

She did not move for a while, as she watched the streak broaden out into a ragged band of daylight which perceptibly clawed its way across the sky, casting a chilly grey light across the miles of rugged moorland that surrounded her. Before long she could make out the ribbon of road which led down from the heights where Blake had stopped the car the night before to the first low stone cottages of Broadley.

'So near yet so far,' she muttered as eventually she staggered to her feet and began to pick her way through rocks and patches of boggy ground. The mud squelched through the toes of her bare foot and soon filled her other shoe. She took it off impatiently and threw it away. Never again, she promised herself, would she venture beyond the paved streets of Bradfield without her walking boots.

It was five-thirty by the time she reached Broadley's single main street. She had passed no one except the driver of an almost ghostly milk-float, who had glanced at her bare feet and tattered tights and given her a knowing grin as he purred past.

'Good party, worrit, love?' he shouted, not waiting to hear what she snarled in response.

The single telephone box was outside the post office in the centre of the village and Laura took shelter there, leaning her head against the glass in an agony of indecision. She knew that Thackeray would be beside himself with worry. She could only guess who else he had told if he thought she was in some sort of trouble.

Even so she felt an intense reluctance to let him see her return home in her present filthy and dishevelled state, which she reckoned was as much her own fault as Blake's. Thackeray's reaction, she knew, would be personally unpredictable at best, professionally dangerous at worst.

Deliberately she punched in the number of the taxi firm which had pinned its card to the board above the phone. She would go, she had decided, to Vicky Mendelson's, where she could shower and borrow some clothes before she faced Thackeray and attempted to make as light as she could of her unexpected night on the moors. But as she stood waiting for her cab to climb the steep hill from the Maze valley, chilled again by the wind now she had stopped walking, she felt as if hundreds of tiny feet were dancing on her grave.

'You take risks,' Michael had once said to her angrily and she knew he was right. But what frightened her was the knowledge that now, if she took risks, she was not the only one who might get hurt. And although she loved Michael with a desperation which overwhelmed her at times, right now, numb with cold, bruised and angry, but safe, she was not sure that responsibility was what she wanted.

# 17

For perhaps the first time in his life, Sergeant Kevin Mower was at a loss. He sat in a corner of the canteen gazing into a cup of cold coffee, trying to reconcile the irreconcilable, ignoring the curious stares of colleagues who knew nothing of his dilemma.

All Mower's instincts told him to obey orders regardless, even apparently absurd orders, because in an unforgiving service to do anything less meant endless and quite possibly terminal trouble. If senior officers wanted to make fools of themselves that was their funeral, canteen wisdom told him. The best course, indeed the only course, for a detective sergeant who nursed ambitions was to keep his head down and hope to ride the inevitable waves which would follow a shipwreck.

But it was Michael Thackeray who Mower reckoned was heading for the rocks, and in spite of himself he felt an over-whelming compulsion to launch a life-boat. Lying in a hospital bed knowing that six pints of your life blood has drained out of you has a remarkable power to concentrate the mind on what is important, he thought wryly. And waking up in intensive care reveals just who is committed enough to be there waiting for you to surface. Thackeray's had been the first face he recognised as the mists cleared, and he would never forget that.

But today he had known there was going to be trouble as soon as he got to the office and learned that Alice Smith had died in the night. Thackeray was already at his desk, dark circles under his eyes and a face so haggard that Mower winced to look at him. The ashtray on his desk was already half full.

'Is Laura all right, Guv?' he asked, although he guessed the question would not be welcome. Thackeray had sent him home to his own flat at two o'clock that morning, still with no news of Laura's whereabouts, and he had slept uneasily, although obviously not as uneasily as Thackeray had.

'She's fine,' Thackeray said shortly. 'I panicked unnecessarily. I'm sorry I dragged you into it. It was just a misunderstanding.'

And my name's Reggie Kray, Mower thought to himself.

'And Kevin . . .'

'Yes, Guv?'

'I'd rather it didn't get all round the nick.'

'Right, Guv,' Mower said.

'Right, now, I want to pin Keith Spencer-Smith to the floor over these deaths,' Thackeray went on. 'And to do that we need to talk to John Blake and his PR woman about his alibi. But first I want to know everything there is to know about Blake. Val Ridley doesn't seem to have got very far so I want you to go down to London and talk to his agent, find out about his career before he went to America, where he worked, where he trained, the lot.'

'Can't the Met . . .?' Mower began before realising his mistake. Val Ridley had not got far, he knew, because he had not pressed her to.

'The Met will take weeks, I want answers tomorrow,' Thackeray snapped. 'And before you go, organise pictures of Spencer-Smith and Blake, and Bonnetti as well if you like. They've all been in the *Gazette* over the last week or so. Ask Ted Grant for prints and get them up to the hospital, see if we can get a positive identification of Danny O'Meara's last visitor. If that fails, get the people who saw him down here to construct a computer impression.'

'None of them are much like the description we've got,' Mower objected. 'The man sounds much older.'

'Just do it, Kevin.'

'You've got new evidence of a link between Blake and O'Meara's death, have you, Guv?' Mower ventured uncertainly.

'Not yet I haven't,' Thackeray said flatly. 'That's what you're going to find in London.'

'Yes, Guv,' Mower said unhappily.

He was no more cheerful half an hour later as he sipped his coffee in the canteen to pass the time before he needed to leave on what he was firmly convinced was a wild goose chase. He could only marvel at the certainty with which a man who had always dismissed hunches as a serious distraction to solid police procedure could ride one so determinedly when his judgement was swayed by emotion. And he was sure that emotion was at the root of Thackeray's irrational obsession with Blake.

Mower was unhappy enough to have toyed with the idea of somehow bringing his London excursion to Superintendent Longley's attention in the hope that he would call it off. But that seemed to risk stabbing Thackeray in the back.

He glanced at his watch. There was just time to do what he now had in mind. He left the police station and walked the couple of hundred yards to Bradfield's rail terminus, a prefabricated sixties replacement for the solid Victorian structure that had once housed a railway of some grandeur. He bought his ticket to King's Cross and then made his way to the glass and scaffolding shanty which served as a waiting room and pulled out his mobile phone.

At the second attempt he located a sleepy Laura Ackroyd at her flat.

'How's your grandmother?' he asked.

'She's fine,' Laura said, obviously surprised at this unexpected concern. 'They're keeping her in until they've finished their tests – a day or two at most.'

'And how are you?' Mower said. 'I hear you had a late night

last night.' This enquiry was greeted with total silence for a moment and when Laura spoke again she sounded strained.

'I'm fine,' she said.

'But off work?'

'I twisted my ankle last night and couldn't get to a phone. A stupid thing to do.' She was obviously not going to expand further and Mower was afraid she would hang up.

'Listen to me, Laura,' he said urgently. 'I'm just about to get on a train for London and you need to know this. Michael's taken it into his head to investigate John Blake, without any justification at all, as far as I can see. I just thought you might know what's behind it. And believe me, if you do, and can think of any way to stop him before he gets in too deep, I think you should do that.'

'I don't think at the moment Michael's going to listen to anything I say about John Blake,' Laura said helplessly. 'Can't you stop him?'

'It's not easy to stop your boss doing something he wants to do in the police force,' Mower said. 'I'm putting my job on the line already talking to you like this.'

'This is all so stupid and unnecessary,' Laura said and Mower could tell she was close to tears. 'He's behaving like an adolescent.'

'Tell me about it,' Mower said bitterly. 'My train's in, Laura, I've got to go. Take care.'

The atmosphere in the CID room was tense when WDC Val Ridley got back from Long Moor Hospital clutching a folder of glossy photographs. She glanced up the corridor at the DCI's door.

'Is he in?' she asked.

A colleague raised an eyebrow. 'He is,' he said. 'But not in a good mood. I reckon he's falling off the waggon at last, is the sainted Thackeray. I'm not sure he's up for an idle chat.'

'Nor am I,' Val said, turning sharply on her heel, knocking on Thackeray's door, putting her head inside and instantly wishing she hadn't. Thackeray was sitting at his desk with the look of a volcano about to erupt. He was facing Superintendent Longley, whose red neck, bulging over his collar, gave the clearest signal possible that the detonation factor in the room was at least double what she could see face-to-face.

Longley spun round in his chair to see who had interrupted the meeting.

'Ah,' he said ominously. 'Just the person we need. Come in, Val, and tell us how you got on.'

'Sir,' Val said neutrally, edging into the room and standing as close to the door as she decently could. 'I got nowhere really, sir.'

Longley eyed the folder she was carrying and held out a hand for it.

'Let's have a look at our line-up, shall we?' he said, opening the folder and spreading the three photographs inside across Thackeray's desk.

'No one seemed familiar, then?' he asked Val and she shook her head.

'I've asked the man on the gate to come in, and the two nurses who saw O'Meara's visitor, when they finish work at five. Then we can see what sort of a picture we get with the computer people.'

'Good,' Longley said. 'That'll be all, Val, thank you.'

He waited until she had closed the door behind her before he turned back to Thackeray angrily.

'What did I tell you? You're all over the place on this one, Michael.'

'It seemed a reasonable sample of pictures at the time,' Thackeray said, his face an impassive mask.

Longley shook his head in disbelief. 'Spencer-Smith, certainly. Bonnetti possibly, if you think O'Meara had something on him. But Blake? What the hell has he got to do with any of this? He's a guest here, invited to a prestigious do, considering a major investment in the area, and all of a sudden you've got him lined up as a murder suspect.'

'He's thicker with Smith than the film museum thing would

indicate. He could have been here in Bradfield at the relevant time . . .' Thackeray shrugged wearily as Longley waved a dismissive hand at him.

'So were a couple of thousand other teenaged boys, I've no doubt. But we're not hawking their photographs round the district. What the hell did the *Gazette* make of it when you asked for this picture?'

'I've no idea,' Thackeray said. 'Val got hold of them.'

'Well you can bet your life Ted Grant's busy putting two and two together and making a hundred and eighty,' Longley said. 'And what about your own personal investigative reporter? Does she know about this?'

'No, sir,' Thackeray said icily.

'Aye, well, she'd better not, an' all,' Longley said flatly. 'Right, now, let's see what we can rescue from this mess. Fetch Mower back, for a start. He's wasting his time and my bloody budget swanning around down there. If I know that beggar, he'll be having a night out clubbing in Soho at our expense if we don't watch him. Concentrate on the murder weapon. I know there's no fingerprints so the beggar must have been wearing gloves. But see if you can trace where the spanner came from. And get your folk from the hospital to come up with some sort of likeness that we can give to the press tomorrow morning to keep their busy little minds occupied. I'll get the Press Office to do a release about the mysterious visitor we want to interview regarding O'Meara's death. What else had you got planned for today?'

'I was going to see the Bonnettis again. In the light of what we've found out from Spencer-Smith and the O'Mearas it's obvious that they were giving us a highly sanitised version of what their daughter got up to that summer,' Thackeray said.

'If they knew owt about it,' Longley said. 'In my experience of daughters they can look as if butter wouldn't melt and all the while their knickers are round their ankles.'

He smiled grimly and Thackeray thought he would not like to have been Longley's daughter caught in that situation.

'Right, talk to Bonnetti if you must,' Longley said grudgingly. 'But think on. That family's a major employer these days and they'll have friends to match. You'll need to be one hundred and ten per cent sure of your ground.'

'And Blake?' Thackeray asked, an obstinate look in his eyes.

'You can ask Mr Blake one question and one question only,' Longley said angrily. 'You can ask him and what's-her-name, his PR woman, to confirm that they were with Spencer-Smith when he says they were. But if all three of 'em vouch for each other, then we're stuck either way, aren't we? The only way you'll crack the alibi is if you can come up with a positive identification – which so far you've not got – or some forensic to put one of them in contact with O'Meara.'

'Right,' Thackeray said.

Longley sat looking at him speculatively for a moment before lumbering to his feet. 'Are you all right, Michael?' he asked. 'You look like you've been run over by a bloody ten-ton truck.'

Thackeray ran a hand through his hair and shrugged slightly.

'I'm all right,' he said. But he knew Longley did not believe him.


The old man, Paolo Bonnetti, had not even attempted to speak since DCI Thackeray and WDC Ridley had arrived. He was sitting in a wheelchair in his spacious conservatory, the first curves of intense magenta on the huge bougainvillaea framing his shock of white hair and leonine face. His son sat close by in a cane chair, his head bowed and his hands clasped as if in prayer.

'Are these really questions we must discuss, Inspector?' he asked Thackeray. 'After all this time it seems like a desecration of my sister's memory.' Thackeray had been conscious of the photograph of Mariella in her white Communion dress as they had come through the living room. A vase of white flowers stood close by it and he guessed that this was how the family had maintained her memory.

'I'm sorry,' he said, and meant it. 'But if we are to have any hope of finding out what happened we need to know the truth about her relationship with the boys in the neighbourhood. Your mother made some terrible allegations last time we were here

165

about the way Mariella was treated by the other children who lived in the road. Now we have a totally contradictory allegation that she was intimate with at least one of the boys she went around with. I need to know whether that is true, and if it is true I need to know whether she was willing – or not.'

The old man in the wheelchair suddenly shouted out unintelligibly and Giuseppe Bonnetti took his clenched fist in his.

'The police have their job to do, Papa,' he said. Hoarsely the old man spoke again in Italian and Thackeray waited patiently for his son to translate.

'My father says his daughter was pure,' Bonnetti said, his voice choking with emotion. 'He says the boys slandered her, that they hated Italians in Bradfield at that time and that all sorts of lies were told.'

'Can you ask your father if he ever suspected for a moment that Mariella might be involved romantically with Keith Smith or Roy Parkinson?'

The old man clutched the arm of his chair with his good hand and the veins in his neck stood out as his colour deepened. It did not need his son to translate the furious denial which he forced from his strangled vocal chords.

'No,' he said. 'No, no, no.'

'I'm sorry, Chief Inspector,' Bonnetti said. 'You've come a long way, I know, but my father's doctor has advised that emotional upsets are very bad for him. A stroke is seldom the end of it, you know? I do think this line of questioning is not good for him.'

Thackeray nodded wearily and Val Ridley wondered whether he or the old man looked more sick.

'Can I come back and talk to your mother at some convenient time?' she asked.

Bonnetti shrugged and his father looked agitated again. The younger man waved them back into the living room out of earshot.

'I suppose so, if you really think it could help.'

'Do you not recall any of this unpleasant racism yourself?' Thackeray asked.

'I told you, Inspector, I was very young.'

166

'There is just one other thing I wanted to ask you, Mr Bonnetti. You said Danny O'Meara had asked you for help recently.'

'That's right,' Bonnetti agreed grudgingly.

'Did he threaten you in any way?'

'Threaten, Inspector? He was hardly in a position to threaten. He was a kitchen porter, briefly, in my restaurant. A pathetic wreck of a man. How could he threaten me?'

Thackeray took his time going home that night. The fear which had dogged him all day threatened to choke him as he got into his car and started the engine. What he craved more than anything was a drink, the one thing he knew that he must not have. One day at a time, he thought to himself. But some days lasted infinitely longer than others. He sat for a moment clutching the steering wheel fiercely to steady himself as he stared the prospect of life without Laura in the face.

She had got back to the flat after six that morning, apologising tearfully for not contacting him. He had been dozing, fully dressed, in a chair, and had let six hours of pent-up anxiety rip. She had answered him in kind, giving him a garbled account of her night on the moors which he had not believed. She had been in no danger, she said, she was quite capable of looking after herself, but when she kicked off her borrowed shoes and flung herself face down on the bed he shuddered at the state of her bruised and blistered feet.

He had left her to sleep an exhausted sleep, showered and shaved and gone straight to work, unsure whether he could bear to return. He was still unsure, but eventually turned the car in the direction of the flat, driving slowly, his perceptions leaden as he steered the car through the late rush-hour traffic.

He found Laura sitting on the sofa in jeans and a T-shirt, her hair in a loose copper cloud around her head and her bruised feet bare. She had a glass in her hand and a vodka bottle on the floor beside her and he could see a dark bruise on her arm just beneath the edge of the white sleeve.

Thackeray stood and looked at her for a moment without

speaking, overcome by anger and despair. He needed to take a deep breath before he could say anything at all.

'You know that's not the answer,' he said, picking up the bottle which had about an inch of spirit left in it. 'How much have you drunk?'

Laura shrugged. 'What the hell's it matter?' she asked, her voice slurred.

'It matters,' Thackeray said, going into the kitchen and tipping the rest of the vodka down the sink as much to defy the temptation to drink it himself as to protect Laura, who was already too drunk for it to make much difference. He put the kettle on and went back into the sitting room.

'Why are you doing this?' he asked.

'Because I don't know what I want any more,' she said miserably.

'Be honest, Laura,' he said quietly. 'You mean you don't want me here any more.'

'Have we ever been honest with each other?' she asked.

He glanced away, unable to answer that question.

'Did you sleep with Blake?'

'No, I didn't. It's nothing to do with Blake. Not really.'

He pounced on her hesitation. 'What does that mean?'

'It means he tried it on, and just for a moment I fancied him too. I thought, oh, God, I don't know what I thought. We'd had a great evening. He's attractive, attentive, fun! I just fancied him. So what happened wasn't his fault. Men always claim women lead them on. Well, this time that was right. I did lead him on. It seemed like a good idea at the time.'

Even in her fuddled state Laura knew that Thackeray sat for a long time without speaking and in the end she turned her head away, burying it in the cushions to hide her tears.

'Blake is at best a womaniser. He's been accused of child abuse. And I still think he could be involved in Danny O'Meara's death,' he said at last.

'That's ridiculous,' she said. 'You're just jealous. You're looking for any excuse to get at him. In any case, nothing happened.' But at the back of her mind was the feeling that something significant had happened which she should tell Thackeray, but in her fuddled state she could not remember what it was.

Thackeray got to his feet and went into the kitchen. After a few minutes he brought her a cup of black coffee and put it on the table beside her.

'I'll pack my things,' he said.

# 18

The new cinema museum frothed with a volatile mixture of Bradfield's solid burghers, its cultural wannabes and a handful of genuine film buffs invited to leaven the mixture. Above the heads of the guests a huge screen endlessly repeated a potted history of the cinema, the climaxes, agonising and hilarious, of Eisenstein and Chaplin, Fellini and Bergman, Coppola and Spielberg. The throng below ignored it and concentrated seriously on the gossip, the champagne and canapés.

Laura Ackroyd, who had hobbled to work that morning in the most comfortable shoes she could find, stood at the back of the room with her colleague, Paddy Stanford, a huge bull of a man in his sixties with a shock of grey hair. Paddy spent his life in the semi-darkness of cinemas or the almost equally dim back bar of the Lamb. There he composed the *Gazette*'s less than searching film reviews with a stubby pencil on the backs of envelopes before persuading a computer-literate secretary at the *Gazette* to translate his scrawl on to a screen.

Laura looked pale and there were violet circles under her eyes. She had never discovered a hangover cure which actually worked and she was fighting off a thumping headache with a brimming glass of Buck's fizz. Paddy Stanford, at a guess, was on his fourth or fifth. At the far end of the room she spotted John Blake, immaculately dressed and, she was slightly relieved to see, coiffed. He was surrounded by an admiring coterie of dignitaries and film buffs, the former, she thought, rather more likely to recall his less than illustrious career than the latter.

Even from a distance she could see the man light up in the warm glow of adulation which surrounded him as he stood framed by a display of blown-up photographs of himself in his most notable roles. A skinny girl in a pastiche of a Busby Berkeley costume waved a tray of canapés in her direction but she shook her head, fighting off her nausea.

'Does anyone really remember John Blake's films?' she asked Stanford.

He shook his head wonderingly. 'He was never what you'd call really big,' he said, selecting five canapés and balancing them carefully on a paper plate on top of his champagne glass. 'He had a certain appeal to women, I think. He made a couple of strong Westerns but we're not talking *The Magnificent Seven*. He wasn't in the Yul Brynner, Clint Eastwood league.'

'Though he likes to think he was,' Laura said waspishly.

'Have you finished your profile?' her colleague asked.

'Pretty well. But I don't think he's going to like it,' she said.

'Ah,' Paddy said thoughtfully. 'That he won't appreciate if he's trying to get this Brontë scheme off the ground.' He grabbed another selection of canapés from a waitress, whose ostrich feather head-dress was beginning to slide over one ear. 'And I hear that's not going too well.'

'Isn't it?' Laura asked. 'I was told that they had someone big lined up to play Jane.'

'I'll believe that when the contracts are signed, darling,' Paddy said. 'In the meantime don't be tempted to put too much faith in that little venture. Or cash. I'll be very surprised if it gets airborne.' Holding his empty champagne glass in front of him like a votive offering, Stanford buffeted away through the crowd towards the bar, leaving Laura to digest that unexpected morsel of intelligence. Above their heads Eisenstein's pram bumped to perdition down the Odessa Steps for the sixth time in an hour.

Laura took another gulp of her own champagne, feeling disoriented. She had been determined to go to work that morning as much to avoid another even more miserable day in the flat as because she felt any obligation to attend the museum opening.

But she was beginning to think it was a mistake. As she watched Lorelie Baum expertly insinuate herself across the room towards her, too fast for her to extricate herself from her crowded corner, she knew she was right.

'Laura, honey,' Lorelie said, throwing a kiss at the air close to each of Laura's pale cheeks. 'Are you enjoying it? Do you have everything you need for your feature? I can let you talk to John for a couple of minutes after he's done his big number.'

'I'm fine,' Laura said.

The American's chilly eyes raked her over and evidently found her wanting.

'Are you?' she said. 'You don't look so fine, honey, I have to say. Do you need to talk to the mayor? I've just been trying to sell the mayor to the man from the *London Globe* but he doesn't want to know.'

'I can talk to the mayor any time, thanks,' Laura said. 'My grandmother dandled him on her knee, I'm told. Don't you worry about me. You concentrate on your man from the *Globe*.'

'John got back very early from your little visit to his mother the other night.' Lorelie said inconsequentially. 'Did that go well for you?'

'It might be very helpful for my grandmother,' Laura said truthfully.

'Yeah, right,' Lorelie said thoughtfully. 'Do you have my mobile number? We're going back to London tomorrow, but call me if there's anything else I can help you with. Anything at all.' She pressed a card into Laura's hand with a list of numbers on both sides of the Atlantic.

'Thank you,' Laura said wearily.

Yet as she watched John Blake make his way to the podium at the front of the room a few minutes later, with Keith Spencer-Smith and Lorelie Baum in obsequious attendance, she felt no more inclination to blame him for what had happened than she had the previous night. The fault, she thought bitterly, was all her own and she could see no way of making amends that Thackeray would ever accept.

She listened to the actor's elegant, witty little speech in a state of suspended admiration. She smiled wanly at the jokes and clapped half-heartedly when he finally declared the Bradfield Cinema Museum officially open. Around her the party sprang instantly into action again. Across the room she could see the spiky figure of Lorelie Baum thow a hostile glance in her direction before turning away to engage a pony-tailed young man in animated conversation beneath the portraits of Blake. Blake himself, with Spencer-Smith smiling ingratiatingly at his shoulder, was soon surrounded by a cohort of civic dignitaries. Laura felt sick.

She was astonished when her arm was squeezed and the familiar voice of Kevin Mower spoke into her ear.

'You've got to believe me, Laura,' he said. 'I tried to postpone this little pantomime. But your feller's not listening to anyone this morning.'

'What do you mean?' Laura asked urgently. 'What are you doing here?'

'I'm with the boss,' Mower said, glancing towards the door where through the swirling crush of people Laura caught a glimpse of Michael Thackeray in animated conversation with Keith Spencer-Smith.

'But why?'

'We need John Blake to answer some questions, apparently.'

'Now?' Laura said, appalled. With Mower close behind her she pushed her way through the crowd to confront Thackeray. She had to shout to make herself heard above the hubbub of the party.

'Michael, you can't be serious,' she said.

Thackeray glanced at her and then turned deliberately back to Spencer-Smith who shrugged angrily and signalled to John Blake, who in turn began to push his way towards them from the other side of the room.

'What in hell's going on?' the actor demanded angrily.

'John, this is Detective Chief Inspector Thackeray and with an unbelievably unacceptable sense of timing he says he wants to ask you some questions,' Spencer-Smith said, his own fury only just under control.

'Can't it wait until this shindig is over, Chief Inspector?' Blake asked.

'I'm afraid not, sir,' Thackeray said.

'Michael, this is petty,' Laura objected loudly into the lull which followed and she caught Blake's eye as he glanced from her to Thackeray and, with a mixture of disbelief and anger, made the connection.

'This is harassment, Mr Thackeray,' Blake said. 'In the States I could sue you for a very great deal of money. And I suppose that it was you who sent someone to see my agent in London to ask intrusive questions? Or was it you, Ms Ackroyd, and your crappy little magazine?'

Laura shook her head in despair and turned away feeling rather than seeing Blake follow Thackeray and Mower out of the room. Behind her a momentary hush fell over the gathering, which instantly turned into a frantic hubbub as those who had seen what had happened at the back of the room made their own lurid interpretation and relayed it to those who had not.

'What in hell's going on?' Lorelie whispered fiercely into Laura's ear, holding her arm in a vice-like grip.

'I really don't know,' Laura said wearily. 'I think we've just witnessed the end of someone's career. But I wouldn't put money on whose.'


Thackeray watched the clock over his office door flick inexorably towards nine. The daylight outside the window had faded to a blue gloom but he had not bothered to switch on the lights. Nor had he paid any regard to Jack Longley's instruction, issued irascibly more than three hours ago, to go home and sort himself out.

Longley had not allowed him to interview John Blake. Some sixth sense seemed to have sent the Superintendent hurrying red-faced down the stairs to the interview room as soon as the party from the museum arrived at police headquarters. With a single imperious gesture the Superintendent had sent a uniformed sergeant into the room to sit with Blake and Spencer-Smith, who had insisted on accompanying his friend, and waved him and Mower out into the corridor.

'Sergeant, did you find any evidence in London to connect

173

John Blake with the Italian girl?' Longley had asked Mower curtly.

'No, sir. I looked through the records at RADA at the right sort of time but they made no mention of Blake and I couldn't find any record of him at a couple of other drama colleges, but that doesn't prove he didn't go somewhere else. Mr Thackeray called me back before I could check them all. I did speak to his English agent but he's only represented him for the last couple of years, since he's been trying to get his career back on the road. He doesn't know much about his early history, certainly nothing before he got to Hollywood. He thought he was an American.'

'And as far as the O'Meara death is concerned, Spencer-Smith claims to have spent the afternoon in question with Blake?'

'Yes, sir,' Mower said impassively, avoiding Thackeray's eyes.

'Right, Michael, I'll talk to your man Blake. And I'll see you in my office as soon as I'm done.'

Thackeray had gone back to his office wondering whether to write out his resignation then or to wait until it was demanded. To have demolished his affair with Laura and put his job on the line, all within twenty-four hours, revealed a talent for self-destruction that even he had rarely achieved before, he thought savagely.

But the interview with Longley, when it came, proved less devastating than he had anticipated. Longley merely eyed him wearily and waved him into a chair.

'I warned you that you were taking this case too personally,' he said, but he seemed to have transferred the brunt of his anger from Thackeray to John Blake during the brief time that he had spent with the actor.

'If you could charge a man for supercilious bloody arrogance, I'd go along with it,' he went on with feeling. 'D'you know what he asked me? He asked me whether we thought it raised our profile to bait celebrity visitors to Bradfield.'

'Did he confirm Spencer-Smith's story?' Thackeray ventured.

'Aye, he did, and that's an end of it,' Longley came back sharply. 'Even if you could come up with summat concrete you'd have to be bloody quick. He's leaving Bradfield tomorrow, and goes back to the States next week. After that you're into extradition and that's not simple.' Longley paused and took a long slow look at the younger man.

'He told me what's bugging you, of course,' he said.

'And what was that?' Thackeray came back, too quickly.

'Getting too close to Laura – his words, not mine,' Longley said.

'Jesus, I'll—'

'You'll do nothing,' Longley snapped. 'Your judgement's gone on this one. You won't talk to him again without my express permission. Understood?'

'Understood, sir,' Thackeray said mutinously.

'Go home, Michael. Take a break. I don't want to take you off these cases but I will if I have to. Get some sleep, review the evidence in the morning and then tell me what we've really got. It's facts we need, not fantasy.'

Thackeray had nodded his acquiescence and gone back to his office. But he went nowhere, because he no longer felt he had a home to go to. His own flat felt less attractive than ever after the sleepless night he had just spent there.

At length he came to the decision he had been avoiding for hours, put on his jacket, picked up a glossy carrier bag from underneath his desk and walked slowly out of the almost deserted police station by the back entrance. He drove quickly up the hill to Laura's house and stopped outside. For the second night running he found that her car was not parked in its usual place and the top floor of the tall building was in darkness. Unsure whether he had wanted her to be in or not, he did not know whether to feel disappointed or relieved. At least it meant that there would not be another confrontation.

He took his carrier bag and went up the steps to the front door but as he put his key in the lock a slight noise to his left beyond the overgrown shrubs at the side of the house attracted his attention, and he froze. Leaving his bag on the doorstep, and walking silently on rubber-soled shoes round the corner of the house, he followed the rustling sound and came up behind the almost indistinguishable figure of a rather small man who seemed to be peering into one of the ground-floor windows. Thackeray reached out a heavy hand for a shoulder.

'What the hell are you doing?' he asked.

The figure spun round and flung a wild punch in Thackeray's direction, which he easily dodged.

'I don't recommend it,' he said, grabbing an arm more firmly.

'Bloody 'ell,' the intruder said. 'You'll give me another bloody heart attack, creeping about like that.'

'I'm a police officer, so don't do anything stupid,' Thackeray said. 'Come out into the light where I can see you.'

The stranger walked in front of Thackeray meekly enough and turned round to face him under the streetlight where he had parked his car.

'I come all this bloody way to deal with a crisis and when I get here no one seems to be expecting me,' he said, taking Thackeray completely by surprise, as the light caught his thinning red hair and bright blue eyes. 'You'll be the boyfriend, I suppose?'

'Good God,' Thackeray said. 'You must be Jack Ackroyd.'

'Right first time,' Ackroyd said. 'And perhaps you can tell me where my daughter is. I've tried her office and they thought she'd gone home. But I got no reply here either. I was just trying to see if there were lights on round the back but it's as dark as a miner's arse back there.'

'You'd better come up to the flat,' Thackeray said. 'I've got a key.' He led the way up to the top floor, moving much faster than Laura's father, who took several rests as he made his way up the stairs.

'By God, she said it was an attic, but this is ridiculous,' he gasped when he finally gained Laura's living room and sank into an armchair, breathing heavily.

'That's why she couldn't bring Joyce here,' Thackeray said.

'Aye, well, I've taken care of Joyce for the moment. I went up to the hospital as soon as I got in from the airport. They obviously wanted her out and she wouldn't hear of a private nursing home, so I've up-graded to a suite at the Clarendon and settled her in there. Last time I saw her she'd got herself down to the bar in the lift, settled herself in the comfiest chair in the place, with her bad leg up on another, and was talking politics nineteen to the dozen with a couple of her old cronies from the town hall. In her element, she was.'

Thackeray allowed himself a small smile at that. He could imagine Joyce's delight at suddenly being translated to the heart of the town again. He put his carrier bag down on the sofa and waved an awkward hand at Laura's collection of bottles.

'I'm not sure what she's got here,' he said. 'I don't drink.'

'My doctor thinks I don't, an' all,' Ackroyd said with a reflective smile. 'If there's any decent Scotch, I'll have that. Just as it comes.'

Thackeray poured him a generous measure and sat down to take stock.

'What's that?' Ackroyd asked, nodding at the parcel Thackeray had almost sat on.

'A mobile phone for Laura,' Thackeray said grimly. 'Contract signed, rental paid. We've been having some communication problems.'

'You're not the only one,' Ackroyd said. 'She doesn't know I got on a flight to Manchester today. Where the hell is she, any road? She doesn't usually work as late as this, surely?'

'I don't know,' Thackeray said. 'She may have gone for a meal after work. She wouldn't have been expecting me tonight.'

'Serious, is it, you and her?' Ackroyd asked bluntly.

Thackeray glanced away with a shrug of his broad shoulders.

'Seriously over, I think,' he said, far more lightly than he felt.

'Aye, well, she can do better than a copper, can Laura,' Ackroyd said. 'What are you? Inspector? Chief inspector?'

'DCI,' Thackeray said with a faint smile. He warmed to Jack Ackroyd in spite of his rudeness.

'But not chief constable material.' It was a statement not a question.

'Hardly,' Thackeray said. 'I think I blew that a long while back.'

'Aye, well, we all blow summat along the way,' Ackroyd said. 'I never could work out what it was I blew with Laura. She was the apple of my eye when she was a little lass, you know? But all I ever got was arguments as she got older. She's as pig-headed as they come. But you must know that by now.'

Thackeray nodded wryly. He could think of a few more epithets for Laura which he did not feel like sharing with her father.

'You're not going to break her heart, are you?' Ackroyd asked belligerently.

Thackeray shrugged. 'I'll try not to,' he said non-committally. 'Now can I ask you some questions about Mariella Bonnetti? I'm delighted you're over here for Laura and Joyce, but I need to talk to you professionally as well.'

'Aye, Laura said,' Jack Ackroyd sipped his Scotch thoughtfully. 'You know, I can remember that lass as if it were yesterday. It's funny how some things stick in your mind. She had all the lads in a right old state, a little cracker like her, but Italian, an Eye-tie. We didn't know whether to love her or hate her.'

'Did she have a boyfriend?'

'We weren't supposed to know about that, us younger ones. Very secretive, they were. And with good reason. Old Bonnetti would have killed any lad he thought had laid a finger on Mariella. But I reckon Keith Smith was laying more than a finger.'

'Smith? Not Roy Parkinson?' Thackeray asked sharply.

'Parky? No, he was more interested in the little lass, what was her name? Danny O'Meara's sister.'

'Bridget?'

'That's right. Bridie. No one was supposed to know about that either but I'd a shrewd idea what was going on in the garden of the old house behind the factory. The four of them used to climb over there and us younger ones weren't supposed to go near. But I climbed on the wall once or twice and got a glimpse of some pretty heavy petting in amongst the bushes.'

'You're sure it was Smith and Mariella?' Thackeray persisted, but Ackroyd was adamant.

'I don't reckon Smithy was sitting watching Parky have it off wi' two lasses, do you?'

'Can you remember what happened on Coronation Day?' Thackeray asked.

'That's what's so odd, if you really reckon she was murdered,' Ackroyd said thoughtfully. 'We all sloped off outside when we got bored with the television. The rain had stopped and we played cricket for a bit. Then Keith and Parky went off with the two girls, over the wall, and Danny O'Meara and I practised bowling for a bit, and went back indoors looking for some more to eat. You won't remember rationing, you're too young, but one of my abiding memories of being a kid just after the war was always being bloody famished. I suppose rationing was all over by fifty-three, but we never reckoned we could let party food go to waste. It must have been an hour or so after that we went outside again and saw those four come back.'

'All four of them?'

'Oh, yes. And then they all went home,' Ackroyd said.

'You mean separately? To their own homes?'

'Yes, that's exactly what I mean. And that's why I never thought Mariella had been murdered. Keith and Parky went off home first, laughing together like they had some big secret. Then Mariella went home. Danny and I saw her go. Then Danny went off with Bridie. The next day, when we were told Mariella had run away, I thought nowt of it. I knew she'd come to no harm that afternoon. We all knew. And later on the rest of us played cricket again till it got dark.'

'But you didn't see her again?' Thackeray said.

'No, she didn't come out to play again. We saw her father going up to his allotment with his spade but he just swore at us and said she wasn't coming out. We didn't see her again. None of us did.'

'And you didn't tell the police all this?'

'I don't think they ever asked,' Jack Ackroyd said.

Thackeray sat for a moment apparently gazing into space, his eyes blank, as he realised how seriously he had gone wrong in this case.

'Do you know who the most dangerous person in a child's life is?' he asked at length.

Ackroyd shook his head.

'The father,' Thackeray said bitterly. 'One way or another, it's usually the father.'

'You think . . . ?'

'Thinking's one thing, proving, after forty odd years, may be something else entirely,' Thackeray said. 'Do you think Mariella's father could have had any idea what was going on between her and the older lads?'

179

Jack Ackroyd sat for a moment, gazing into his drink. Then he nodded slowly.

'Most of the time we either ignored Mr Bonnetti or tried to make his life hell,' he said. 'Do you remember that daft song they sang around that time? "Papa Piccolino, Papa Piccolino?" No, I don't suppose you would. You're too bloody young for that, an' all, aren't you? Any road, it was a silly Italian thing and naturally we latched on to it. We used to run after him in the street singing it at the top of our voices till he lost his rag and ran after us, ranting and raving in Italian. We thought it was a huge joke. I can't remember whether it was before or after Mariella went missing we took to singing after him. But I do remember speaking to him one day before she went. The four of them had gone off together and I was left on my own. There was no one else around and I was kicking my heels, pretty pissed off with it all. Old Bonnetti came past on his way to his allotment and asked where Mariella was.'

'And you told him?' Thackeray asked softly.

'I don't suppose I told him in so many words,' Ackroyd said. 'You know what honour amongst lads is like. But I was angry enough to have given him a hint.'

'And that would probably be enough,' Thackeray said. 'It'll be almost impossible to prove, but thanks anyway, Jack. You've got me back on track, if nothing else.' He got up and moved towards the door.

'You're not waiting for Laura?' Ackroyd asked.

'She knows where to find me,' Thackeray said, nodding at the package he had left on the sofa. 'And she's got no excuse now, has she?'


19


Maria Bonnetti hit Michael Thackeray hard across the face. She had to stand on tiptoe to do it but she was solidly built and the blow seemed to lose none of its force by describing a rising arc. Taken completely by surprise, Thackeray could only take a step backwards to avoid what would undoubtedly have been a second strike if Sergeant Mower had not grabbed the old woman's arms from behind and held them tightly to her sides until her rage had subsided slightly.

Hearing the blow the group of tall, dark-haired young men who had clustered at the foot of the stairs in the spacious tiled Bonnetti hallway turned suddenly to fix unsmiling eyes on the two policemen.

'You are pigs,' Mrs Bonnetti hissed, her ample bosom heaving. 'To come here when my husband is sick. Get out of my house, you pigs.' One of the young men moved forward uncertainly to put an arm around her shoulders and Mower gradually released his grip.

'Grandmama?' the boy said.

'I'm sorry that we have come at such a bad time,' Thackeray said, feeling his reddening cheek gingerly and fighting down the mixture of embarrassment and anger which had seized him ever since he and Mower had been let into the house. 'But assaulting a police officer isn't a good idea, whatever the provocation.'

The sound of footsteps on the landing above them attracted the attention of the assembly in the hall. Giuseppe Bonnetti came to the half-landing and gestured his mother up to join him.

'There is no prospect of speaking to my father, Inspector,' he said coldly as Maria edged her way towards him, holding tightly to the banisters to take the weight off inflexible knees. 'I could have told you that if you had bothered to telephone.'

'Then I must insist on speaking to you,' Thackeray said, aware of a dozen dark unfriendly eyes fixing themselves on him again as he spoke. The atmosphere was frigid and Bonnetti did not deign to reply until he had helped his mother up the last few stairs and through a door on the landing which they could see stood ajar and from which they could hear the murmur of voices. Having seen his mother safely inside and drawn the door closed behind her, Bonnetti came directly to the top of the stairs again – it was obvious that he too was almost beside himself with anger.

'You will do me the courtesy of waiting,' he said. 'The priest is with my father administering the last rites, if that means anything to you. I *will* be there.'

Even as Thackeray nodded his acquiescence, Bonnetti waved the group of young men up the stairs and turned his back. Paolo Bonnetti's grandsons cast a final collective glare in the direction of the police presence and then filed upstairs and disappeared into the old man's room.

Mower glanced round the hall with a shrug. 'We could have chosen a better moment, Guv,' he said.

'Is there a better moment to ask a father if he killed his daughter?' Thackeray said, following the Sergeant into the small sitting room to one side of the front door and flinging himself irritably into a deeply upholstered sofa.

'Chance'll be a fine thing,' Mower said. 'If he really is dying, we may never discover what happened.'

'Giuseppe knows,' Thackeray said flatly. 'His mother may not, but he does. And you've just seen the passion he brings to bear when he thinks his family's being threatened. And if you're sure Kay O'Meara will identify him as the man she saw her father talking to before he died then we've also got evidence of a confrontation between Giuseppe and O'Meara before O'Meara was killed.'

'You think O'Meara realised what had happened when Mariella's body was found?' Mower countered doubtfully.

'Jack Ackroyd said as much. He said he and Danny saw Mariella go home. At the time the parents said she never arrived. When the body turned up, even after all those years, Danny put two and two together and threatened to expose Giuseppe's father. Giuseppe went up to Long Moor and killed him.'

'It's very thin, Guv. Will it stand up in court?' Mower asked. 'Kay O'Meara's sure of her identification now, this morning, but in seven or eight months' time? A good defence brief could shake her. She didn't recognise the photograph initially and the computer impression is not that like Bonnetti. Vaguely, perhaps, but hardly a perfect fit. She could be wrong.'

It had been Kay O'Meara's identification of Bonnetti which had sent Thackeray to the family's home that morning only to discover that the old man had suffered another stroke during the night and was not expected to survive.

They became aware of footsteps on the stairs and Thackeray moved quickly to the door to meet a tall, angular priest who was already halfway across the hall and heading for the front door.

'A word, please, Father,' he said in a tone which offered no opportunity of denial. He glanced at Mower. 'Go and make it clear to Mr Bonnetti that I must speak to him urgently, Kevin,' he said.

The priest, a middle-aged man with a thin ascetic face and weary eyes, followed Thackeray back into the sitting room and closed the door gently behind himself.

'Chief Inspector Thackeray, I assume,' he said, putting his black leather briefcase on the coffee table and taking a pack of Gaulloise from one of the sagging pockets of his dark suit. He did not offer them to Thackeray. 'I am Gerard McVeay from St Augustine's. You seem to have chosen a particularly inappropriate moment to call.'

Thackeray ignored the criticism. 'Father McVeay, I think you know what I have to ask you,' he said.

'And I think you know what the answer will be,' McVeay said with equal formality, drawing deeply on his pungent cigarette. The two men eyed each other through the smoke for a moment, each in his own way implacable and weighing the other's implacability.

'There is no risk now that Paolo Bonnetti will ever stand trial for his daughter's murder,' Thackeray said. 'It would be well-nigh impossible to prove.'

'No risk at all,' McVeay said. 'Paolo Bonnetti died ten minutes ago. But I am still bound by the confidentiality of the confessional. If you were a Catholic you would not even bother to ask a question which cannot be answered.'

Thackeray smiled grimly as McVeay's words hurled him back to boyhood hours spent on his knees trying frantically to invent enough venial transgressions to keep his confessor convinced that he was not trying to conceal some mortal sin. But the distraction was momentary and he certainly did not intend to share it with this censorious priest.

'If I were to speak to your bishop about the waste of public money involved in my continuing an investigation which a word from you could bring to a speedy conclusion . . .' he said.

Father McVeay smiled a frosty smile, revealing small, crooked, nicotine-stained teeth. 'Then you must feel free to talk to the bishop, Chief Inspector,' he said.

'And pursue my questions with the bereaved? Is that really what you want?'

'This is an unhappy family,' Father McVeay said. 'It has been unhappy for a long time. If you feel you must add to that burden at this moment that is something for your conscience, not mine. I suppose it depends how you see your duty.'

'My duty is to discover who killed a young girl over forty years ago and a sick man just a few days ago. I have good reason to think the murders are connected.'

'Then I wish you well, Chief Inspector,' McVeay said, picking up his case. 'But I can't help you in the way you think I should. I'm sorry.'

On the floor above, Sergeant Kevin Mower was having rather more success in persuading Giuseppe Bonnetti that his interests lay in co-operating with the police. The grey-haired restaurateur stood with his back against his father's bedroom door and an expression of disbelief on a face that had become haggard since the last time the two men had met.

'You wouldn't dare,' he said hoarsely.

'Mr Bonnetti,' Mower said, with every expression of sorrow in his dark eyes, 'I know how difficult this must be for you. But your mother assaulted a senior police officer. I know. I was there. I saw her. That is a serious charge.'

'You wouldn't charge her,' Bonnetti said.

'That would be for the Duty Inspector to decide after she had been interviewed at the police station,' Mower said kindly. 'He might opt for a caution or he might not. The magistrates, of course, don't take kindly to assaults on the police . . .'

'My family will not stand for it,' Bonnetti said, glancing over his shoulder to the murmur of voices which came from the room behind him.

Mower raised an eyebrow. 'It would be a pity to have to send for a police van . . .'

'Mother of God,' Bonnetti muttered, his confidence palpably ebbing away. 'And if I come with you, to answer your questions?' he asked.

'Oh, I think Mr Thackeray would be much more interested in that than he is in your mother's little temper tantrum,' Mower said, allowing himself the smallest of satisfied smiles as he spun on his heel and preceded Bonnetti down the stairs to the hallway where Michael Thackeray was waiting.


Beattie Baker stood for a moment to ease her aching back before she picked up the pile of clean sheets and towels and knocked on the door of the Brontë Suite on the first floor of the Clarendon Hotel. When there was no reply she used her pass key to unlock the door, went into the vestibule and put her burden of clean linen down on the shelf outside the bathroom door.

She was not surprised to hear water running inside, so she knocked on the sitting-room door and went in. Breakfast dishes still stood on the central table and a heap of folders and papers were scattered on a side-table next to a briefcase. It was a lived-in room where everything appeared normal except for the fact that the coffee pot had been knocked over and brown liquid with a sprinkling of coffee grounds in it had run off the edge of the table and was soaking into the beige carpet. Clicking her teeth in annoyance Beattie took a cloth from the pocket of her overall, set the pot upright and began to clean up the mess.

It was not until she had finished clearing the dishes and restoring the table to its normal high sheen that she became uneasy. The water continued running in the bathroom behind her, but with a regularity which did not seem quite normal for someone engaged in a bath or a shower. Apart from that the suite seemed almost eerily silent.

Moving soundlessly across the thick pile of the carpet she

knocked first on one bedroom door and then on the other. There was no reply from either. She wiped her square dark hands on her overall, as anxious not to intrude as she was about the heavy silence which enveloped her. Making up her mind at last she knocked again and opened the first of the bedroom doors, only to find the room empty, the bed in rumpled disarray.

The second bedroom, when she inched open the door, was similarly deserted, although a suitcase lay open on the bed and various items of female clothing lay scattered about as if someone had been interrupted in the middle of packing. Clicking her teeth again Beattie marched to the bathroom door and knocked more firmly.

'Good morning,' she called. 'Are you all right in there, sir? Madam?'

There was no reply and the water continued to run unchecked. Thoroughly alarmed now she tried the door handle gently. It was not locked and swung back quickly revealing what Beattie, brought up on Hollywood movies, half feared. A woman's body lay crumpled on the tiled floor, her towelling robe twisted around her as if she had fallen awkwardly while trying to pull it on as she had stepped out of the shower, which was still running behind her. Through the clouds of steam which misted every surface, Beattie could see that her eyes were open and her face unblemished, though distorted in what looked uncannily like a smile. But the unnatural angle at which the head lay against the side of the bath told Beattie all too clearly that Lorelie Baum was dead.


Sergeant Kevin Mower had learned long ago when to keep his head down and this afternoon was one when he could only wish that the earth would kindly open up and receive him into its bosom. Not that Michael Thackeray's anger was aimed in his direction specifically. But as the closest member of the bemused team to the DCI, he felt more exposed than most.

'There are times when you should trust your instincts,' Thackeray said flatly to no one in particular. 'I knew that bastard was dangerous.'

'I've put out a call for the Merc,' Mower said tentatively.

'He could be out of the country by now,' Thackeray predicted ominously. 'If Amos is right about the time of death, he had two or three hours to play with before the chambermaid found her.'

'I've alerted the ports and airports,' Mower said.

'And Interpol?'

'And Interpol,' Mower confimed, wondering if there was in fact anything he had forgotten. He had been as shaken as Thackeray when they had been called to the Clarendon to examine the crumpled body of Lorelie Baum which, Amos Atherton had assured them, must have been lying there for several hours, long enough for rigor mortis to begin to affect the muscles of her face and jaw, although she was still damply warm from the hot shower water that had cascaded down behind her for hours.

Beneath the towelling robe her body was a mottled blue and red around the shoulders and back, as if someone had rained blows down on her from behind. Her neck was broken, whether by a direct blow or through a fall as she tried to escape from her attacker on the wet tiled bathroom floor was impossible to tell.

Of John Blake there had been no sign. His room was empty, his suitcases and personal belongings gone. The Mercedes which the porter said had been parked in the street behind the hotel since the previous evening had also disappeared. The forensic team were still conducting their meticulous search of the suite when Thackeray and Mower left, but so far there had been no indication of why Blake had apparently turned so viciously on his companion and, it appeared to be generally assumed at the hotel, his lover.

They had brought Lorelie's abandoned paperwork back to the office with them and Mower had been meticulously sifting through everything that had been left behind. But it was not until he tipped the contents of a plastic bag, into which the suite's wastepaper basket contents had been placed, that he smoothed out a crumpled piece of flimsy paper and whistled in surprise.

Thackeray glanced across at him bleakly.

'Something?' he asked.

'A fax from some finance company in London, Guv,' Mower said, scanning quickly. 'Dated this morning too, and not good news. It says that the American backers of *Jane Eyre* have pulled out. The deal is off. The film's on hold.'

'That must have been a blow to Blake, after all the hype in the *Gazette*,' Thackeray said.

'Surely not enough to blow Lorelie Baum away,' Mower said incredulously. 'It was hardly her fault.'

'We know nothing about this man,' Thackeray came back angrily. 'We've never known anything about him. I said to Laura he was hiding as much as he was revealing in his interviews with her. But she took no notice. She switched off her critical faculties where Blake was concerned.'

'You still think he might have been involved with Mariella?'

Thackeray shrugged dispiritedly and the sick feeling of foreboding which had dogged Mower ever since they had gone to the Clarendon tightened its grip on his stomach. Giuseppe Bonnetti was still languishing in a basement cell waiting for a further round of questioning about his father's past and his own more recent contacts with Danny O'Meara, while his family solicitor pulled every lever of power in West Yorkshire to get his client released. Whether they charged Bonnetti with O'Meara's murder or eventually had to let him go, Mower could see little joy in the encounter. Bonnetti was steadfastly denying everything and the evidence for his involvement was weak, and would get weaker as time passed and memories began to fade. He had no alibi for the time of O'Meara's death, but the murder weapon had been without fingerprints and Kay O'Meara's identification, based on a brief encounter in the street, was the only one they could get.

Thackeray and Mower were roused from their separate and unhappy thoughts by Superintendent Longley, who burst into the office unannounced.

'Have you had a call from a lad called Gary, a nurse up at Long Moor?' he asked brusquely.

Mower glanced at the Chief Inspector, who seemed to have suddenly turned to stone.

'No, sir,' the Sergeant said quickly. 'Should we have?'

'He came through to me and then the bloody switchboard seems to have lost him,' Longley said irritably. 'And he's throwing several sorts of nasty stuff at the fan.'

'He was one of the nurses looking after O'Meara,' Mower said.

'Aye, that's right, and he reckons we should know by now who O'Meara's visitor was that day. Says he noticed the resemblance to Blake from the photographs at the museum opening. It was just a casual thing, he said. He wasn't sure. But he mentioned it to Miss Baum, who was standing just by him, almost as a joke, he says, but she promised to pass it on to the police.'

Thackeray looked at Longley for a moment before comprehension began to dawn and he realised the full enormity of the mistake he had made.

'Bloody fool,' he said. 'What made him think she'd do that? Lorelie wouldn't pass it on in a million years.'

'But she might threaten to, Guv, if Blake was giving her grief over the problems the film had run into,' Kevin Mower said. 'Blake must have been pretty pissed off if she tried that.'

'Kevin, get hold of all those photographs of Blake that were up on the walls at the museum,' he said. 'The man's an actor, for God's sake, and we never took on board what that meant.'

Longley nodded.

'Gary says the photograph of Blake made up as an older man, with grey hair, for some film or other, looked familiar,' Longley said. 'Very like the man who came to visit O'Meara – though quite what the connection was between the two of them I can't imagine.'

'I can,' Thackeray said quietly. 'Bridie was the connection.'

'Aye, well, some evidence would come in handy, Michael,' Longley said. 'But never mind O'Meara. The publicity woman's death's enough to be going on with and the chances are Blake's swanning around the country right now made-up much the same way. You'd better get Gary in here PDQ to give us a new description of the beggar. And circulate the picture, if he confirms that's what he looked like when he visited the hospital. Minus the bloody Stetson. Let's not make ourselves look completely ridiculous.'

'Poor Lorelie,' Mower said. 'She can't have had any idea, but if Blake had killed once, perhaps twice, the next time wouldn't have seemed like a big deal.'

He glanced at Thackeray, who was still sitting transfixed. Longley followed his gaze and met Thackeray's dazed blue eyes.

'You'd best pack Bonnetti back to his grieving family before his solicitor has heart failure,' Longley said. 'Tell him we've a new lead to follow up. We can always have him back in if we need to.'

'You told me I was letting emotion cloud my judgement,' Thackeray said quietly to Longley. 'And I bloody well listened to you and backed off Blake.'

'Aye, well, everyone makes mistakes, Michael,' Longley said and they all three knew that was as close to an apology as Thackeray would get.

Mower was about to follow the Superintendent out of the room when the telephone rang. Thackeray picked it up and Mower saw his grip on the receiver tighten until his knuckles turned white. Mower picked up his own receiver and punched into Thackeray's line to pick up on a voice he did not recognise.

'. . .where the bloody hell is she? Do you know?'

'I've no idea, Jack,' Thackeray said, his voice tight and controlled. 'You're quite sure about the Mercedes?'

'Her neighbour seemed sure,' Jack Ackroyd said. 'Early on, it was, she said. About nine-thirty. But she never arrived here at the hotel – and they haven't seen her at work.'

'I'll get back to you,' Thackeray said, putting the receiver down as if it might explode if it jarred against its rest.

'Laura?' Mower whispered.

Thackeray nodded, unable to speak.

'Oh, Jesus,' Mower said, and he knew that the abyss Thackeray was looking into was deeper than he could ever imagine.

# 20

With one hand John Blake kept a firm grip on Laura Ackroyd's wrists and swept up her long pony-tail of red hair into a knot on the top of her head with the other. His touch was gentle enough but it was all she could do to repress a shudder as his hand brushed the nape of her neck.

'I knew as soon as I saw you that you should be my Jane,' he whispered over her shoulder. 'Maybe we'll have to dye this blonde. A pity really, but I don't think we can get away with a red-head in the part. You know how devoted people are to the Brontë stories. But you've that milky skin, that English look. Perfect.'

Laura swallowed hard. Her throat was dry and her heart seemed to be beating so fast that it should have been possible to see it fluttering against the light blue T-shirt she had slipped on over her jeans that morning. She had arranged to take the day off work so as to spend time with her father and Joyce, who was being reluctantly and slowly persuaded to convalesce in Portugal with her son.

John Blake had intervened, turning up outside the flat in the Merc with an apparently innocuous request that she accompany him down to the movie museum in town to look at some clips from his early films which, he said, would help her with her profile.

She had not invited him in but had gone downstairs to talk to him in the street, greeting him frostily but allowing herself to be convinced. She had time before she was due to meet Jack at the Clarendon and seeing the films, she thought, might give her some feeling for why this man had set the hearts of her mother's generation beating so hard.

'Come on, Laura,' he had said, giving her his most attractive smile. 'We had a little misunderstanding last time, but there was no harm done. This is business, for both of us. And you're going on into town anyway. I can drop you at the Clarendon by eleven to see your folks. No problem.'

It was not until Blake turned left instead of right on to the dual carriageway which linked Bradfield with the smaller towns higher up the valley of the Maze that Laura felt any apprehension.

'You're going the wrong way,' she said mildly, not worried yet, but Blake merely glanced at her with a half-smile which she could not interpret and put his foot down hard on the accelerator.

'You and I still have that unfinished business to attend to, Laura,' he said. He drove fast and determinedly, not fast enough to attract the attention of the law but far too fast for her to make any attempt to interfere with his driving or to try to jump out of the car. Furious with herself, she sat back in her seat watching Milford, Eckersley and eventually Arnedale flash past as the hills rose more steeply on either side of the river and wondering whether her impulsiveness had finally led her into complete disaster.

'Where the hell are we going?' she asked eventually as Blake signalled a left turn and swung the car off the main road and on to a narrower country lane.

'You'll see,' he said. He had locked the car doors and even when he slowed infrequently at junctions she knew that trying to get out would be difficult and dangerous. In any case, as the road snaked up on to open moorland where the only signs of life were scattered sheep and an occasional hovering curlew, she knew that there was nowhere to run. She had got away from Blake once, in the dark, more by luck than judgement and at a heavy cost. But she would not be able to outrun him in daylight, for all the difference in their ages, over rough and boggy terrain where a single false step could lead to a fall. He was tall and strong and, she guessed, California fit. The safest course still seemed to be to humour him until she could be sure what his intentions were. But a small voice at the back of her head told her that by that point she might have left it too late. She thought longingly of Michael Thackeray's gift of the mobile phone which she had unpacked and thrown irritably back on to her sofa the previous evening.

She had an idea of their destination a few minutes before they arrived. Avoiding the village where they had shared a pub lunch, Blake had taken a narrow back road, little more than a track, to the empty farmhouse they had visited and which he had hoped would provide one of the locations for his film. He drove into the deserted, overgrown farmyard and parked the car in a narrow space between the house and a derelict barn.

He had helped her out of the car and led her inside, keeping a firm hold on her wrist. Standing looking out of one of the windows down the long deserted stretch of the hillside they had just climbed he had moved behind her and begun to rearrange her hair. So it was to be sex after all, she thought to herself bitterly, wondering how she could ever have even half welcomed the prospect. She pulled her head away and her hair spilled down her back again. Blake let go of her wrists and pulled her round to face him.

'Why did you lie to me, Laura?' he asked angrily, holding her shoulders.

'I don't know what you mean,' she said.

'Oh, come on, honey,' Blake said. 'All this reporter nonsense to gain my confidence and dig up my past. What are you? An undercover cop? Or just doing your boyfriend a favour?'

'I'm a journalist,' Laura said. 'I was commissioned to do a profile.'

'You're good, I'll grant you that,' Blake said. 'I thought you were going to go all the way that night in the Merc. That's devotion beyond the call of duty in my book.'

Laura felt her cheeks flame and she looked away.

'Pity you're not really my type,' Blake said, pulling her back to face him again. 'Still, I guess you can call me master before we're finished. That's what Jane called Rochester, you know? My dear master. Let's hear it, Laura.'

Laura shook her head angrily and tried to pull away but Blake's grip was too tight. He ran a finger gently down her cheek and laughed at the revulsion in her eyes.

'You know, you could turn me on without my having to hurt you at all,' he said. 'What a pity we haven't much time. Come along, my dear. Unlike little Jane, you're not wandering off over the moors without me.' He pulled her into the second of the main rooms of the farmhouse, which was still sparsely furnished, sat her down firmly on a wooden chair and tied her hands to the back with thick twine.

Laura shook her head in bewilderment. 'What are you doing?' she asked desperately. 'If this gets out, your films plans will be ruined.'

Blake looked at her coldly.

'You really don't get it, do you?' he said. 'I suppose you can't have, or you wouldn't have fallen for my spiel this morning and come along for the ride. The film's dead and buried, honey. And so am I unless I can get out of this Goddamned country. For the moment, just regard yourself as my insurance. All you need to worry about is whether your boyfriend will trade for you, if the need arises.'

'They'll come looking for me,' Laura said desperately.

'Oh, I guess they will,' Blake said. 'But they'll have one hell of a job finding this place.'

'Lorelie knows where it is.'

'Lorelie won't be telling,' Blake said shortly. 'Lorelie turned out like you in the end: a bitch who asked too many questions. Now shut up. I've some calls to make.' He pulled a mobile phone from his jacket and went into the other room where she could hear him only indistinctly.

Laura sat uncomfortably on her wooden chair, testing her bonds, which did not give a fraction of an inch, and trying to work out the implications of what Blake had said although she was sure she would not like the conclusions she was being driven to. If the film was off and Blake was talking about Lorelie in the past tense, she had an uneasy feeling that what he was evidently running from was not just the wreck of his plans but something far more serious. I am, she thought grimly, a lousy judge of character.

Blake came back into the room looking pleased with himself.

'Right,' he said with satisfaction. 'If there's one thing to be said for the film business, it's that it harbours more than its share of fools with loads of money and no sense at all. We'll move on when it gets dark.'

194

'My friends will have found us long before that,' Laura said, hoping that she sounded confident rather than desperate.

'I don't think so,' Blake said comfortably. 'And now let's think what we can do to entertain ourselves for a long afternoon in the country.'

The Assistant Chief Constable swept into Bradfield police station with his entourage at two o'clock that afternoon to take charge of the investigation. He found an operations room buzzing with determined activity but when he moved on to Superintendent Longley's office there was little cheer to report. There had been no sightings since early that morning of the silver-grey Mercedes in which it was assumed Blake had fled Bradfield with Laura Ackroyd. A news black-out was in force, which was normal in cases of abduction and with which even Ted Grant had reluctantly agreed to comply, though he seemed to regard access to information about Laura's disappearance as his personal prerogative. Every police officer in the country had been instructed to look urgently for a car which was by no means unobtrusive.

'Where's Thackeray?' the ACC asked Longley brusquely.

'I tried to get him to go home,' Longley said. 'He's doing no good here. But he refused, of course. He's in his office as far as I know. I told Mower to keep an eye on him – unofficially of course.'

'And the reporter girl's family?'

'They're at the Clarendon. Jack Ackroyd's ringing up every half-hour demanding that we send in the SAS, Special Branch – even the FBI, as Blake's officially an American. But unless we get a sighting, or some sort of demand from Blake, we're stymied. As far as I can see, they've disappeared off the face of the earth.' Longley's normally rubicund face was grey and creased with anxiety.

'This isn't the bloody *X-Files*,' the ACC snapped. 'If the car's not been seen the chances are he's not gone far and he's undercover somewhere. But why take the girl? What's the point of a hostage if he's not trying to bargain with her?'

Longley shrugged. He had no answers and the longer the silence over Laura's whereabouts continued the more his conviction grew that she was in serious danger, although that was not something he wanted to admit to himself, to the ACC and least of all to Michael Thackeray.

One floor below Thackeray stared unseeingly out of his office window. He had already filled the room with a thick haze as he tried to chain-smoke his way out of the gnawing fear which had seized him the moment he had been told that Laura had driven away with Blake. Mower watched him anxiously, glancing up every few minutes from the papers on his desk – the random pile of documents which had been removed from Blake's suite at the Clarendon. He could see Thackeray's hand shake as he lit another cigarette and knew he was at the end of his tether. He was aware that all had not been well between Thackeray and Laura over the last few days and guessed that made the fierceness of Thackeray's self-recrimination all the sharper. If she had not been alone at the flat that morning, Laura might not have made the decision she had evidently made.

'Did you come up with any more ideas, Guv?' he asked. 'Anywhere else she went with him, apart from these posh restaurants?'

Thackeray did not turn round.

'They went to the country one day, looking at locations for the bloody film,' he said. There was a moment's silence as both men seemed to find it difficult to absorb what Thackeray had just said. Then Mower picked up a small red book from beneath the jumble of papers on his desk and flicked through it.

'The fifth,' he said. 'It's in Lorelie's engagement diary.'

Thackeray spun round.

'Does it say where?' he asked.

Mower shook his head. 'Just "Location recce". Did Laura not say where she'd been?'

'Somewhere up beyond Arnedale, I think,' he said. 'Some farm . . .' He and Mower looked at each other for a long moment.

'Do you think . . .?' Thackeray said.

'A long shot but worth checking out, Guv,' Mower said. 'If they got the chopper up there . . .'

'Then for Christ's sake do it, Kevin. Do it now.'

*

196

'If I'd been Rochester, I'd never have let Jane run off,' John Blake said conversationally. 'I'd have kept her there. Locked her up in the attic with the first wife. She'd have come round in the end. Just like you will.'

He had been striding around the dusty room where he had imprisoned Laura for what seemed like hours now, becoming increasingly irrational and frightening as he did so. The suave mask with which he normally faced the world appeared to be flaking away, ageing him even as he spoke, and making his obsession with playing a romantic hero more unimaginable by the minute. The only Victorian hero appropriate now, Laura thought, would be Dorian Gray.

She could not see her watch but guessed from the slanting light of the sun which filtered in through the grimy window that it was now well into the afternoon. She was hungry and desperately thirsty and her hands and arms had gone numb where the twine had slowed the circulation. It seemed like hours since she had asked Blake for a drink of water.

'Say "Please, Master",' he had said but she had shaken her head angrily at that and turned away to hide the tears in her eyes.

'You remind me of a bolshie red-headed woman called Ackroyd I knew once when I was a kid,' Blake said. 'Any relation?'

She shook her head furiously, realising at last that John Blake must be the Roy Parkinson who had played in the street with her own father all those years ago. And she remembered what she should have told Thackeray: Blake's mother had called her Pam. And that, Joyce had thought, was Roy Parkinson's sister's name. Guessing just how much he had to hide, she slipped closer to despair.

What was happening, she thought, had little or nothing to do with her intervention in John Blake's life. She was no more than an intruder at the end of the Italian girl's long, interrupted story. She might have felt an affinity with the outsider who had been teased and tormented all those years ago. She might have once been where Mariella had been and uncovered memories of her own childhood which still stung more sharply than she could have believed possible. But those were random ironies she knew she was unlikely to share, if she became, as she was sure she would, the latest victim in a line which must have begun with Mariella. Worse, Michael Thackeray would never know how sorry she was for the mistakes she had made in the last few days.

'What was she?' Blake insisted, breaking in on her thoughts. 'Your grandmother? She was an interfering bitch too, as I remember.'

'You killed Mariella,' Laura said. 'Your name was Roy Parkinson and you killed the Italian girl.'

'Wrong, and you don't collect two hundred pounds,' Blake snapped back. 'I never touched Mariella. She was Keith Smith's girlfriend, not mine.'

'Then what's all this about?' Laura cried out in desperation. 'You are Roy Parkinson. Your mother called me Pam. What have you been trying to hide all this time? What are you running away from?'

'That cursed year we spent in Peter Street, and it looks as if it's caught up with me in the end,' Blake said. 'I knew I should never have come back to Yorkshire. Do you know how that bastard O'Meara recognised me? After all those years? With dark hair and all the expensive work I've had done? I'll tell you how. He heard me doing an interview on the radio, that's how. They say voices never change and he recognised mine. Called me at the Clarendon. Called me Roy and said he remembered I'd wanted to be an actor. Threatened me. Demanded money or he'd drag up his snivelling little sister after all that time. Disinter little Bridie, another embarrassing corpse. Under-age Bridie I put in the family way. If anything was guaranteed to kill the film project, that was it. John Blake and an under-age girl. Again! My backers take funds from the Christian Right, for God's sake . . .'

'So you killed him,' Laura said softly. 'But they pulled the plug on the film anyway.'

'I underestimated Lorelie,' Blake said angrily, his face flushed. 'The bitch was off her head with jealousy. She told the backers I was being investigated by the police.'

'Jealous?' Laura said in surprise.

'Jealous of you. Thought I was paying too much attention to

my little Jane.' Laura turned away in disgust from Blake, who was staring at her with glittering eyes. During the time that John Blake's overweening ambition had been cutting a destructive swathe through Bradfield, she thought, it seemed that the only people to see him clearly enough not to be deceived by his abundant charm had been the two people moved by jealousy – Lorelie Baum and Michael Thackeray.

The thought of Michael Thackeray dissolved in her mind into a silent scream and she closed her eyes to blot out Blake's looming presence. As the afternoon wore on her head gradually sank on to her chest and she felt herself losing touch with reality. At some point she must have moaned or cried out, although she was not aware of it, because the next thing she knew Blake had taken her head in his hands quite gently.

'Jane,' he said hoarsely. 'My little Jane. You know I'd do anything for you if only you'd ask me to be your master.' She shook her head again, and Blake turned on his heel angrily and went out of the room. She heard a car door slam. He came back within minutes holding a bottle of mineral water. He stood in front of her and took a long swig.

'Bastard,' Laura whispered and was rewarded with a sharp slap across the cheek.

She let her head sink forward again and closed her eyes. Blake gave a grunt of frustration and she heard him sit down at the other side of the room, taking an occasional gulp from his bottle. But this time Laura was not asleep. She was awake and forcing herself to think hard.

Her conclusions were grim. The longer she remained a prisoner, she thought, the less chance there was of being rescued, especially if Blake had made firm plans to get out of the country after dark. She did not imagine that he would take her with him or leave her behind alive to tell this story. If Michael Thackeray had remembered her mentioning this place the police would have arrived long ago, she thought. So she was on her own.

So far she had sustained herself by defying Blake but if she continued on that tack much longer what little strength she had remaining would drain away and she would find herself as helpless as she was now when he finally released her from her chair. The only chance of salvation, she concluded, and she was not sure whether the bitter taste in her mouth was real or imaginary, lay in capitulation.

She half opened her eyes. Blake was still slumped in a sagging armchair against the far wall, his bottle of water, now almost empty, in one hand, his eyes closed.

She moaned faintly and wriggled on her chair, moving it slightly with a grating sound on the dirty stone-flagged floor. She saw Blake's eyes open and he sat up, instantly alert, like the predator she now knew he was.

'Water,' she muttered.

He got up and came closer. 'What did you say?'

'Water,' she said again. 'Please.'

Blake's eyes brightened with excitement. 'Please, master,' he insisted.

'Please, master,' Laura croaked.

'Dear little Jane,' he said, kissing her cheek before holding the water bottle to her mouth and letting her drink. When she had finished, he wiped her lips with a handkerchief and eyed her speculatively.

'Would you like to be untied?' he asked. She nodded but he frowned and waited, his head on one side.

'Please, master,' she said again.

'You promise not to run away, dearest Jane?'

'Of course not ... master.' She hesitated before adding truthfully, 'Where would I run to?'

He cut the twine which held her wrists to the chair, but when she tried to stand she found that impossible and she quickly doubled up in pain as the blood began to pump normally again into her hands and arms. Blake put an arm around her and she willed herself not to pull away.

'Sweet Jane,' he said. 'Such a silly girl to get her hands into such a state.' He took hold of one of her wrists but instead of stroking it, as Laura expected, he gave it a sudden vicious twist which made her cry out in agony.

'There are no sweet girls left in America, you know,' Blake went on, oblivious to her distress. 'They're all assertive, manipulative bitches like Lorelie. They go to training classes for it.'

200

'What happened to Lorelie?' Laura whispered but Blake did not reply. He seemed to be listening and it was a moment before Laura too heard the faint clatter of a helicopter, coming closer. Blake was on his feet in an instant, hurrying towards the door.

'Don't move,' he said. 'I promise I'll kill you before they get here if you try anything stupid. I'm going to move the car out of sight.'

Laura believed him, and although the buzz of the approaching aircraft filled her with hope she knew that the moment to run had not yet arrived. Blake came back very quickly, with the car keys in one hand. But it was what he held in the other which filled Laura with horror. He waved a petrol can and a cigarette lighter in her direction and gave her a wolfish smile.

'I don't think they saw me,' he said. 'I've put the car in the barn. But I brought this just in case. I'm not waiting here for your boyfriend. If they come mob-handed, we'll go together, you and I, just like Rochester nearly did with his crazy woman in the attic.'

Deliberately he unscrewed the cap of the petrol can and began to sprinkle it liberally around the room and then in the hallway outside as far as the front door. Laura choked as the fumes filled her nostrils and throat.

'You're mad,' she said, but she did not think he heard her. Outside the noise of the helicopter seemed to be fading away. Desperately she looked around the room. The cap of the petrol can lay on the window-sill where Blake had left it and beside it was the cigarette lighter. Barely thinking about what she was doing, she pushed at the rotting window frame, which fell out with a crash as she scrambled on to the sill and out into the overgrown garden beyond. She heard Blake's angry yell somewhere in the house as she turned, flicked the lighter, tossed it into the room behind her and ran from the explosive roar of flames at her back.


From the helicopter above Kevin Mower, who was sitting beside the pilot, spotted the sudden eruption of smoke from a huddle of farm buildings a mile or so away and peered anxiously out of the window as the machine swung round in a tight arc to come in low over the fire. The pilot skimmed over the burning farmhouse and then turned sharply again, gesturing downwards to the track where he had spotted a silver car bumping down the hill towards the valley. They gave chase, but the driver ignored their loudspeaker instructions to stop and accelerated even faster along the rutted lane, cornering wildly.

'The tractor,' the pilot said, gesturing further down the lane to a farm vehicle with a trailer which was climbing laboriously up the hill.

'He'll not be able to see him,' Mower said. In a final desperate effort to persuade the Mercedes to stop the pilot swooped low in front of the speeding car. But they were too late. As the Mercedes met the tractor head-on the driver swerved wildly for the last time, lost control and careered down a steep bank into a rocky gulley where the car overturned and came to rest on its roof, wheels spinning. Eventually even that movement ceased and the Mercedes lay like a broken toy amongst the jagged boulders.

When Kevin Mower eventually scrambled down to the wreck from the flat patch of moorland half a mile away where the chopper had landed, the distraught farm-worker who had been driving the tractor had pushed the car on to its side and John Blake had almost clawed his way out through the shattered windscreen. He lay doubled up across the bonnet, the lower half of his body still inside the car, his eyes half closed, his hair missing, his face ashen, and his shirt and jacket sodden with blood. He glanced at Mower with the faintest flicker of recognition before he lost consciousness, a trickle of blood leaking from his mouth. Mower could never be completely sure, and could make no sense of it, but he thought that the actor's dying word was 'Jane'.

'Is he the only one in there?' he asked the tractor driver, who looked at him uncomprehendingly and shook his head.

'Is there anyone else in the bloody car?'

Mower did not wait for an answer. Regardless of the damage he might do Blake or anyone else, he put all his weight against the roof of the vehicle and rocked it until it tipped back over on to its wheels so that he could see into the crumpled passenger compartment. His relief that there was not another body inside was quickly overwhelmed with a new fear.

'Stay there till the ambulance comes,' he said to the bemused tractor driver before he scrambled back up the rocky incline to where the chopper was waiting, rotors idling.

'Laura Ackroyd wasn't in the car,' he said to the pilot as he hastily strapped himself into his seat. 'Come on, move it. We've got to find her.' And he pointed his companion back towards the clouds of black smoke which were still drifting from the farmhouse into the clear upland air. As the chopper flew in low again over the moor, he did not think he had ever seen a more welcome sight than Laura standing on a rocky outcrop above the smoking ruin waving wildly to attract their attention, her red hair streaming out behind her and catching the dying rays of the sun like a banner in the wind.

'Thank Christ for that,' Mower said to the pilot. 'Tell him we've found her alive and well, would you? I'm not sure I can manage it.'


Thackeray slowed his car at the summit of the M62 motorway and let it roll gently enough along the slow lane for them both to take in the glory of the high Pennines which spread for miles on either side. Beneath them, the waters of a man-made lake glittered like beaten gold in the late afternoon sunshine while beyond the water-filled valley the hills rolled away to a faint purple horizon. The drive back from Manchester airport, where they had seen Jack Ackroyd off to Portugal with his mother, had so far been silent. He had not wanted to break into Laura's evident melancholy, but now she looked at him and flashed one of the brilliant smiles that was guaranteed to clutch at his heart.

'I'm all right, you know,' she said, although the dark shadows under her eyes gave the lie to her words. 'I'll go home tonight.' Since she had been brought back to Bradfield for a medical check and the taking of detailed statements at police headquarters, she had been staying at the Clarendon with her father.

203

'Are you sure?' he asked.

Laura nodded again. 'I'm all right,' she said. 'Really.'

'Did that bastard ...?' Thackeray stopped, not able to finish the question.

'He hit me, he tied me up, he humiliated me and I hated it,' Laura said quietly. 'But he didn't rape me, Michael. You've read my statement. And even if I'd left it out of that, do you think I wouldn't have told you?'

Thackeray glanced away, no longer sure what Laura was prepared to tell him.

'Blake died without regaining consciousness, so we'll never be sure, but I think Lorelie's death was probably an accident,' Thackeray said. 'She shopped him with the backers in America, of course. Faxed them to say he would be involved in a police investigation here within days. She went along with his alibi for O'Meara's death until he threatened to sack her.'

'He as good as offered me her job in Los Angeles,' Laura said.

Thackeray glanced at her, horrified. 'She was black and blue,' he said. 'He must have attacked her but she probably slipped on the bathroom floor ... That's what killed her.'

Laura pushed up the sleeve of her cream shirt to display the blue and yellow bruise above her elbow.

'I've had more than one taste of John Blake's efforts at persuasion,' she said. 'But how did poor Lorelie discover what Blake had been up to?'

'She met the nurse from Long Moor at the museum opening and he told her what a joke it was that Danny's visitor was the spitting image of Blake made up for a character part in some 1970s Western. She must have guessed then that he had killed O'Meara to cover up what had been going on here all those years ago and decided that was something she didn't want to be involved in. She must have thought he killed Mariella. When the American backers for the film faxed back to London to say they were withdrawing their support – we found that fax – Blake must have gone crazy and Lorelie ended up dead.'

'I guessed he must be Roy Parkinson,' Laura said. 'His mother called me Pamela but it wasn't till later I remember Joyce saying that she thought his sister was called Pam.'

'Yes, we've traced the sister. She's been living a blameless life in York for years. Took her mother out to California regularly to see her brother, but was too young to remember what went on that Coronation summer.'

'So who killed the Italian girl?' Laura said.

'Keith Spencer-Smith thought Blake did, and it's quite possible that Blake thought Smith did. Either way they both had too much to lose to risk having people in Bradfield recognise them when they found themselves back in the town. And their mutual cover-up became even more crucial to them both when Mariella's body turned up.'

'But you don't think either of them did it?'

'Spencer-Smith insists your father's version of events that day is right. Mariella went home that afternoon and none of them saw her again. I'm convinced Mariella was killed by her father. Her mother is saying nothing and it's impossible to know whether or not she knew what had happened. I think probably not. But Giuseppe Bonnetti admits now that the old man often called Mariella a whore when her name came up. But there was no way any of the family was going to tell us that while the old man was alive and insisting publicly that Mariella was innocence itself.

'Of course, I was completely wrong about Giuseppe Bonnetti and O'Meara. It was Blake O'Meara's daughter saw talking to her father in the street. Blake with the same grey wig he used when he went up to the hospital to visit O'Meara. What I always left out of account was the fact that Blake was an actor.'

'The last thing he could have tolerated when he was about to star in *Jane Eyre* with a young actress was a revival of allegations that he preyed on little girls,' Laura said. 'He said as much. O'Meara threatened him so he killed him.'

'And he persuaded Lorelie Baum and Keith Spencer-Smith to cover for him,' Thackeray said. 'They both knew how much they had to lose if Blake's project collapsed. Blake went up to the hospital with his hair greyed up and a bloody great spanner in his pocket, intent on shutting O'Meara up for good. The spanner comes from a set we found in the boot of the Mercedes.'

Laura shuddered. 'So both your murderers are dead.'

'Maybe it's better that way,' Thackeray said. 'But I won't be letting Spencer-Smith and Betty Johns off the hook. Poor old Alice didn't deserve to die like that.'

'I'm sorry, Michael,' Laura said. 'I should have listened to you. But you didn't seem to me to be very rational about Blake. I just thought you were jealous.'

'I wasn't rational and I was jealous,' Thackeray said, with a faint smile. 'I had no evidence at all to link him with Mariella and her friends. It was just a feeling.'

'Intuition,' Laura said with a grin. 'It's a women's thing.'

Thackeray let the car drift down the steep incline from Lancashire into Yorkshire as the sun dropped slowly behind them and they slipped out of its golden light into the gathering dusk. As he accelerated Laura reached out and put a hand on his shoulder.

'Michael, I'm sorry I hurt you. I do try,' Laura said, suddenly anguished. 'But you must know how I am. Sometimes I feel my independence slipping away from me and I panic.'

'I've never tried to tie you down,' Thackeray said. 'I have no right.'

'Come home with me,' she said. 'Let's try again.'

Thackeray did not reply for a moment and then not directly. 'You asked me the other day if we had ever been honest with each other,' he said. Unexpectedly he swung the car off the motorway and away from Bradfield on to a country road she did not recognise.

'Where are we going?' she asked, suddenly afraid.

'To Long Moor Hospital,' he said. 'I want you to meet Aileen, my wife.'